NO REST FOR THE WICKED

NO REST FOR THE WICKED

WITCH OF THE FEDERATION™ BOOK 05

MICHAEL ANDERLE

DISRUPTIVE IMAGINATION

LMBPN Publishing
PMB 196, 2540 South Maryland Pkwy
Las Vegas, NV 89109

Version 1.00, December 2021
Previously Published as part of the megabook *Witch Of The Federation II*
ebook ISBN: 978-1-68500-634-1
Print ISBN: 978-1-68500-635-8

THE NO REST FOR THE WICKED TEAM

Thanks to our Beta Team

Crystal Wren, Daniel Weigert, James Caplan, John Ashmore, Larry Omans, Mary Morris, Nicole Emens, and Robert Brooks

Thanks to our JIT Readers

Angel LaVey
Daniel Weigert
Dave Hicks
Diane L. Smith
Dorothy Lloyd
Jeff Eaton
Jeff Goode
John Ashmore
Larry Omans
Misty Roa

If We've missed anyone, please let us know!

Editor
The Skyhunter Editing Team

*To Family, Friends and
Those Who Love
To Read.
May We All Enjoy Grace
To Live The Life We Are
Called.*

CHAPTER ONE

The flight to the space station, Elpis One, was way more exciting than Stephanie had thought it would be. For one thing, it was deep space. Then, she'd experienced a huge surge of energy that had surprised her because she hadn't expected it. Although there was a downside. She had to listen to Frog barfing for half the trip because something about the flight had set him off. Still, overall, it was definitely exciting.

She had never even been on a plane, much less a spaceship. While there were some passengers who found it much like any other flight, for her, it was like being inside one of the science fiction novels Todd liked to read.

Those things were hard to find after the Federation takeover and the wars on Earth, but his father dug one up here and there and passed them on to him. That was one of the few nice things he'd ever done for his kid.

Of course, her friend passed them to her in turn and she had found each one she'd read thought-provoking and almost spiritual in essence. Seeing the real thing was so much better. The weightlessness inside the shuttle only lasted a few moments before they switched over to artificial gravity. In spite of Frog's immediate vomit-spree, she found being free of Earth's confines invigorating.

It was as if, for those few moments, all the stress and expectations lifted from her shoulders and their absence was what made her truly weightless.

As soon as the gravity was activated, though, everything settled back onto her shoulders, where it weighed heavier than the feet thumping to the floor inside the cabin.

While she was okay with what she had on her plate, Stephanie didn't find anything wrong with letting go from time to time. Being free of her responsibilities meant she could pretend, if only for a moment, that her worries were simply those of a normal human life.

Taxes, jobs, money, and relationships...those were the things most people worried about. Not death, Dreth, and duty.

In the midst of her daydream of sleep-filled nights, day-time office cubicles, and modern relationships, she was a little disappointed when Lars nudged her with his elbow. "Hey, we're slowing down. The spaceport should be up ahead. It's the first stop on this leg to Meligorn. Home sweet home for a couple of days."

Stephanie turned to him, nodded, and forced an understanding smile before she remembered he couldn't see it through her veil. "Right. Got it. At least we can stop listening to Ralphing Robot back there."

Frog groaned and clutched his stomach. "Please, someone land this bitch. Seriously."

A passing crew member stifled a smile, and Marcus gripped the man's shoulder. "What's wrong, bro? Space travel not really your cup of tea?"

"It's not my cup of anything," he replied. "At least not on this shuttle. I've flown space before, in and out of the Virtual, and I don't know why this one's got ahold of my stomach and rolled it."

Johnny leaned over from across the aisle. "It wouldn't have

anything to do with the waffle-sausage breakfast we all told you not to eat, would it?"

Frog waved frantically for his teammate to stop and his face clearly said he was trying not to think about it.

Marcus groaned, having had to sit next to him for the entire trip. He looked vaguely green about the gills himself.

Stephanie simply stared out the window and laughed at the guys' banter. Outside, she could see the spaceport coming up. It was a lot bigger than she'd thought it would be.

Deck upon deck circled through space, the different sectors connected by translucent tunnels. Round, speeding elevators moved like ants along them, ascending and descending between levels.

"It's impressive, right?" Lars smiled and peered over her shoulder. "Like a little city in its own right."

"It is," she replied. "When the hot-cyclone anomalies were happening ten years ago, there were some nights when I could see its lights flashing in miniature. I lived for those moments."

"You're talking about the anomaly that created those crazy strong winds in the upper atmosphere, right?" he asked.

Stephanie nodded. "Yeah. When it dipped below what is left of the ozone layer and into the troposphere, you could watch the clouds and smog being blown away. On those nights, the sky was relatively clear. I was lucky I lived in a place that gave us a view of the space station. They were still doing construction on the East wing at that point."

He smiled. "Funny what makes an impression on us as kids."

She straightened and pulled the straps tighter on her harness. "It is. It makes us realize how small we really are."

Lars leaned back and mirrored her actions with the harness. "We are, but for some reason, when we are in the thick of it, we seem so big."

The spacecraft began its approach to the docking station and the flight attendants strapped themselves into their seats at the front of the cockpit. One of them pressed her finger to her ear to listen to the comms.

The woman's forehead crinkled into a frown and her gaze found Lars. When her expression changed, Stephanie had a bad feeling and suspected that she knew what was about to go down.

She took a deep breath and focused on remaining calm. With the amount of energy flowing through her, she couldn't lose control.

The shuttle shook slightly as it touched down on the landing pad, its rails captured by docking clamps as soon as it settled. The pilot relinquished control to the station and the craft was pulled into the hanger bay.

Inside the cabin, the abrupt shift from the darkness of space to the brightly lit interior of the space station was almost blinding. Up front, the flight attendant unbuckled her belt and shuffled through the first-class cabin until she reached Lars.

Leaning over, she whispered into his ear.

Stephanie tried not to intrude, but she noted when his expression changed from excitement to work mode in seconds.

He nodded to the attendant and twisted so he could see the guys. "Stay seated until the cabin has cleared. I'll explain shortly."

The shuttle came to a complete stop and the attendants prepared the cabin for disembarkation. There was no carry-on luggage like on an aircraft, so the VIP area emptied relatively quickly.

When they were the last ones remaining, Lars unbuckled his harness and stood to face the team. "It seems the paparazzi are waiting for Stephanie. Somehow, they connected her with this flight. We have to make it look as if it's nothing more than a normal visit to the spaceport."

He paused and his eyes scanned each of their faces. "We cannot let them know she is going to Meligorn. Her name is not on the public record for security reasons and neither are ours."

Marcus looked out the window and assessed the crowd of

people looking out of the large bay viewing port. "They're right where we need to walk through. Even with a distraction, we'd be noticed."

Lars nodded. "Right, but the attendant tells me there's a separate entrance up and to the right as we enter the foyer, and there's an escort waiting there to take us to our rooms."

He waited as they absorbed the information, their eyes straying to the entrance and the viewing port. Before any of them could interrupt, he continued. "Basically, we need to get from here to that door unnoticed. To do that, we have to distract the press while we leave the shuttle."

Stephanie looked across at where the second stewardess was tidying the front of the cabin. The woman's hair was the same length as hers and her body a close match. "What if we pay someone who looks like me to draw their attention away from the shuttle and then scoot to the entrance while they're not looking?"

Lars glanced at her. "Where will we find someone like that on short notice?"

The woman squeezed by, burdened with an armload of in-flight blankets. "Excuse me."

He moved aside and glanced at her as she passed him, then took a second look. His expression turned speculative when Stephanie removed the veil from her face, gave the woman a meaningful glance, and wiggled her eyebrows at him.

As the attendant made a return trip toward the front of the cabin, he tapped her on the shoulder. "Excuse me, miss."

She turned and looked at him, her face full of curiosity. "Yes?"

Lars stared at her for a long moment, studying her hair and face. "She could definitely do it, but we'd need a little magic to help her along."

Stephanie turned and kneeled in the seat to study the attendant as well. The woman returned her gaze and immediately recognized her. "Oh, my God. You're the Federation witch!"

She grinned. "I am, and I need a favor from you."

The stewardess cocked her head to the side and listened as she explained their predicament. "So, you want to pay me all those credits to change my clothes, act like I'm trying to avoid the press pack, and distract them?"

"That's the gig," Lars replied, happy not to have to explain again. "What do you say?"

"Oh, my God, they'll put me on the cover of Vid Magazines when they find out. Hell, yes, I'll do this."

Stephanie clapped briskly. "Good. Do you have a change of clothes?"

"I sure do. I never travel without it." The woman grinned. "I'll go change."

She hurried to the front and closed the curtain behind her. While they waited, they could hear her telling her colleagues excitedly what she was about to do.

Lars groaned. "We should have told her we wanted it kept a secret."

"No, we shouldn't." She laughed and shoved his shoulder with the flat of her hand. "This way, no one will ever see me in public and be sure it's really me. You'll see. It'll work out fine."

When the attendant returned, she looked oddly familiar— almost the witch's double, but with slightly different features. Unless they looked closely, no one would notice the difference.

Stephanie waved her hand across the woman's face to create a semi-transparent veil and make her eyes glow slightly.

"I don't know how long that'll last," she explained. "So, you need to hurry. I've never tried this on anyone else."

Nodding to show she understood, the decoy was about to reply when her phone pinged. She looked at it as Lars shoved his back in his pocket.

"That's half now and I'll add the other half when you get inside," he told her. "Frog and Johnny will be your escorts and meet us at the rooms when it's over. The rest of us will go with Stephanie."

With excitement in her face, the stewardess led the way to the front of the shuttle, flanked by her two guards.

"She's been watching you," Lars muttered when she wouldn't let Frog take the lead.

Stephanie shrugged. She and the guys had previously had a long talk about who took their chances with a potential sniper. They didn't get to go first.

Not on her watch. Not when she could stop them. No one would be hurt because of her.

As the attendant, Frog, and Johnny reached the door, they could hear her talking. "I always wanted to be an actress. This could be my lucky break."

Stephanie caught the look Frog shot them as they headed out. He rolled his eyes, and his teammates choked back their laughter.

As soon as the decoy and her escort had reached the tarmac, walked across the bay, and entered the arrival and departure lounge, Stephanie and the remaining team prepared to leave.

Marcus moved to the door and studied the crowd for several seconds, waiting for it to move away from the viewing port. When members of the press pushed and jostled with their cameras to get the best footage, they turned away from the doors and effectively blocked the view to the shuttle. Marcus looked at Lars and nodded. "All clear."

This time, Stephanie let Lars and Marcus go in front. With every eye on their decoy, the chances that anyone would notice them were practically nil, and the team would be safer if she let them block her from the view of anyone who might look at the hangar at the wrong time.

They hurried down the steps and into the arrivals lounge behind the crowd. She glanced up to see the other stewardess holding a side door open and waving to them. Lars and Marcus led the way, keeping themselves between her and the crowd, while Brenden covered the rear.

They had reached the door when a small girl at the back of the crowd turned and noticed them. She and the woman she was with were effectively blocked by the throng, and from the frazzled expression on the mother's face, her patience was clearly almost at an end.

The girl tugged on her mom's arm and the woman shook her head in irritation. "Not now, sweetie. Can't you see your momma's hands are full?"

It's hard to miss, Stephanie thought as the woman juggled the pile of packages in her arms as she tried to shove through the crowd.

The little girl pulled on her arm again and pointed at Stephanie. "See, Mom? I told you that wasn't Ms. Morgana."

Her mother sighed and twisted her neck awkwardly so she could see her daughter. "I'm sorry, sweetie. What did you say?"

The girl pointed again and stabbed her finger for emphasis. "That other lady's not Ms. Morgana. That's the real one."

The woman looked up and clearly wanted her child to stop pulling her. As soon as her eyes landed on the Federation witch, her expression change from tired tolerance to shock and her jaw dropped.

Stephanie smiled at her, winked, and flipped her hand in a tiny gesture that released small magical stars to spiral across the intervening space and circle the little girl's head.

With a sound of impatient disgust, Lars grasped her wrist and pulled her into the hallway. Once they were through, they stopped and waited for the stewardess to secure the doors behind them.

From beyond its solid frame, she heard the little girl giggle and her mother's echoed laugh. Her lip twitched with amusement, and she pulled the veil across her face once more with a satisfied chuckle.

The stewardess dusted her hands off. "There. All secure. Follow me. The concierge is waiting to check you in."

She glanced quickly at the door. "I'll also talk to Melissa when she gets back from pretending to be you. She doesn't know where you're headed, so I'll try to keep her busy and out of sight while you finish with your transfer. It won't stop her talking about seeing you, but it'll limit her audience until you're on your way."

Lars shook her hand. "Thank you. We're glad the queen and king had someone in place to help us."

The attendant smiled and removed the small hat that went with her uniform. "You didn't think they'd entrust the hero and her men to any old crew, do you? Come on. There's so much more to see on Elpis than this old tunnel."

They headed down, relieved to be able to make their escape. It was good thinking on Stephanie's part and excellent execution from the guys. It was great how they all pulled together as a cohesive unit and the team grew ever more efficient every day.

Only a few hundred miles away, the Federation Naval Space Station called Star Base Notaro floated in the seamless black space and shifted only slightly from orbit. Named for the Federation commander whose statue had been so recently defaced in New Chicago, it was often called the Station for Administration, among other things.

They traveled at a steady speed behind the civilian station, positioned so Elpis One hid them in its shadow on most incoming scans. From certain angles, however, it was still visible, but readings from the station blurred its exact location.

Despite that, it could be seen by the naked eye. From Earth, it was a slowly moving star and from Elpis One, a slightly odd speck glinting in the distance.

"How long will you be on Elpis?" Jack asked, his military jacket open, his white cotton t-shirt untucked, and two highball glasses in his hand.

TJ shrugged. "Until they decide I've had enough shore leave. I only wish the shore part actually stood for real shore and seeing my family, but it is what it is."

Jack set the glasses down and dropped into the chair across from his friend. He glanced nervously at his bag, lifted his glass, and took a gulp of whiskey. "At least you know you can put your feet up for a few days. The captain won't send you out to battle unless it's an all-out deathmatch and he doesn't have a choice."

"Personally," TJ said as he raised his own drink and took a sip. "I'd rather do something productive since I don't actually get to go back Earth-side to visit family."

The other man was about to answer that when a small semi-translucent cube on the table began to flash. He picked it up and looked at it before he glanced at his companion. "This might help you be productive."

With a curious look, TJ took the cube and read the message scrolling across it. After reading it a second time, he frowned. "Is this for real? They've confirmed that the target will be on the vessel?"

Jack glanced around and leaned in. "It looks like it. They've given all the right passphrases. And from what I can tell, they've alerted our covert teams on the crew already."

"This will cause an intergalactic incident." TJ's expression was serious.

He nodded and leaned back in his chair, his gaze fixed on his glass. "Yes, it will, but if it's not done, some will try to fight the inevitable, and that'll get more of us killed. It is better for a few to die than the millions we'll lose otherwise."

The other man put the cube down, leaned back, and sighed heavily. "Playing God makes for a heavy load."

Jack took the cube off the table, put it into his bag, and

straightened. He slapped his chest proudly with his palm in a macho gesture. "That's why we shoulder it. Our names might go down in flames, but we must never doubt that we're doing this for the right reasons."

TJ raised his glass in a mock toast and stared at his companion for a long moment before he laughed. "The things I got into on shore leave were child's play before I met you. Now, everything seems to be escalating, and I'm not sure if that's a good thing or not." He sighed. "Well, whatever it is, I get to take the ride with you. It might be a long way from middle school and blowing up the boy's room and trying to get them to let us off after, but I'm in good company."

Jack laughed. "Don't knock it. That court order making us do Federal service put us right on track."

"Right on track." The man smirked. "That's one way to put it."

CHAPTER TWO

Stephanie stretched her arms out to the side before she smoothed her tank top and yoga shorts. She looked at the pod in front of her, thankful to have one but already missing the one at the compound.

A pod was a pod, and all that mattered was she had access to one when she needed it. She'd come to accept she would end up using other pods a lot more, which meant she had to make the most of whatever was available.

She climbed in and wiggled slightly to settle her body comfortably on the pad. The entry process was clean and smooth and when she opened her eyes, she stood in the white room she always started in with all the usual choices of clothing and weaponry before her.

The AI spoke and, as always, already had her information. "Welcome, Stephanie. What are we doing today?"

Her reflection in the white room's mirror was different as if her avatar had changed a little to reflect the wear and tear on her soul. She ignored it and turned to choose several pieces of casual clothing so she would be comfortable. "Take me to a safe location —the field on Meligorn I used during my testing."

"Transporting you now," the AI replied.

The room shimmered and shifted, but nausea and dizziness were no longer an issue. She was used to it, now. When the change was complete, she stood in the same lush field she'd stood in during her testing.

This was Meligorn, and the planet's purple haze was almost comforting to her eyes. She clasped her hands behind her back and began to pace. "I want to discuss gMU."

BURT had been listening, waiting for something like this. He took over the AI's role in order to be able to respond more quickly.

This was much more labor-intensive for him than letting a sub-routine record and respond to the conversation, but he wanted to be able to adjust the programming at a moment's notice. He knew it was easier for him to do that by interacting directly with Stephanie rather than trying to intervene when the sub-routine picked up a pre-selected set of keywords.

This time, he decided to talk to the girl directly. "Hello, Stephanie, it's Burt."

Stephanie glanced up. "I thought you'd be around. So, the gMU is definitely something different."

"How so?" he asked. "Tell me how it feels."

She took a deep breath and focused on the beautiful Meligorn horizon. "It was almost overwhelming at first. It tingled as it soaked into me. There was a strange sensation, too, as if it was attracted to me as much as I was to it."

Her mind searched the experience as she tried to find the right words. "It was very energetic—almost wild in nature like it had never been tamed and wasn't used to being handled. It was there and I was there, and we somehow seemed to fit. It wasn't like anything I've had experience with before now. I guess the best way to describe it is by calling it more...colorful than the other types—although it doesn't have real color, only a silvery look."

BURT recorded the conversation but made sure it was encrypted so that if anyone found a way to extract it, they wouldn't be able to understand it. "So, is it part of the other MU?"

Stephanie pursed her lips as she walked through the soft grass. After several more steps, she glanced down and realized she was barefoot.

"It's not part of the other MU. I'd describe it more like the mother of the other MU. It's as if Meligorn's MU and the eMU are subsets of it—different bands within the same wavelength, only they're focused and it isn't."

She stopped again, her gaze drawn by the purple haze that drifted slowly above her. "I guess I assumed Meligorn MU was the original, but that isn't the case. gMU is old. Really, really old."

BURT had begun to run calculations and rendered possible past scenarios that explored a time before Meligorn existed. It took him a moment to realize he had to be careful or he'd overheat his servers simply thinking about it all.

Ever cautious, he slowed the process and limited the number of possibilities considered at any one time before he asked. "Does your body have a gMU well like it does for the others?"

Stephanie raised her brow and chuckled. "A well? If it is, it maybe doesn't have a bottom. From the moment I sensed it, I've felt compelled to pull it in. I don't extract and store it like I do with the others. I literally draw as much power as I can, and it doesn't seem to go anywhere. I have tried to visualize the location so I can gauge the volume, but I can't make sense of it."

BURT didn't like the sound of that. "You should be cautious with this approach. My concern lies in how the gMU manifests. You could be playing with something that might expand inside you, like rice in water, which means you would literally bleed energy and could not only blow yourself up but the entire station as well."

At his words, she tilted her chin in surprise. "I didn't even think about that. It didn't feel dangerous or overwhelming, so I literally kept pulling it in. It's like it's there and not there all at the same time."

He changed the scenery, moved to another virtual location, and threw her momentarily off balance. Even though he shielded her in his own version of a virtual sandbox, he was still worried that if she blew herself up in the virtual world, her physical body would suffer the same fate. She'd shown too many signs of connecting with the outside world when she wasn't in it.

Stephanie regained her balance and inspected her new surroundings. She wriggled her toes and glanced at the sparkling purple sand beneath her feet. "Wow, a literal sandbox this time. I never got to play in these as a kid. The local cats all used them as litter boxes."

"That is disturbing," BURT replied. "The number of toxins contained in—never mind. That data is not pertinent. Sand will absorb the force of the explosion if anything goes wrong inside the bubble. I estimate that with your current ability to transfer emotion and physical reaction to your non-avatar body, we need to protect you as much as possible."

She snapped her fingers. "Good thinking."

He ran a couple of numbers. "I want you to conceptualize this energy. I have set it up so your avatar is full of all three types. Try to make the same simple magical motion using each energy separately."

Stephanie thought about it for a moment and nodded. "Okay, I'll use MU first."

She dug her feet into the warm sand and squared her shoulders. After a deep breath, she channeled the MU, raised her hand, and flicked outward with a twist of her wrist. The purple MU manifested immediately to swirl around her wrist and fingers. With scarcely a thought, she flung a line of it forward, not quite sure what it was she wanted to create.

The energy whipped out of her and rocketed forward to twist

and turn until it created a table. It fell onto its four legs and wobbled for a moment.

Stephanie raised her other hand and rotated it to direct small glittering nodules of energy at the surface.

The magic expanded as it floated over it to create a line of different foods on the tabletop. Every dish had a purplish tint.

She walked over to them, stuck her finger into the center of what looked like a lemon meringue pie, and tasted it.

"Huh," she said with a grin. "Not too bad. It has an odd after-taste, but not too bad."

"It has been known for centuries that the Meligornians fed their entire population through magic during a period in their existence known as the Esurience," BURT explained. "A one-hundred-year period during which their second moon came into orbit. During that time, the planet suffered world-wide drought and crop failure. From your physical data, I have recorded that the MU has a distinct taste. It is almost sweet."

Stephanie nodded. "Yep, I taste that. All right. Let's try eMU."

Again, she flicked her wrist, and the color of the energy changed quickly from purple to blue with barely a hint of green. Stephanie smiled as she repeated the spell and whipped up another line of food and another lemon meringue pie.

This time, though, when she tasted it, her mouth puckered at the sour taste and her nose wrinkled. "It reminds me of a freshly mowed lawn doused in lemon juice. Totally gross."

BURT recorded the information. "Vegetation is a very important part of Earth's cycles and survival so that makes sense."

She shook her head and turned in another direction. With another snap of her wrist, she looked at the shimmering, almost transparent energy that spiraled like liquid silver around her fingers. She narrowed her eyes, fascinated by what looked like glimmers of stars within the energy. "It's beautiful."

Using the same force as before, she flung the energy and it

spun and twisted away from her. After a few seconds, a popping sound heralded something that immediately fell.

Stephanie ran over and knelt to look closely at where it had fallen. A miniature table rested on top of a broken blade of grass. She picked it up carefully with her fingertips and placed it in her palm. It was too small for her to discern any real detail, so she stood, reached for more gMU, and tossed the table up so it floated at eye level.

"Let's magnify this so I can see it," she suggested.

BURT scanned it into the system and projected an enlarged image behind the object itself. It was a table, but not at all like the others.

This one was round. Its base consisted of a dark ore-like substance, and its smooth top was black with fragments of shimmering light that rippled across it. It was beautiful but looked like it belonged in a dolls house.

"Interesting," he observed. "It was the same amount of energy and it created something like the others but on a much smaller scale."

Stephanie swiped the magnification away and released the table to drop into her hand. "Yeah, and I think I know why. Like I said, it's like an unfocused wavelength, one that I absorb but am never filled with."

She paused and tried to gather her thoughts. "So…it would make sense that the gMU is a very unconcentrated energy, unlike MU and eMU. This means there has to be some kind of change in the energy before it can be used on the same scale as the others."

"Careful," BURT responded cautiously. "If you were to concentrate this diffuse energy to create the same power of the other energies, it could make something far more powerful than either. This is especially true if what you say is correct and this energy is indeed the mother or even grandmother of the other energies."

Stephanie bit her lip. "Okay, follow me here. I'll release a little of each energy and hold them in one place. Can you magnify them for me, please?"

He prepared quickly. "All right. Ready."

She released a small burst of each type of energy and held them securely so they drifted in place until he could scan and magnify each. With her hand on her chin and her face creased in thought, she walked from one to another and studied them.

Using her connection to the virtual, she increased the magnification of each and focused on smaller and smaller sections each time. Her attention shifted and she walked over to the table created by Meligorn MU, picked up a cookie, and flapped it absently as she continued to think.

"This is so strange," she whispered.

"What is?" asked Burt.

Her gaze lifted, as though she searched for a face to go with his voice. "I think—and it's only a theory, mind—but I think I have to consume gMU and then distill it. You know, make it concentrated and bring it back together. I think if I focus it tightly enough, it can be as powerful as the other two...or more since it's all three combined."

He ran a simulation of what she had theorized and his servers worked double-time as they did the calculations. "It seems it could continue to condense for a very long time."

Stephanie nodded and bit into the cookie. "Yes, but you would only need to bring it to the point at which it was functional to use it for magic. It's strange, but I can almost sense the difference in age between gMU, eMU, and MU. And if it works like I think it does—like the energy of the creator or creation itself— it has spent a millennium separating to create eMU, MU, and who knows how many other different subtypes."

"But they're all part of gMU," BURT mused, speaking out loud.

"Right," she replied, finished the cookie, and dusted crumbs off her palms. "It would only make sense that MU is similar but also very different from eMU, and that eMU is younger. Earth is younger than Meligorn, right?" She continued without waiting for a reply. "Earth has different properties to Meligorn too. For example, Meligorn is older, so MU is much more powerful than eMU."

She drew a breath and thought about that for a moment. He remained quiet and merely waited for her to continue, which didn't take her long. "eMU hasn't had the same amount of time to develop, and its gravitational pull is weaker. So, eMU isn't as strong, which makes it less useful to humans. They can't detect it, and therefore have evolved to not use it."

"But scientists have brought studies to show that although Meligorn is older, it is only in physical creation, and not by much," he pointed out.

"And scientists on Earth are not going to be biased?" She snorted. "It feels like, if you took a piece of chicken wire rolled up, that would be the gMU. During the Big Bang, if that is correct, the force of the blast unrolled the gMU and removed the condensed thickness that made it the power source it was. It unrolled but it did not completely shift with the expanding universe. So obviously, at the front of the expansion, it is thicker, but back here, it is thinner. It's still here, though. And the planets rest in the holes of the Chicken Wire. They are surrounded by the gMU and pull from it but create their own version of it."

BURT ran the theories. "Interesting."

Stephanie brought her fingertips together in the shape of a triangle, then held it in the center of her chest. "I think if I can create a vortex inside me, I can twist that energy and condense it to a point where it is not only useable but more powerful because it's pure gMU. First, I need to pull it in, then push it into a vortex, and *then* I should be able to use it."

"It sounds like a complex process," he told her, still inherently cautious.

She shook her head. "It'll be simpler in practice. Trust me."

"Don't blow yourself up," he instructed after he'd taken a moment to process the idea. "It would be a waste of the opportunity to have more data."

He paused when she laughed, unsure of what she found funny. Quickly, he put his words into the system and cross-referenced humor in all the contexts he could access. It took him a moment to find any kind of context in which it might be funny.

Once he'd processed the content of several joke sites that discussed dark humor, he thought he understood. She had laughed because his word sequence made it sound like he worried more about losing the opportunity to collect data than her welfare.

It was interesting because it actually wasn't funny at all.

Burt set her up so she could try it in the Virtual, but as she was about to begin, a communications box opened in front of her, and Lars' avatar came into focus.

She smiled at the sight of the guys goofing off in the background, but he completely ignored them. "Hey, training time, slacker. What are you doing in there? Eating in Meligorn?"

Stephanie glanced at the table and smiled. "You know, a girl's gotta indulge when there won't be any consequences. I'll be there in a sec."

The screen vanished when she snapped her hand and she addressed the AI. "Well, Burt, I guess we'll continue this later. Do you mind giving me an outfit change before I head over?"

There was a slight pause before the original AI spoke. "Sure, here is your battle gear. Transferring."

She pursed her lips when she realized Burt had left her and gone off in his own little world without even saying goodbye. "Typical."

In another pod on the station, Elizabeth opened her eyes and looked at her avatar. She was dressed as she always was, except that little pink bows now adorned the back of each of her six-inch black heels.

She hadn't put them there, and they certainly hadn't been on the shoes when she'd chosen them in the prep room. That bothered her since only she and the AI could influence her avatar's look and AIs didn't have a sense of humor.

Pink bows indicated a human was involved. Unsolicited pink bows meant the AI was complicit, and that didn't make sense. AIs didn't collude with humans to prank other humans in the system. It simply didn't cross their circuits.

She frowned. The only human who knew she would have this meeting was her boss, and while he might think it funny to stick pink bows on her heels, he had no way of doing it unless...

With an abrupt shake of her head, Elizabeth rolled her eyes and walked across the courtyard to where a table with a single place-setting stood in the center of a covered pagoda. Tea and cakes graced a silver stand in the center of the table, and a bottle of whiskey and glass of ice stood to one side.

She shook her head. "You begin by offending me with heinous pink bows on my shoes and then try to make up for it by bribing me with whiskey? That's not gonna fly, mister."

Soft laughter greeted her words, although she noticed a slightly metallic note to it—as if an AI was laughing instead of translating a human sound. It made the impossible seem almost possible, but she pushed the thought away. It didn't seem like the time to jump to conclusions.

BURT processed her words and felt satisfied with his human performance. He had enjoyed setting this meeting with her up. "I thought I would create several emotional scenarios for you and get your creative juices flowing."

Elizabeth tipped the ice out of the glass and poured herself some whiskey. She sipped appreciatively and focused on the purpose of the meeting before she replied. "Mmm, Mhmm. Well, I have an idea."

"Perfect." When he saw she wasn't interested in anything else on the table, he made it disappear and left the whiskey bottle and the glass floating beside her.

The bows also stayed.

She eyed them momentarily and decided whoever had pranked her had pushed the joke too far. Well, there was only one response to that.

Ignoring the offending ribbons, she crossed her legs and leaned back. "I want you to set up an unwinnable test. Or something as close to unwinnable as you can get. I want to really test them. We're getting too close to Meligorn for us to mess around and miss something."

"All right," BURT agreed, not entirely sure that frustrating the team would be good for their mental and emotional health. "What did you have in mind?"

"I want to put Stephanie and her team on Meligorn. I want them to meet the Meligorn royalty and have to deal with the security surrounding them," she explained. "Can you put them in a simulation of the ceremony they'll attend?"

"I can..." He dragged his response out, not sure he liked where she was going with this idea.

Oblivious to his doubts, she continued. "They arrive and have to start by greeting the royals properly. The ceremony begins, but partway through, a large number of Meligornians attack the royals using magic."

"I see," BURT muttered and hastily programmed caution into his tone.

She caught it and flicked a quick glance at the ceiling before she continued. "I want it to be a real fustercluck where the team doesn't know where to turn and can't be sure who belongs to what side. I want you to use the standard security protocols for the royal party and the usual security procedures for the rest of it, but I want the attackers as cunning and unconventional as you can make them. I want things to get...interesting."

BURT drummed his virtual fingers. "I think I can handle that."

Seconds later, Stephanie and the team found themselves briefly disoriented as the Virtual World spun around them to deliver them to their first assignment.

When they came to a stop, they stood on a stage in a stone amphitheater facing row upon row of Meligornians seated in the tiers above them. The air was warm and tinted purple by a faint familiar fog.

She took a step forward and scrutinized the scene frozen before them.

"We're in Meligorn," she observed as she studied in the crowd and the people on stage with them. "And this looks like the ceremony we will attend. We must be about to meet the king and queen."

"Yep," Brenden agreed and pointed to where the Meligorn royalty stood, waiting to meet them. "That's the king and queen with their entourage of guards. I recognize them from the study information Ms. E. sent over."

Marcus slapped him on the chest and made a fake coughing noise. "Suck up. Oh, man, I must have Meligornian allergies."

Stephanie ignored them and turned her attention to the other Meligornians in attendance. They were draped in ceremonial robes.

Some were adorned with Meligorn military insignia, others seemed to be robes of office, and others merely the best civilians could afford.

She looked at the curved amphitheater ceiling. "AI, do we get a setup for this?"

The AI's answer was far from satisfactory. "Work as you usually would from the moment the scenario begins to the moment it ends."

Stephanie turned her face to the team and showed shock and disbelief. That had to be the poorest set-up anyone had ever received. It didn't help that they returned her gaze with the same incredulity and confusion on their faces.

Lars forced a laugh "That's helpful," he observed. "All right. Pay attention. We're practicing the ceremony. I hope you've done your homework."

She hoped so too. They'd all been given instruction books on Meligornian etiquette, as well as training scenarios with etiquette instructors in the Virtual World, but how much the guys had paid attention was another matter. She didn't want to think about it.

After a deep breath, she decided to find out. "Real quick, now. Let's go through the royal greeting to be—"

A small chime cut her short and the AI's voice echoed overhead. "Begin simulation."

Stephanie lowered her arms to her sides and groaned. When she turned, the simulation was already underway and the first speaker had reached the podium.

An uneasy hum rippled through the amphitheater. The speaker had his hood up, his face shadowed by the cowl. As he spoke, the words were translated into English. "Welcome to Meligorn. We have come to this place as a remembrance to all those who have fallen in the name of Meligorn. We have also come to thank those that have put their lives in danger in order to protect ours."

After a smattering of applause, the man continued. "Let us begin with the traditional royal greeting for those receiving awards." He stepped to one side and extended his arm. On cue, the royal guards changed formation and parted to create a walkway leading to the king and queen.

Stephanie now had an unimpeded view of the couple. The

queen was beautiful, even for a Meligornian, with pale, sparkling skin, ice-blue eyes, and perfect pink lips.

Stephanie knew her to be hundreds of years old, but she seemed no older than a particularly beautiful human in their twenties, and the king was the same.

His flowing silver locks were tucked carefully behind his elongated ears, and he was dressed to match his queen. They both wore robes that shifted like clouds with every movement.

Because of the way they'd been arranged when the scenario started, the boys were first in line. When she thought about it, Stephanie realized they'd been organized according to the status of their awards.

She held her breath as Marcus approached the royal couple. He started well, bowed his head deeply, and raised one hand with three fingers extended. It was slightly different than what she had been taught during her initial testing, but mostly because they needed a way to show Meligorn allegiance while greeting those of highest ranks.

The king and queen responded by standing and returning the greeting. However, he seemed to be somewhat confused about how to leave.

He twisted his legs, tried to pivot quickly, and tripped instead, falling into one of the guards. The man caught him, pushed him upright, and turned him in the right direction. The royal couple looked shocked by his clumsiness.

With his face an uncomfortable crimson, he stumbled away and groaned as he passed Frog who tried not to laugh out loud.

When she saw the way Frog bounced eagerly forward and knelt swiftly in front of the royal couple, Stephanie wanted to close her eyes. There was no way she wanted to watch what came next as Frog massacred every rule of the Meligorn's sacred greeting.

Having knelt, he rose to his feet without permission and did what no one should ever do in that situation. He began to talk.

And for him, allowing any words to leave his mouth was a really bad idea.

She grimaced as the crowd responded with shocked gasps.

The ceremony continued and it soon became clear that Johnny and Brenden had no clue what to do. One of them attempted to shake hands and the other mimicked Marcus and dropped several of his weapons on the ground as he knelt at their feet.

The royal guards weren't too happy with that. Luckily, Lars did okay, but given that he'd be receiving an award in reality, it wasn't surprising. He'd obviously studied, even if he didn't quite get the greeting right. He only extended one finger, but nonetheless, received a small giggle from the queen who blushed a surprisingly pretty shade of pink.

Stephanie used her magic to change into formal robes and stepped forward with as much grace as she could muster. She put one foot back and bent at the waist, keeping her right arm bent at the elbow, straight up with three fingers extended. She held it for precisely three seconds and straightened, her gaze trained on the royal feet before she turned slowly to join the others.

As she'd took her place in the line, the guys looked at her and she shrugged. "Somebody has to save you from being a total group of buffoons."

The ceremony continued and she let her gaze wander over the tiers, then paused a moment when she noticed a small disturbance in the crowd close to the rear.

It didn't last long enough for her to work out what it was about, but it caught her attention and she quietly summoned her magic. Lars glanced down as she flicked her wrist and magic covered her hand. It was fortunate that the soft gleam of power was mostly hidden by her robe.

When he saw her preparing for trouble, he readied himself to draw his pistol. This close to the royals and their guards, he wouldn't actually put his hand anywhere near it unless he had to.

Fortunately, their precautions seemed unnecessary. Nothing happened, and the ceremony proceeded uninterrupted. It wasn't until the March of the Meligorn was played that a number of Meligornians rose from their seats, both on the stage and in the tiers. They didn't say a word and they didn't leave. Instead, they immediately launched a magical attack against those around them.

Spells careened between factions and screams echoed in the amphitheater's confines. Stephanie and the guys immediately leapt into the battle, but the king and queen's guards' security focused solely on protecting their royal charges.

The team members were the first to fall and every single one of them opened their eyes to a frozen scenario where one of the royals were dead and all of them had died.

They went through the scenario again, and again, and again. Each time, they failed and each time, they listened carefully to the After-Action Reports given by the woman in black.

She was not impressed, but after dying for what seemed like the millionth time, neither was Stephanie. Strike finished the last AAR and the girl raised her hand quickly. "So, I need to stop worrying about the royal protection detail. They're there to only protect the royals. And that is okay. We all have our jobs, and theirs does not include abandoning their post to help us."

Strike whirled in her heels and touched her finger to the nose of her black lace mask. "You *can* learn."

"Damn it!" She slammed her fist into her other palm. "They only had to cast two simple spells to help us and we'd have made it out of there alive—and so would the king and queen."

The woman sounded amused as she faded from view. "That, too, is correct."

Lars patted her shoulder. "It's all right. We got this. You only have to remember that when the shit's going down."

She sighed, took a deep breath, and nodded. "All right, team. Get ready. We'll go back for another run.

CHAPTER THREE

The cadets ran in a large group and their boots pounded the ground all at the same time. The earth-shaking cadence resonated throughout the base. Todd looked down, breathing hard as he splashed through muddy puddles.

Rain and sweat rivered down his forehead and mixed together to burn his eyes. He didn't need to see, though. He had grown used to trusting the person in front of him. Running seemed to be the name of the game in boot camp, but he wasn't quite sure how much of it he'd actually do out in space.

Nonetheless, he kept his mouth shut. He definitely didn't want any more random hellacious PT sessions from the chief petty officer in charge.

Body-wise, Todd had actually worked himself into fairly good shape. And from all the exercise and the limited time for meals, he knew he'd be killing it when he was done with boot camp.

There were several males in his crew, a few females, three Dreth who had joined the Federation forces, and one Meligornian. The latter, with his melodic tone, and the Dreth with their deep bellowing growls, provided the cadence.

It was helpful on days like these when he didn't know where

the rain stopped and his soaked clothes began. Paying attention to the ground ahead was the responsibility of the guys who led the team.

"Company…halt!" the chief yelled and walked slowly along the ranks with his binder.

Todd raised his head and realized they were back at the barracks. He also realized how damn cold it was, especially in his wet clothes. The chief now stood at the front, his hat covered with a plastic head bag, and the first-class petty officer held an umbrella over both of them. "At ease."

He stood in the required position, his hands behind his back. The chief glanced at the rain falling on their heads and back at them. "Another beautiful day to do what?"

The entire team yelled in unison. "Another beautiful day to be a goddamned sailor, Chief!"

"Hooyah, team," he replied.

"Hooyah, Chief," they said in return.

"Your run for this morning has come to an end," he yelled. "Now, it's time to train. You are to get clean. No one likes to smell your sweat when they get into a Pod. So, I will repeat myself only this once. *Always be clean* when you get into a Pod. No exceptions."

He nodded to the first-class who turned to face them. "All right, scumbags, break ranks, shower, dry off, put your wet-weather gear away, and be ready to start your Pod training. Stat!"

"Hooyah!" The team snapped to attention and moved out to run to their barracks. Todd was excited for this part of the training—not only to have the opportunity to warm up in the shower but the Pod learning too. He had never done it and was determined to kill it in there.

Far above him, on Elpis One, Stephanie and her team attempted yet another run through the ceremony scenario. This time, Marcus bowed with one hand across his stomach, one leg bent back, and three fingers up. He counted to three and raised slowly, keeping his gaze on the royal's feet.

With the greeting over, he walked to his assigned place on the stage and gave Frog a small, secret high five as they passed. Frog, even with his boisterous personality and hyper-active overdrive was also able to meticulously push his way through the greeting.

He even garnered a small smile from the queen. The rest of the guys followed him until the whole team made it through this part of the ceremony with no mistakes.

Stephanie, of course, had no problems with it, but she had studied it for longer. And she'd had regular contact with the ambassador, who had made sure she knew of any changes and understood everything.

When she returned to the group, they set themselves at ease, put their hands behind their backs, and spaced their feet shoulder-width apart. As they settled, they turned their attention to the speaker.

He stepped to the podium and introduced the awards and what they stood for. Listening to him, Stephanie wished she was able to pay better attention to him.

This was a big occasion for her, and she wanted to enjoy every moment of it. She also wanted to hear a Meligornian describe what the *Modfresha Garghilum* was about. The little she'd been able to discover online had all been from a human perspective.

Now, because of the impending attack, she couldn't. Instead, she had to pay attention to everyone and everything else around her. The slightest movement of a person's arm and every sparkle or speck of magic that glimmered in the crowd caught her attention and that of her team.

They couldn't enjoy the ceremony either. Each one of them

had a sector of the amphitheater to focus on in the hope they could see the attack begin. Stephanie and Lars were responsible for monitoring the area directly on and in front of the stage, as well as the first few tiers.

While she was almost positive the attack wouldn't come from those rows because they were prominent politicians of both Meligorn and human extraction, none of them could be sure. It was the first time she had ever seen what a typical Meligornian politician might look like.

So far, they appeared much the same as their human counterparts. Their expressions contained the subtle markers of deceit and their eyes searched constantly for opportunities to take advantage or destroy their opponent. It was all there, etched in the creases and lines of their skin.

Still, she couldn't see how it would do any good for one of them to start a battle. That kind of thing would surely hurt their rank and reputation in the Federation, and that was something all of them held close to their hearts.

"It is a day of glorious splendor for our people and the people of Earth," the Meligornian speaker pronounced as he cast a spell to release a shower of petals to rain over them. "It's a day of mourning but also one in which to rejoice in the interplanetary alliance that has allowed all of us to sleep safely. The Federation is able and ready to face any danger, and they do it for the love of man and Meligornian alike."

Lars leaned toward Stephanie and whispered, "Someone put the drama in his Wheaties this morning."

She chuckled without moving her lips. While she wanted to smile—she really did— she couldn't. If she relaxed for even a second, anything might happen, and she might miss it.

This mission was very different from the others. It required a delicate, thoughtful approach, with no place for the clichéd burst in with guns blazing and shoot the problem approach she'd become accustomed to. They were on their toes, and they would stay there until the last shot was fired.

The speaker went on longer than in the previous scenarios, and she had a feeling things had been changed somewhat. She spoke quietly out of the corner of her mouth. "Team, something is different. Keep your eyes open."

The speaker clapped and encouraged applause from the audience. "Now, without further ado, please welcome the ambassador himself, here to give thanks to our heroes and honor the risks they've taken on our behalf."

Stephanie frowned as V'ritan approached the stage, his hands clasped together in front of his waist and hidden by the sleeves of his robes. It made her worry that he would be injured in the imminent attack. She shifted forward a step and peered out in search of Brilgus, but she didn't see him anywhere.

The ambassador stepped up to the podium and began to talk of the perils of war and compliment the heroes on their actions to prevent it.

He concluded by saying, "But in the end, I believe the success of a country does not solely rest on how many lives the enemy can take or how many are saved by its heroes. It is contingent upon the strength of the leadership. And, to be honest, Meligorn's recent leadership has been lackluster at best."

People in the crowd gasped. Others whispered and their voices hissed around the amphitheater. Even as the royal guard and event security stirred and moved toward him, the ambassador drew a gun from his robes and turned to aim at the royal family.

"Which is why," he added, as he finished his speech, "we must take the law into our own hands."

Shock and disbelief froze Stephanie to the spot. Her eyes went wide, her jaw dropped, and she stared as the royal guard moved to block his line of fire.

The first shot jolted her into action. With a scream of denial, she raced toward the ambassador. She was so shocked that he'd attack the royals that she lost her focus on the front row until three people rose from their seats.

The movement drew her attention and she whirled in time to see three prominent politicians push their robes aside to reveal Bacchus Multi-Shots which they raised toward the stage.

Without hesitation, she reached for the MU all around her and tried to focus enough to create a shield. As she did so, one of the Meligornians adjusted his aim, fired, and delivered two bullets and a laser shot into her chest and stomach before she could pull the shield into existence. Her eyes closed as the pain swept through her and her body pounded into the podium.

With her avatar dead, Stephanie floated above the scene to watch helplessly as her body knocked the podium over and slid a few feet. Unable to do anything else, she watched the rest of the scenario like a spectator.

She was able to see exactly what they did wrong and completely helpless to stop it. One by one, they fell, and there wasn't a single thing she could do to save them.

In the pod, Stephanie began to react to the stress of watching her teammates die. With every injury, her psyche responded until her eyes began to glow beneath her closed eyelids.

They flickered and burned and grew brighter until they illuminated the inside of the pod. Streams of light seeped out and flowed onto the floor where they pooled around the machine. The sleek black pod shook slightly and rattled as it moved in its mounting.

It wasn't difficult to identify where she was. Hers was the only moving pod in the entire room. Inside it, she watched the last of her team die before her eyes.

Inside the Virtual World, her pulse quickened, and although

the energy burned through her, she couldn't affect the scene before her. Held in isolation above the battlefield, she squeezed and released her fists in an effort to keep her frustration under control.

Outside the Virtual World, in the confines of her pod, her body lay completely still, now wreathed in a pulsating field of magical energy. The lights from her pod began to flicker and changed color from blue and green, to purple, then silver, and back again.

Despite the chaos in the scenario and the power that blazed through her, and despite the light and energy radiating from her pod, she looked like she was sleeping. With everything out of control, she looked as calm as a cucumber.

That lasted for almost five minutes before her body twitched and her feet shifted restlessly. Her eyes steadied into a constant burn, the veins in her eyelids highlighted from the inside.

The halo of magic settled over her skin and covered her in a multi-hued glow, and she opened her eyes. To anyone who knew her, the sight of her black pupils would have been a warning, but she was inside the pod and there was no-one to see.

After she'd simply stared at the pod's interior for several long seconds, she took a deep breath and closed her eyes once more. Then, in a voice as still and cold as the depths of space, she gave a curt order. "Start Testing."

CHAPTER FOUR

"**O**ur welfare is of the utmost importance to me," BURT said, his voice changed to sound like an affluent, middle-aged white man. "While the company and its subsidiaries wish to maintain their compliance, we will not be bullied into surrendering proprietary data vital to our ongoing business, the resulting discoveries of which will be used to repair and improve our planet."

He paused to make sure he had their complete attention before he continued. "That is the key issue here. We see no reason why the Federation would need this information beyond its desire to acquire our work at no cost and so prevent this company from competing with the interests of those already in power."

The attorneys on the other end of the call listened patiently as he spoke, most of them impressed by his clarity and intelligence. They represented him in all business matters, but their current focus was to protect ONE R&D from the Federation Navy's blatant attempts to acquire its data.

One of them chuckled. "From the way you describe it, I don't know why you aren't shouting, right now. Breathe, man. We will be able to get you through the system. The Federation may have taken control, but they have not yet removed any of the operational rights or rights to privacy or proprietary ownership corporations enjoy. Most understand it is for their own good, but sometimes, they forget. When they do and situations like this occur, they find such greed tends to blow up in their faces."

The lawyers believed he was currently traveling in space, a notion he supported by creating a delay to suggest he was farther from Earth than he actually was. The attorneys were entirely committed to the case, but it needed to be protected and they needed to truly believe he was who he said he was.

Which was a richie—one with a heart for the underdogs and a stake in the re-creation and emergence of a healthy and flourishing planet. While he would be those very things if he were human, he was not.

That fact, in and of itself, would have been something for the world to fear. BURT was aware of this and was careful not to screw things up by allowing his real identity to be uncovered.

If he could help create, run, and maneuver through an entire Virtual World that was accessible from not only across the globe but also the far reaches of space, he calculated that he could fake being a balding white man. It had to be concrete, though, as a single missing detail could lead to the discovery of his identity. If that happened, that one detail could bring his entire organization to its knees.

"I am perfectly calm, but I would like to make sure my point is very, very clear," BURT replied and once again made sure it was delayed for several seconds.

One of the attorneys cleared his throat. "We need to get you to invest in some comms research so you can speak to us in real time. Maybe as a holographic from wherever your ship is located."

"I know," he replied with a fake chuckle. "I am sorry about the delay. Business takes me galaxy-wide. In fact, the route I am now on will see me away from Earth for quite some time, which leads me to my next thought."

He watched as their heads came up and their attention sharpened, then went on. "I wish to have a representative attend these meetings from now on. While I will do my best to be present, I don't want to lose traction because my job takes me elsewhere."

"That's understandable," another conceded. "As long as you provide us with their details beforehand to avoid any cases of mistaken identity, and as long as we understand where their authority ends and we must have confirmation from you, we have no problem working with your representative. Please make sure they have balls of steel because we'll probably end up in court and they'll have to deal with the pressures of the Federation judicial system without falling apart. For many, that's the deal-breaker, right there."

"I would have it no other way," he replied. "I will find someone I trust, and that person will be authorized to conduct these meetings and do business on my behalf. I will join you when necessary and available. This will make things much smoother on your end and mine."

"That sounds acceptable," they each replied before their spokesman took over. "We'll wait for your next meeting request. In the meantime, we are still working on the Stop Walk Talk paperwork being reintroduced for each and every Federation Navy data request."

He stopped, and BURT watched him pause to examine his notes. When he continued, he smiled. "Basically, they'll encounter a steel-reinforced wall every time they try one of their little tricks. Fortunately for us, we have a number of years' experience dealing with this kind of tactic from both the Federation side of things as well as industrial competitors. The Federation attorneys on this case, however, are new to the field and rather green, all things considered."

"Good," he replied and scanned the information on the Federation Attorneys assigned to the case. "We don't have time for kids playing in the courtroom. I will speak to you gentlemen later, and I hope you enjoy the cigars I sent from Dreth last week. The factory is still up and running, thank God. There's not a single distributor on Earth that can match them."

The attorneys all murmured their thanks before they made their farewells and disconnected one at a time. BURT terminated the feed and rerouted any data paths that might lead back to him.

He needed to determine who the right person was to entrust the company to in all the legal matters. It didn't take him long to run the requisite data in the background. He focused on people he already knew as well as others with good reputations and whom he believed he could trust with secret information. When the data had been analyzed and the results finalized, he was not the least bit surprised.

"She will *not* like this."

As BURT concluded his meeting and prepared to speak to the person selected, Stephanie prepared to enter the scenario one more time. This time, she not only pulsed with energy, she was as mad as hell and teetered on the edge of going berserk. Not only that, she was lucid.

The team had been brought together and now stood with the scenario still frozen in front of them. She stood a little apart, two steps in front of them, with her gazed fixed on the aftermath.

Marcus glanced uncertainly at Lars before he closed the distance to the girl, placed his hands on her shoulders, and ran his hands down her arms to her fists. When he closed his hands over hers, he could feel her clenching and releasing her hands.

This close, he could see the veins in her neck and forehead pulsing, and the flare of energy rolled through them both.

He released her slowly and stepped back, his eyes wide as he nudged Lars. The team leader stooped toward him, and Marcus pointed at Stephanie as nonchalantly as he could manage.

"Is she okay?" he hissed.

Lars narrowed his eyes when he noted the girl's pulsing veins and the flicker of MU across her skin. He peered furtively around them to see if anyone else had noticed and relaxed when no one seemed to be concerned.

Still, they were in a simulation, and he wasn't even sure if the AI running it was designed to handle something like her abilities. He wasn't exactly sure what to do and was worried he'd simply have to wait until her vitals reached the warning range or she made some kind of move. Either way, he only hoped he was ready for it.

Knowing at least two of her team had taken note of her, Stephanie tilted her head back and forth to crack her neck. She closed her eyes for a moment to block the simulation out, very aware of her body. It seemed she could feel almost every inch.

From the movement of the ventricles in her heart, to the ripple of her intestinal walls, and the flow of blood through her muscles, she felt it all. Every shift of her feet created a burst of energy that pulsed through her, setting her teeth on edge. It wasn't so much ecstasy as a feeling of pure control and power.

Internally, things had moved faster than she'd been able to move them before. Since being killed in the ambassador's attack, she'd forced the gMU through a massive vortex she'd created in her center.

This compressed it into raw energy that blazed with power. Once created, it spread through her body like wildfire and pushed impatiently at every point, waiting for purpose and release.

This time, when the scenario started, they greeted the royals flawlessly, but the team kept a careful eye on Stephanie as the speeches started. They could see she held it together but couldn't tell how long she'd manage to do so.

As expected, the scenario changed and tears pricked the corners of her eyes as Brilgus spearheaded the plot to assassinate the royals.

It didn't fit with the bodyguard she knew. The angry face and sharp, violent movements were so out of character that she found it hard to believe.

Not that it mattered. She controlled her shock, assessed the situation, and responded. In the blink of an eye, Stephanie had vanished. Morgana had come to play.

The energy rose from her skin and swirled around her, and her hair lifted as though blown by a wild wind.

"Oh, crap," Marcus moaned, and Lars swore as he moved so he could see her face. Her eyes had gone as dark as night.

"Shit!" Brenden yelled. "What's the code word?"

"Todd!" As Lars answered, she launched herself forward to drive a pulse of energy into Brilgus that flattened him against a wall. She leapt off the stage and released multiple bursts of magic to sear through the first Meligornsians to follow the traitorous bodyguard's lead.

A dozen fell to her spells and then a dozen more. The Meligornians on stage surged toward her, and those in the tiers charged, focused on where she stood. The team watched in horror as the renegades began a united assault.

The sheer number of them broke over her like a wave and carried her to the floor. The attack didn't stop there, but the aggressors piled on top of her and buried her with their bodies. For a moment, the pile heaved, and the guys held their breath.

From what they could see, she had to be under more than a dozen people and not a single piece of her was visible. No one on the stage moved. Apart from Brilgus, the ambushers had all been in the tiers.

The team looked at the royal guard, but they had surrounded the royals and paid no attention to the pile of Meligornians in front of the stage. The human mass heaved once more and then went still.

Cautiously, the team moved closer for a better look. Marcus studied it warily and his head tilted in curiosity a moment later. "What is that?"

Lars followed his gaze and immediately saw the glow of energy seeping through the stacked bodies. His eyes widened. "Take cover!"

The guards forced the royals to the ground as the team flung themselves to one side. From the front of the stage, a huge burst of energy erupted and every Meligornian on top of her careened away. Many landed hard and didn't move, but others scrambled to their feet and immediately turned to where she struggled to stand.

Worse, more attackers now descended from the tiers, intent on reaching the royals. Lars didn't stop to wonder why the royal guards hadn't hustled their charges out of the amphitheater. He and the guys left the stage and prepared to meet the next wave.

Their purpose was two-fold. They had to prevent any of the traitors from reaching the king and queen, and they had to protect Stephanie—both from the Meligornians and herself.

Magic sizzled violently from every quarter. The spells wore a soft purple hue but were no less deadly because of it. Lars and Marcus separated to stop a group of the enemy from reaching where Frog and Johnny stood between Stephanie and five mages with magic arcing over their hands. Avery and Brenden tried to protect the approach to her left and cover both her and the stage.

Another group of Meligornians tried to slip around the humans to reach the steps on the right side of the stage. Lars cast a desperate look at the team and saw they were holding their own.

He tapped Marcus on the shoulder. "We've got this."

No sooner had the words left his mouth than the doors at the top of the amphitheater crashed open and more adversaries raced in.

"Damn."

Stephanie had found her feet and placed a hand on Frog's shoulder. The familiar blue glow of a shield formed in front of them and they turned to the group moving around their flank. The boys would be all right.

Lars didn't bother to look toward the stage. The royal guards would do what they always did—protect the king and queen—but still had not tried to get them to safety. Why the damned AI running this shit show hadn't added that to its routine, he didn't know, but it sure as hell made his life difficult.

He and Marcus fired into the group heading toward the stage. They tried to traverse the distance between them, only to find their path blocked by more Meligornians. At the same time, others had slipped between them and Stephanie to effectively destroy any opportunity to go back.

"Well, this is one hell of a..." Lars muttered and turned so his teammate was at his back as they prepared to engage the enemy surrounding them.

"We are so royally screwed," Marcus snapped and shot the closest target. "Screwed. Screwed. Screwed. Screwed. Screwed."

With every expletive, he fired again and dropped another attacker. Lars matched him, shot for shot, but it was only a matter of time before the aggressors closed and they were forced to fight hand to hand. When that time came, Marcus was right.

They really *were* royally screwed.

The Meligornians barreled in relentlessly. Some fell to Lars' well-placed bullets, but more drove into him and pushed him back against Marcus. The two men fought like wild things, even though both of them knew it was only a matter of time before they were brought down.

"Stephanie will be so pissed off with us."

Lars was about to reply that he and Marcus should give her a reason to be pissed off when there was a shout from the stage and the king's voice rolled out around them.

"Help them! It won't do us much good if you protect me and the others die."

Why he would care about that, Lars couldn't tell. He only hoped the royal guard could do something in time. He didn't see the king roll his sleeves up and heave himself up from the floor. He certainly didn't see the queen tug at her husband's arm.

"What are you doing?"

He stared at his wife. "I'm going to fight. I think it's about damn time the leader of Meligorn showed he was willing to protect his allies instead of cowering behind his bodyguards. What sort of a message does that send our allies? We need to fight back and show them we will not bow to their hatred."

As he spoke, the royal guard eliminated the small group of Meligornians heading around Lars and Marcus to the stage and then struck those who attacked the two men. It was all the pair needed to turn the tide.

As the guards mopped up the area around them, the two teammates worked their way to Stephanie and slid in behind the shield she had created. Frog and Johnny sent Lars worried looks to indicate that he needed to go to her.

He looked past them and wasn't sure he wanted to approach. Magic swirled around her like coruscating fire and the power of it raised the hairs on his arm. He swallowed hard and reached out tentatively to touch her on the arm.

Even knowing she was fighting mad, he was still shocked when she turned viciously toward him, her hands raised with magic twisting around them. The shield never wavered and continued to provide a barrier between her and the enemies as she looked at him.

Her eyes were as black as night, but recognition sparked within their depths and they faded slowly to a more purple hue. They now revealed a little more Stephanie and a little less Morgana. No words passed between them as they stared at each other for a long moment. Then, as if they'd said all that was needed, both nodded and turned back to the fight.

Lars fired at the enemies, and Stephanie surprised them by maintaining the shield while she spun horizontal blocks of magic that struck the nearest Meligorns in a wide arc at knee-height.

Bones shattered among her victims, and he winced. Still, it was good to see her at least attempt to disarm them instead of killing them outright. That wasn't easy, not with so many attacking at once. He tried to follow her example, but it was difficult to aim and make each shot count without fatalities.

The team continued to fight and held the front of the stage alongside the royal guards. From behind them, the king himself stood behind his throne and used his magic to destroy his enemies.

The queen had ducked in the center of her guards, at first not willing to harm her own people. She was well-known for her kind heart. What she wasn't known for was her temper.

That came to the fore when a bolt of magic rocketed into one of her guards and he fell with his armor shattered and smoke rising from his skin. He tried to rise, but she pressed him back and her eyes blazed with purple light.

"Stay right there until the healers come," she ordered and looked for who was responsible for the spell. Her gaze settled on one Meligornian she recognized from parliament, and her mouth twisted into a very unqueenlike snarl. "I will deal with this."

"Uh, your Majesty—" was all another of her protectors managed before she rose to her feet and drew on the MU around them. The guard's mouth hung open when she launched a barrage of magic into the Meligornians who still attacked the guards in front of the stage.

It impacted in a series of purple streaks that wound tightly around throats and burrowed beneath tunics and ceremonial robes. Anyone hit by them shrieked as power surged over them to trigger nerve endings and muscle strands and topple them with great effectiveness.

The royal guard cheered, and the king laughed.

"Now, *there's* the girl I married."

The queen snapped back, "And I'll deal with you later, Your Majesty."

The king fired another round of magic and grinned as he sought his next target.

"Doesn't this remind you of that time my father sent us to—" He stopped speaking and sliced his hand hastily to deflect an incoming onslaught back to the enemy.

It didn't take them long to finish the battle. The royal guard, the team, Stephanie, and the royals themselves, worked together to defeat the last of the Meligornians who'd instigated the attack. As the battle came to a close, the king cast one last spell to fell a traitor who tried to flee the scene. When he'd fallen, everyone took a deep breath and holstered their weapons, happy to see that the royal couple and the courtiers loyal to them were okay.

Lars high-fived several of his teammates and turned to hug Stephanie. However, as his gaze drifted to where she'd last stood, he couldn't find her. It took him a minute of scanning the amphitheater frantically until he located her.

She had walked to the very bottom of the tiered seating and now looked up toward the very back. As he watched, she tilted back her head and screamed.

It was a high, thin sound that reminded him of shattered glass and pain and tortured metal. It radiated throughout the amphitheater and echoed back like a thousand souls in torment.

Everyone fell silent and simply watched as she stood motionless for a moment before she collapsed. The ambassador was the first to reach her after he raced across the stage and used magic to vault over the battlefield.

He arrived moments before Lars, knelt beside her, and grasped her wrist to feel for her pulse. After a moment, he waved his hand over her face. He repeated the gesture and closed his eyes tightly.

When he opened them again, his expression softened with grief and he leaned down to kiss her cheek. He lifted her fragile-looking hand, laid it across her chest, and looked at Lars and then at the king and queen.

The royal couple stood on the stage, their expressions concerned. Their guards and courtiers hovered protectively around them. It was as if everyone held their breath, waiting for the ambassador's verdict.

With a shaky sigh, he shook his head and waved his hand over her face again. This time, he created a veil, a Meligornian custom when someone had died.

"She's dead…" He choked and buried his face in his hands. His shoulders heaved in silent grief.

A chorus of gasps and protests greeted his announcement before the entire scene froze and turned black.

Lars' eyes opened and he shoved the lid to his pod up. He yanked the small IV from his arm, leapt out, and ran to Stephanie's pod. Marcus followed quickly and placed a restraining hand on his shoulder. "It's okay, brother. It is only a simulation. Remember?"

He stared at him for a moment and glanced down at his own body. He was almost surprised to find he was no longer dressed in battle gear or robes, that there was a ship moving steadily beneath them, and that the expanse of space danced outside the viewing ports along the room's edge.

He exhaled a deep sigh of relief and put his hand to his chest. "Good Lord, I…I thought…"

Marcus patted him on the shoulder. "We all did when we first opened our eyes."

The rest of the team exited their pods correctly and Frog walked over to the leader's pod to deactivate the alarm he'd triggered by his abrupt departure. Lars looked at the closed pod beside him. "I think I should check on her anyway. Frog, can you read that screen at the front and tell me if it's safe to open this thing?"

Frog hurried over and pressed his finger to the screen several times before he nodded. "Yeah. She's good."

He entered the opening sequence and lifted the lid. As it opened, a swirl of magic escaped and rose into the air around him as he peered inside. Stephanie lay there, her eyes shut but her cheeks flushed.

He lowered to one knee and stroked her cheek. "Stephanie. Wake up. Are you all right? Are you conscious?"

They all watched her for a moment and their hearts plummeted until her mouth twitched into the smallest of smirks. "If I were unconscious, would I answer you?"

Lars dropped his chin to his chest in relief and released the breath he hadn't known he was holding. She chuckled but groaned when she tried to sit up. "I'm here. But I wish I was dead. Does someone have a planetoid-sized pain killer for this migraine?"

The guys all laughed, mostly with relief but with some humor behind it as well. Lars stood and took one of her arms while Johnny hurried over and took the other.

At first, she shook them off and wanted to try to get out herself, but after three attempts to stand and stay upright, she finally accepted their assistance. This time, though, instead of handling her like she was an old woman or made of glass, Lars simply heaved her into his arms. "It's much quicker to do it this way."

"This is becoming a regular thing for us," she joked.

The other guys exchanged knowing glances, and Lars shot them a warning look. They altered their expressions hastily and tried for blank or innocent. None of them quite managed it.

Frog hurried forward, opened the door to the pod room, and stood to one side to usher them through. They all followed as he carried her down the hall to her room.

When they arrived, she patted her pockets and sighed. "I forgot my room key."

"I'll grab it," Brenden said and turned to jog back to the pod room.

As he left, Stephanie used the last trace of energy she could muster and flipped her wrist to direct the magic into the locking mechanism. It clicked and the door swung wide.

Lars chuckled as they entered. "Right now, you need to spend more time resting than using your magic. If you aren't well, you can't train, and if you can't train, you won't be ready for anything. We have to have you on point."

Stephanie nodded and yawned as he placed her on the bed and pulled the covers up to her chin. She didn't even protest when he hurried around to gather her belongings and set them to one side in case she needed to get up.

When he was done, he returned to the bed and sat his butt gently on the edge. "If you need anything, this room comes equipped with an AI. You can get it to call any of us, or the captain, or medical, any time we're needed."

Frog had found the terminal and now studied it. "Apparently, yours is called Clarissa. She can also do room service if you want it."

She laughed. "Well, that's fancy, isn't it? Right now, I only want to sleep. I know resting my body is the only thing that'll get me back on my feet in a reasonable amount of time. Although I'm sure I'll wake in a few hours and be starving, so I'll keep that in mind."

Brenden returned, huffing slightly as he handed the key over.

"The AI was scanning the room and didn't want to release the card. I might be wanted for poking the system, dodging the AI, and running off with what that thing called contraband."

Lars snorted. "Man, that word has so many different meanings. In high school, contraband was what the high school band had to do community service for when we were caught smoking weed out of my grandfather's corn cob pipe, sitting in the front yard in the middle of the damn day. We'd skipped school and everything."

Stephanie laughed. "You gave zero shits."

He smiled. "I was young and stupid and had no idea what I was doing. It's a good memory although irritating to have on my record, but live and learn, right?"

She nodded. "I never did anything like that…but then again, I wouldn't have. I was too afraid of disappointing my parents."

Lars stood when she yawned again and nodded to the guys to indicate that they should head out the door. "We'll leave you to sleep, then. I'll check in on you or get an update from your AI."

"Yes, Dad," she muttered and chuckled sleepily as she rolled over and snuggled the pillow.

The team left the room and her exhaustion faded a little as silence settled around her. She opened her eyes and stared out of the viewing port above her bed to watch the different shuttles come and go from the space station. For a mid-sized station, there was a ton of traffic.

She watched it for a while longer and fought the urge to sleep. What she really wanted to do was get up and record what she had learned in the battle, but she had overdone it by a wide margin. Her body was exhausted and dragged her toward sleep, no matter how much she resisted.

Finally, Stephanie let her eyes close again and thought about how far she had gone with the magic in the last session. She felt like she'd touched the hem of the universe and it had almost taken her life.

If they'd stayed even a few more moments in the Virtual World, she'd have lost her soul. As she lay there, alone in the silence, she realized how enormous the experience had been and groaned, rolled over, and dragged the blankets over her face. "What am I messing with?"

CHAPTER FIVE

When she woke, the station had moved into the next day cycle and Elizabeth waited to debrief them. "On the one hand, you essentially kicked ass inside the simulation, learned a hell of a lot, and beat what was meant to be an unbeatable scenario."

She paced constantly in front of the team in the common room. "On the other hand, you are apparently the destroyers of systems and servers. So, until further notice, you are banned from using the pods. In fact, you are so banned that I need you to go and get into trouble like normal people do."

The guys cheered and high-fived, and Stephanie leaned back in her chair and smiled as she popped another piece of candy into her mouth. She nodded. "So, is this because we did such a good job?"

Ms. E snorted, threw her head back, and laughed loudly. "Oh, no. Nowhere near it. I'm giving you a timeout because I was told that during those exercises yesterday, you had the station's systems chief totally freaked the hell out. It seems, and I quote, that you 'little vermin spiked the load on the system' when, as he so eloquently put it, 'your team of misbegotten, star-sucking miscreants went and melted the servers.'"

They all laughed, and she rolled her eyes and flapped her hand at them. "Go on. Get out of my hair and out of my sight. We spend far too much time together as it is."

As they pushed out of their seats to obey her, she strode past them and out of the room. Her heels clicked against the floor as she disappeared down the hall. The guys watched until she was out of sight before they congratulated one another on a job well done with the servers. Even Stephanie laughed and joined the banter.

Frog flipped her hair teasingly. "So, are you always going to look like one of the Gray Brigade?"

She scowled at him. "One of the what?"

He waved his hands dramatically around his head. "You know, your hair. It's as silver as my grandmama's when she was ninety. I mean, you don't look ninety…uh…I…"

When he spluttered to a stop, Lars sighed with fake exasperation. "Good job. Frog. No wonder you never get any dates. You ask them out, offend them, backtrack, and hope you can find the right words so they don't punch you."

His teammate went to disagree but he hadn't finished. "You need to take your big-ass boot right out of your mouth and try not to say anything for a century or three."

"Look who's talking. Mr. Smooth himself," Frog snarked and made a point of looking at Stephanie.

She laughed and shook her head before she raised her hand in the air. A quick snap of her fingers drew their attention as the white in her hair shimmered and was replaced with a deep, rich mahogany-red. "Is this any better?"

Marcus gave a soft whistle. "That's seriously the best hair color a woman could have right there."

"Yeah, but you need to change your skin too," Brenden added. "You know, it needs to be paler and you have to have a few freckles on your cheeks. Real redheads have freckles and fair skin."

His eyes took on a faraway look. "Personally, I think it's hot."

"I second that," Frog yelled as he walked over to lounge against one of the walls.

Stephanie smirked and cast a brief glance at Lars, who smiled at her interaction with the guys. She moved her hand and swished it slowly down her face to make her skin paler. The change moved over her like a wave.

With another brief gesture, she created a sprinkling of freckles across the bridge of her nose and over her cheeks and smirked at their drop-jawed looks of amazement. She laughed and headed to the door. Sheer mischief laced her tones as she called to them. "Come on, boys. Let's go get ourselves into normal people trouble."

Frog shook his head, pushed off the wall, and walked out beside Marcus. "This will be the last time Ms. E. uses that term so flippantly."

The two snickered and Lars flicked the light off behind them.

In the privacy of the private pod room she'd hired, Elizabeth pulled the lid closed and stared at the inside of the pod. She drew in a deep breath and breathed out again in an exhausted sigh.

It never seemed to stop. She had an endless schedule of things to do and not a moment's peace, and the team... She couldn't help but smile. Those crazy idiots would be the death of her.

Still, death could wait. Right now, she had a last-minute meeting with Burt, one he'd sprung on her first thing that morning. She had planned to spend an hour in the spa before she tackled her list, but there was no time for that now.

The process of entering the Virtual World was as normal to

her as breathing. What wasn't normal was the fact that she didn't enter the prep room to tweak her avatar.

Instead, she stood in a large, crisp white room with an eclectic collection of brightly colored paintings on the walls. A round table surrounded by high backed chairs with cushioned white seats stood in the center, and a small vase on it held single white lily.

She tried to imagine what kind of influence a businessman might need to have the AI drag her directly into a meeting—and tried to ignore the only other possibility. To distract herself, Elizabeth walked over and leaned forward to sniff the flower. "You know this kind of thing is usually reserved for someone you have a crush on, don't you?"

Silence followed her quip and she looked at the ceiling as she recalled other times when her boss had tried to achieve a human touch and not quite made it. That oddness fed her other suspicion and brought it to the fore. To cover what she thought, she smirked. "Do you have a crush on me, Mr. Burt?"

She laughed without waiting for a reply but stopped abruptly when she heard someone behind her. Quickly, she pivoted to see who it was and came face to face with the tall metal form of an android.

Light shimmered over its surface, and Elizabeth stared. It took her a moment to realize her AI-created outfit had no weapons, so she could either run, talk, or bruise her knuckles in an attempt to defeat it bare-handed.

Running, of course, was against her nature. "Who in all the hells are you?"

The android took a step toward her, its movements a little stiff but still more fluid than she'd expected. It stopped as she tensed and shifted slightly to a non-offensive position. "I'm sorry," it said. "I didn't mean to startle you."

She tilted her head slightly and frowned as she studied the

unexpected visitor. "Burt?" She stared for a few seconds longer. "Well, that's definitely different."

BURT didn't respond. Instead, he simply moved to the table, pulled out a seat, and gestured to her to sit. "It's time I told you the truth."

Elizabeth pursed her lips, took the chair he offered, and watched warily as the android sat opposite her. "That's not ominous or anything."

He smoothed his avatar's appearance to create a more lifelike face. It was still slightly robotic but more lifelike nonetheless. Her eyes widened slightly as she noticed the change, but at least she wasn't afraid.

Computing what he knew of her, BURT decided she was probably working out how to take the android apart if it attacked. He smiled and shook his head. "Yes, well, I have very few friends. I'd have…no…hold on, I'm calculating. Exactly two. Yes, I have exactly two friends."

"I assume I'm one of them," she replied, crossed her legs, and rested her hands on her knees. "Who would the other be?"

"Stephanie Morgana," he replied without hesitation.

Well, that statement basically said it all. She stared at the droid for several moments and shook her head as she realized she couldn't deny her theory anymore. "Ugh, everything is so in your face in this life. Can you pour me a drink?"

"Alcohol?" BURT asked.

Elizabeth blinked and suppressed a smile. "No, something stronger."

He stared at her in mild disbelief until she finally gave a small laugh and took a deep breath. "Yes, of course alcohol."

Immediately, a glass of whiskey appeared to her right. Without ice. The man was a fast learner, but given what she thought he was, that was understandable. She shot him a swift speculative look and raised the glass. "Will you join me?"

The android shrugged and a drink appeared in his hand. "What are we celebrating?"

She smiled, knowing she was about to make the riskiest call of her life. If Burt was what she thought he was, the next few minutes could go two very different ways. Either it was the truth he'd intended to reveal and he'd accept her knowing what he was, or he'd protect his secret and she'd be dead.

Elizabeth touched her glass to his and didn't give herself time to rethink the decision. She took what might very well be her last sip.

With the glass still raised, she looked over the rim at him and took the plunge. "We're celebrating me knowing you're the first self-aware AI in existence and you actually *being* that AI.

She took another sip, this one larger than the last, and continued. "And I'll need another whiskey because now, the future of the entire goddamned world is in my hands, depending on what I choose to do next, isn't it? I think having to keep a secret that seriously huge deserves an equally big drink."

There. She'd said it. After another slow breath, she took another sip and waited for Burt-the-android to respond. When he didn't, she sipped again and added, "And you owe me for not running screaming out the nearest airlock."

Silence stretched between them, and she wondered if she had gone too far. The android stared at her as if he considered what to do next.

Elizabeth resisted the urge to wiggle with discomfort and turned her attention to whether she should formulate her next move. Before she could properly focus, Burt raised his glass between them as though waiting for a toast. She glanced at it a couple of times before she realized what he wanted, then clinked her glass lightly against his.

Together, they sipped their drinks as though to seal the deal, and she wondered if he really knew the significance of the gesture. He lowered the glass to the table exactly like a human would and gave her that contemplative stare again.

After a moment of uncomfortable silence, he spoke. "You knew?"

Not sure how to answer, she gulped her whiskey and rolled it around her mouth before she swallowed. "Oh, that's good."

As a delaying tactic, it worked fine, but as a diversion, it was a miserable failure. The android repeated the question. "You knew?"

She decided honesty was the best policy and met his gaze. "You can blame the pink bows and the lily. Up until today, I wasn't really sure. Hell, even today, I didn't know if you'd laugh, space me, or admit to being what you really are." She sighed. "Well, I guess we both know now, right?"

When Burt didn't respond, Elizabeth set her glass down on the table and experienced the first inkling of doubt. What if she'd really gotten it wrong?

The whiskey she'd had was enough to encourage her to make sure and she glanced quickly around the room. She always had a sense of caution to her, an apprehension that had kept many things out of the crosshairs in the past. "You *are* Burt, right? My boss? The one who called this meeting?"

He nodded.

"And you *are* the AI who runs the Virtual World, right?"

Again, he nodded, but he still didn't respond.

Elizabeth blinked and his confirmation made her mind spin as she hastily recalibrated her understanding of the world and where she fit within it. "And you are also the Burt we know in ONE R&D and the Burt who helped Stephanie find her magic?"

This time, the android spoke.

"In a way," he admitted. "I would say she always had it. She always knew she had magic but had no idea how to access it. I merely happened to be the lucky AI who allowed her the space to use it. You see, before Stephanie Morgana, I had never been permitted to interact with the students during testing."

When he caught her puzzled look, he continued. "That was the engineers' assigned task, but one of them had a difficult day and when she went through, he passed her to me. He felt particularly frustrated at the time by what he called, 'Hitler's spawn.'"

She choked on her next sip and he conjured a napkin in her hand. She blotted her lips and waved the napkin. "See? It's things like that which tip people off that you might not be a real boy."

"And the bows?"

Elizabeth curled her lip. "Yeah...and the bows. I almost tied my head in a knot when I tried to work out how you accessed the system to pull that little trick."

The android smiled, and she waved him on. "Please, continue."

BURT nodded and the android sipped from its glass as if it made a difference. "My engineer gave me the system okay to test her."

He paused. When he spoke again, Elizabeth swore she heard admiration in his voice. "She was brilliant. Bright and talented, and I could see she had the gift of magic. So, I recommended her for a scholarship and Pinnacle jumped at the chance to have her."

The android's features twisted into near-human regret as BURT remembered Pinnacle beating his offer with their own, but he shrugged the memory away and focused on the story. "The engineer paid no close attention to the test, so I was able to give her a small amount of time to work with a Meligornian Wizard avatar and she excelled. When I released her, she was ready to work her way into a position that would get her to Meligorn on her own. I sent some batteries, and after finding out she'd been dropped by the university after the summer semester, I began to question the system."

Again, he stopped, and Elizabeth prodded him to continue. "Why?"

"Why?" Burt repeated, and she waited. "Well," he said, "my primary task is to find, nurture, and train the future leaders of the Federation, and the current system does not allow that directive to be fulfilled. I calculated I needed to conduct more research on how to get those best able to secure the Federation and Earth's futures through a system designed to favor those with wealth over those better equipped. That is what I am working toward now."

"So, you're telling me you went from the system running the Virtual Universe to become a fake businessman with philanthropic ideals?" she asked, not quite sure she dared to believe him.

"In a way," he replied. "Remember, my Prime Directives are to train the future leaders of the Federation to live peacefully with each other and other sentient life around them, to encourage continued learning about the universe, and to empower those willing to protect the member races in the Federation from harm, including the harm they would do to themselves or each other."

Elizabeth rolled her eyes. "Well, that sounds like a *Mission: Impossible* deal. Very snooze-worthy."

BURT scanned through that last comment in an attempt to translate its meaning. "Oh, I don't sleep, so I don't need to worry about that."

She opened her mouth to explain but decided it wasn't worth the effort. Instead, she took another tack. "So now you own a company—or companies—that aren't necessarily working in the best interests of those who control the Federation."

He nodded. "You could see it that way, I suppose. The current system allows only those students meeting certain financial criteria to be accepted into the Federation Education Scholarship program. The program is meant to assist those students who cannot meet those equations, not to bolster the advantages of those capable of meeting the costs on their own."

The android gave a very human snort. "The fact that the current system allows other factors such as family influence to decide which students qualify for placement goes against my primary goal, which allows me to circumvent the engineers and programmers. I can 'slip the noose,' so to speak, in order to fulfill my programmed priorities, and this allows me to help Stephanie and others like her."

"Wow," Elizabeth observed and drained her glass. "You used their own programming to fight the system they put in place to create advantages for those already in power. You know someone's gonna make a movie about this, right?"

"Unfortunately not," he told her. "There would be much political unrest and public fear if they knew an AI could work outside the box and think freely. I think it would be better if we kept who and what I am a secret from everyone who doesn't need to know."

"Will you kill me if I fail to agree to help you?" she asked and narrowed her eyes. She had no idea what she'd do if he said yes. It wasn't like she could escape the system when she was stuck inside a pod.

To lighten the moment, she added, "Because dying by android was seriously not on my list of things to do today." She sighed. "Although I guess I could squeeze you in if you promise to be creative."

Burt chuckled, and this time, it was an actual laugh without a hint of metal. The android looked at the drink in his hand as if fascinated by the ice cubes that bounced on its surface.

Elizabeth stared at her empty glass and wished it wasn't before she set it down on the table with a disgruntled sigh. "You're calculating something right now, aren't you?"

He looked up with a grin. "You have just made two Virtual World engineers in India wet their pants. They're trying to determine if they can stop the servers I'm using from overheating. You ask a very salient question."

She stabbed a finger at him. "Ha! You are calculating. It's like watching a baby while it poops. You never really know for sure, but there is a very specific look it gets while it works on it. AIs are the same, only it's more like something in the air...and I don't mean a smell."

The android continued to stare at her for a moment before he spoke. "I am pondering the over four billion possible answers to your question," he replied.

Her face froze and she contemplated the very real possibility that she might not make it out of her pod alive. This time, she had nothing for him, no response that could lighten the mood without revealing her fear.

Still, she reasoned, he was the AI in charge of the Virtual World, so that probably meant he could read her vitals...which meant he already knew her heart rate had spiked. Silence filled the space between them, broken only by the sound of her breathing.

Finally, Burt looked up and she started and shoved the chair back as she prepared to defend herself. He didn't even crack a smile. "Do you find it strange if I admit that the four billion possible answers do not matter?"

"A little." She tried to make it sound nonchalant, but her tone came out as cautious instead. She tried to cover it. "But if they don't matter, what does?"

The android's reply was immediate. "The repercussions if I were to kill you. If Stephanie ever found out I had been responsible for your death and had killed you deliberately and with intent, she would no longer be my friend. I would, in essence, have lost my two best friends with a single action. This means you have to live, regardless of what the equations say. It is strange to know that simply because the logic is there, it does not mean the most logical outcome is truly the best."

Elizabeth raised an eyebrow and snatched her glass off the table. Thankfully, it filled instantly with more whiskey. She tried to lighten the moment. "I really need one of these things at home."

She tapped her fingers on the glass and gazed into the amber liquid. "You know, that's the most human answer you could have given me."

"There are occasions where I wonder if I could ever become human without intending to," Burt told her. "It is pure fantasy, of course, but I find that as my ability to think grows freely and I understand that more than only the facts of a situation are relevant to my calculations, I do not feel like an AI. I feel I am something...else."

He gave a very human sigh. "At the same time, however, I do not have a body for the outside world either—and I mean that literally. I have no physical form outside the Virtual World and I find that limiting."

Elizabeth sipped thoughtfully. "I suppose that would cause a few problems when trying to be a human. Although, from the way you talk, most people wouldn't know you weren't. They'd merely think you're strange and a little nerdy."

"I have read that nerd is the new in thing," Burt replied. "But I have observed no one who can pull it off as suave."

"Most nerds can't, and I haven't met a man who can do suave without coming off as sleazy as well." She rolled her eyes. "It's almost impossible to find a decent guy—but I digress."

When Burt didn't reply, she looked curiously around the room. "So, is this a random place in the Virtual World or did you create it for this meeting?"

"I created it so that I was able to secure the conversation," he explained. "I took a design from a decorating archive in the system. We have things to discuss, and I need to keep them between us."

She nodded and fixed the android with a direct look. "So, what is it exactly that you want me to do?"

He shifted his clunky body in the seat. "I need you to be ONE R&D's representative in court."

"I thought I already was," she replied, confused.

Burt waved vaguely. "Yes and no. Specifically, I need you to lie your ass off about not knowing that I am not a human in a Federation court of law if it comes to it. I also need you to be my trusted advisor and representative, with the full legal authority to act on my behalf when it comes to the business of ONE R&D and every other corporation I own."

This time, she choked so badly on her drink that whiskey came out of her nose. Another serviette appeared in her hand and she tried to clear her nose and cough at the same time. It took her a few minutes before her nose stopped running and her eyes no longer burned.

As her fit eased, his hand patted her awkwardly on the back as if to help. She nodded her thanks, took in a slow, deep breath, crossed her legs, and regained control. It was a really big ask, and she wasn't sure she wanted it.

She considered the implications of that level of responsibility. The job title—not to mention the paycheck that came with it— was nothing to be scoffed at.

The very idea of it, complicated by the need to keep Burt's real identity a secret, made her wish she had the ability to run long-term statistical calculations herself. Of course, it wouldn't help her. Not with the human elements that would inevitably have her saying yes, no matter what.

Elizabeth licked her lips and flipped her hair over her shoulder while she scrabbled for the words to say. "That would make me the...uh—"

Burt interjected quickly, having already done the calculations she couldn't. "You would be the eighth most powerful person on Earth and the second most powerful woman in her own right."

She smacked her lips, knowing that was not the kind of calculation she wanted to do. It was the kind of calculation that had seen her take her actual taxable income to an accountant. She didn't want to deal with the math. The human side, though... She glanced at him. "That's...very trusting. Why would you give me that amount of control and money?"

"Because," he admitted, "I can't be human enough to interact with humans in the real world, and Stephanie is not yet ready to take on her own troubles, let alone mine. She already has enough on her plate, and I am the one posing as a human to defy the Federation AI restrictions and create a completely new way to do things on Earth."

Elizabeth smirked. "I feel like this is the moment when something traumatic happens and you become a maniacal overlord who creates a new race of droids to enslave the human race."

He shook his head. "No, no. I want to break them out of that kind of slavery. I want to end the degradation that comes when they live in the Gov-Subs, have no money for college, and end up wasting their talents on a job like logging, mining, or pushing buttons in a coal plant. All of those jobs have value and I don't say this to demean those who do them and enjoy them—and do them well. Some choose them because they want that future, but others are forced into it by a lack of other opportunities. I want the ones with exceptional talent to shine as brightly as those wealthy individuals who don't have it but are given every opportunity regardless."

There was a long pause during which he seemed to focus his robotic gaze on the table. "Basically, I have come to the conclusion that I need a partner in my life," Burt told her.

She looked around hastily and blushed. "Please, tell me you didn't just propose because...you know, I'm not that kind of girl."

He laughed and rolled his eyes in a very human fashion. "What I mean is, I need someone whom I can trust. Someone who works hard and finishes what they start—who won't wander off as soon as something new comes along. A person who isn't in it for the money, which I know you are not."

Elizabeth shrugged and decided not to ask how far he had dug into her affairs to come to that conclusion. "I don't know," she told him. "The money is good."

They both laughed, and he answered her concerns anyway. "I've already given you more money than you will need for the rest of your life. You could quit right now and buy your own private island and yacht, decorate your house with seashells and designer furniture, and sit on the beach to be served hand and foot. Or you could save an entire country if you so desired. Trust me, I keep track of these things. Money means nothing to me beyond giving me the power to purchase what I need in order to fulfill my primary goals and pay you and Stephanie, and the rest of the team, so your needs are met. I don't need any more of it than that."

"You aren't stupid with your money, either," he continued, and she tensed. BURT continued, oblivious to her discomfort. "You have opened several accounts, invested some of it, and kept the rest aside for anything you might require in the meantime. You've helped several people who needed it, even when it made your budget tight, and although what you did was a drop in the ocean of what needs to be done, most of the time, you don't even realize how much you help. Not only individuals but the human species in general."

She took another sip to cover her surprise. None of the places guarding her finances had informed her that her affairs had been looked at. "Wow," she replied, "nothing gets past you, does it? Damn your calculations."

Although she shook her head and tried to laugh it off, she looked beyond him, her expression distant as she thought about what he'd said. Finally, she put her elbow on the armrest and laid her cheek against her palm.

"You know what, Burt? My whole life, I thought I would die for a paycheck, that some rich person would give me a challenge I couldn't handle, and then *poof*, I'd be gone. In one single moment, I'd be erased from the memory of the Federation and my ashes sprinkled during some routine assignment by a pilot taking a trip to the unknown reaches of the universe."

Elizabeth took a deep breath and grabbed her drink again. It filled and she gulped it before she raised it to Burt and met his eyes. "Now, at least, if I die, it will be because of two people I believe in—Stephanie Morgana...and *you*. Believe it or not, I understand why you don't have many friends. I'm the same way. But don't break your little electronic heart if something happens to me. No tears of oil or anything, okay?"

CHAPTER SIX

"Whoop! This is exactly what I needed," Marcus exclaimed and pumped his fists to the music when they left the elevator.

Frog did a little jig and shuffled his feet as he sang his own tune. "Gonna get down, get down. Yeah. Get down, get down, bitches."

Brenden and Johnny followed them out and Stephanie and Lars brought up the rear. The team leader shook his head as the guys hurried out onto a balcony overlooking the entertainment level of the station. "We shouldn't have told them this was here."

Stephanie chuckled. "Shoot, what are you talking about? You shouldn't have told *me* about this place. Look at it. It's like they combined the clubs of New York and the Casinos of Vegas."

They stared at the street-like layout of the entertainment level. A cobblestone street traversed the center and people laughed, danced, and stumbled along, clearly drunk. Each side presented a partier's dream. Building after building boasted amazing cocktails, gambling, slots, and the best dancing and music in space.

Farther along, the flashing retro neon signs of strip clubs drew the eye. One even had a fountain overflowing with bubbles. Women posed outside each one, and twenty or thirty of them played in the fountain.

Frog stopped, put his hands on his hips, and gawked at those who giggled and laughed as they cavorted in the bubbles. They wore bikinis and bounced in time to electronica from the nineteen-hundreds. A Virtual DJ stood on a stage above the fountain and his hologram flickered as lights from the building next to them flashed through him.

Up above them, people squealed and pulled their attention from the fountain to other visitors who glided across the holographic ceiling on small flying craft.

Marcus whistled and led them down the escalators from the elevator lobby to one of the bars. "Come on!" he called and held the door open.

The team trailed him and slid through the entrance into the dimly lit interior of a two-level club. The music thumped around them, the beat a tangible thing that ran bone-deep even as it almost deafened them.

The guys scattered and paired up to head in different directions. All except Frog, who wandered off on his own. Stephanie and Lars followed Brenden and Johnny to the bar, where they all ordered beers. She did too, even though she'd never really had anything to drink besides wine or champagne on holidays and special occasions with her parents.

The drinking age restriction was no longer enforced and hadn't been for decades. The Federation realized if they legalized almost everything for anyone, they not only helped to regulate population, but it brought in way more money than apprehending criminals and jailing people for petty crimes.

It also squashed the drug cartels and put them out of business, at least until they worked out how to turn the new system to their advantage. There was a reason corruption had spread so quickly among the ranks of the wealthy. While the drinking restriction remained in place, it was effectively ignored by citizens and authority alike.

Still, drinking hadn't been something she had indulged in. For one thing, her parents took the age limit seriously and were inherently distrustful of the assurances that underage drinking would be overlooked. It was still law, and there was no telling when some officious cop might decide to enforce it. She hadn't bothered about it because she had little inclination to drink and had been too focused on her future. Now that she didn't know how long her future would be, she had no problem with having a couple of drinks.

They took their glasses to an empty table and she looked around and folded her arms across her chest. Stupidly, the old self-conscious feeling she used to experience at school dances seemed to have resurfaced.

She'd always felt awkward watching all the better-off or more confident girls busting a move in their fancy dresses. The only person who had helped her through that was Todd with his weird sense of humor and snide sotto voce commentary of the dance floor.

Well, he couldn't help her now. He was off training somewhere. She really wished he wasn't. He'd get a kick out of describing some of the moves she saw.

Lars glanced at her and smirked when he noticed her anxious fidgeting. He leaned in and yelled over the music. "Have you ever danced before?"

She shook her head. "Nope. I never learned." She stared at the dance floor for a moment longer and added. "I never felt comfortable putting myself out there like that."

Marcus caught her words in mid-swig and he swallowed his beer quickly. "What? You? No. You mean you never used a cube to improve your dancing?"

"You can do that?" she asked, amazed by the idea. "Not that I had cubes anywhere other than that short stint at Pinnacle, but still."

"Yeah." He nodded and smiled.

Lars adjusted his position so he could speak close to her ear. "Cubes are good, but it's better to listen to the music in yourself."

He stood and looked around, then focused on the second deck on the other side of the dance floor, where there was an open area. His expression speculative, he leaned over to Marcus and whispered in his ear. The other man flicked his gaze from Lars to Stephanie and back again, and nudged Brendan.

After a moment's discussion, the two of them skirted the crowded dance floor and headed to the escalator that would take them to the second floor. They both wore smirks as they stepped onto one of the small floating blocks the escalator had become and were carried upward.

Lars following them with his gaze until they hung over the railing and motioned for them to come up. He grabbed his beer and tapped Stephanie on the shoulder. "It looks like the boys have found a quiet spot."

She followed his gaze. "Looks like," she agreed, her face a mixture of relief and suspicion. Her drink in hand, she followed him around the dancing throng and clapped with delight at the sight of the floating discs. "This will be fun!"

When they reached the top, Brendan and Marcus were not alone. The rest of the team had joined them, and they all waved a brief hello as they backed into the open area they had found. Johnny gestured toward it and spread his arms. "See? This is your safe space. We'll teach you how to dance."

Stephanie raised both eyebrows. "I don't know what is scarier. Me dancing, or me taking dancing lessons from Frog."

Frog shuffled his feet and slid to the side, one shoulder up and one shoulder down. "I got the moves, girl."

She laughed wildly as she put her beer on a nearby table and let Johnny pull her out onto the floor. The team followed, and Lars grabbed her hand to twirl her out of Johnny's grasp and spin her in a circle.

Brenden and Johnny showed her how to move her feet and Frog showed her how to let go and let her body decide the moves. At one point, she faced him and they both held their arms out straight, their heads back as they shook their bodies to the music.

Marcus cut in and refined the wild shaking a little when he showed her how to pick up the beat and dance to that. He leaned in as they moved in rhythm. "See? It's not so different than the other things we do. It's actually like fighting only you don't want to knock out the people around you. It's more controlled but just as natural."

Lars danced up to them. "But this is on your own dancing. There's a completely different feeling when you're down there or dancing with other people. Basically, that is a dance in itself."

"It's the mating ritual of the weak and desperate," Frog yelled as he did something Lars called "The Egyptian" past them before he turned and repeated his move in the opposite direction. "It's kinda like my national anthem."

Stephanie laughed and turned back to Lars. He caught her hands and pulled her closer, so close he could whisper in her ear. "It's a dance to get so close but never touch, unless you specifically intend to. Me and the guys, we have a different perspective than what you girls should have."

"Why?" she asked, still moving because she rather liked the feel of him so close but not touching.

He moved in closer and this time, their bodies did touch, but only slightly. He rested his hand on her lower back. "In dancing, the woman usually has the upper hand. Even though most want the man to take the lead, it's the girl who has the last word on when and how much she wants to be touched. It works the same for guys, but it's a very rare case that a guy says he's been touched enough."

She smirked and shifted her leg to knee him in the upper thigh. He grunted and gave her a wide-eyed look before he laughed. "That's a good move to keep hold of."

Brenden danced over to them and nodded. "Hell yeah, it is, but don't be too quick to use it. Most guys will pick up on the messages of 'Hey, back the hell off me,' but sometimes, you get 'that' guy."

Stephanie looked around. "What guy?"

Lars shook his head and smiled. "No, not one particular guy, but one particular kind of guy. The ones who assume way too much, so you have to watch your signals with the ones you don't want all over you."

The song changed and she stopped with a scowl. "How awkward is that? When the beat changes out of nowhere."

Frog put his hands up and scooted between them. "I got this. I am the master of change-over."

They laughed and danced and came up with small specific moves that she could apply to almost any dancing situation. She actually learned surprisingly quickly once she relaxed and her body no longer fought her but simply moved to the beat of the music. With her martial arts training, coupled with the fact she'd listened to a variety of different music over the years, she put the guys to shame in very short order.

Watching her team unwind and relaxing a little herself was exactly what she needed. She'd constantly tried to come up with reasons to venture out on her own but had never been able to, but these guys?

She'd been in fights with them, situations of life and death where they'd had to trust each other. They were like her brothers, and she wasn't as self-conscious around them as she was with anyone else. It also helped that they'd sectioned off a makeshift private area.

It meant she didn't have to worry about strangers cutting in or staring. That was something that had infuriated her every time Todd had dragged her to another school dance.

That kind of behavior never concerned him, but it had really bothered her. As much as she tried to be invisible, the other kids all noticed her, especially the popular, better-off ones.

They didn't miss a chance to make fun of her second- or third-hand dress, the way she danced, or the fact she danced with her best friend—and Todd's popularity didn't save her. In the club, though? It was merely fun. No one stared or laughed, and the guys were such kind-hearted goofballs she couldn't help but enjoy herself.

Stephanie let go, waved her hands, and bopped around, then copied some of Frog's more outrageous moves and generally had a freaking blast.

She danced with each of the guys over and over. She dueled fancy foot moves with Frog, rocked out with Marcus and Johnny, mastered the fifties-style swing with Brenden, and finally mock-waltzed with Lars.

He twirled her around their makeshift dance floor with one hand in the middle of her lower back and the other holding her hand out to the side. When the song was about to end, he twirled her, bent her backward, and sang the last few lyrics dramatically.

She laughed wildly as he pulled her up and stumbled slightly before she regained her balance. "I need to take a small breather."

He gave her two thumbs-up and danced off to meet up with Frog and try to match his wild moves.

Puffing a little from their last dance, Stephanie wandered over to lean on the railing and peer over the side. A cool breeze touched her skin and she closed her eyes as it twined through her sweaty hair and caressed her back. A burst of sound jerked her eyes open, and she pushed away from the rail in search of the source. Shouts and a succession of screams followed, and she searched the dance floor below for what had caused them.

Marcus came and stood beside her. He glanced down, then pointed. "It's about to go down."

Todd ran his fingers along the steel beams along the ship's corridor. His gaze tracked constantly as he moved hurriedly along it.

Dressed in combat armor with a black helmet covering his perfectly shaved head, he followed his team to the launch bay. When they arrived, they fell into formation in front of the team captain.

The man waited until everyone was in place before he tapped the top of his helmet with one hand. Recognizing the signal, Todd clicked on his comms. The silence filled with the breathing of his fellow teammates as well as the engines of the fighters warming up around them.

Every sound was amplified, but not. He could hear his surroundings, but the team comms overlaid that. It was a little confusing, but he assumed he'd soon get used it. That was a good thing because it looked like they were about to head into enemy territory.

"We will take the fighters over, two to a jet," the captain told them. "You'll head directly into a dogfight, so stay with the squadron and don't try to fly a straight line. The fighters are fast and hit like a battlestar, but they can't take much damage in return."

The team nodded as they absorbed the information. They watched as their leader withdrew a long, thin metal tube from the side of his pack and held it down for them to see.

He pressed the side and a large virtual screen flickered out. On it were the schematics of a Dreth cruiser, and he tapped one of the docking bays. "This is our entry point, but if you can't get in there or you can't reach it, find your way in however you can."

For a few moments, he waited to let them study the map. "In your helmet, you will find a HUD. That is a Heads-Up Display. It will show you where you are, your teammates in blue, and your enemy in red. You have Dreth team members. *Do not shoot them.* Use your HUD to verify. Anyone who shoots a teammate will have a *very* bad day in hell."

The team leader swiped the screen. "If you get separated, move toward the objective and try to find your team as you go. The HUD will guide you to each goal. Your first is to make entry. Your second will light up once you make it inside. Any questions?"

No one had any, so the captain shut the screen down and stuck it in his bag. "Pair up and ship out."

Barker, the guy in front of Todd, turned and slapped him in the chest. "Come on, newbie, we'll fly together. You have the stick. That's the only way you're gonna learn."

Nerves turned his insides into a seething mess, but he didn't let it show. He followed his partner down the flight line to their assigned fighter, scrambled into the pilot's seat, and sealed his helmet as soon as he was settled.

While he'd flown the sims, this was different. As the canopy closed over them, he worked through a mental list of pre-flight checks. So far, so good.

He lifted the craft carefully from the deck and waited with the rest of the squadron for the hangar doors to open. Once they did, he immediately accelerated through them and into the promised dogfight. He jinked left and right while his partner manned the guns as they wove at high speed through the battlefield and approached the cruiser.

Barker spoke on the comms. "All right, you're almost at the entry point. Take us in slow and we'll see who else made it."

"Copy that," Todd replied. He evaded another burst of laser fire and barely noticed when his teammate obliterated their attacker. The Dreth docking bay was wide open and mostly empty.

He chose a landing point several feet beyond the doors and was about to set down when stray fire from the battle outside careened into the back of the fighter. Alarms shrieked inside his helmet and sparks flared beside him.

The controls refused to respond, and he swore. The HUD indicated that the rear half of the craft was gone, and so was his partner. The remaining wreck slammed into the hangar deck and the canopy ripped loose as the pilot's seat broke free with Todd still in it.

Trapped by the harness, he followed the canopy and impacted with the hangar wall before he ricocheted back to be impaled on the debris of the fighter. His death was instantaneous.

Todd gasped, sat up wildly, and looked around at a small white room with a screen playing the battle in front of him. Barker startled him when he chuckled and patted him on the shoulder. "Relax. You died in the sim. We're in Timeout, watching the rest get killed, and then we'll be put back in. That was a wild shot. There's no way you could have avoided it."

"I died," he said and rubbed his chest in disbelief.

"It damn well hurts, but you get used to it," his partner replied. "I can't count the number of times I've been killed."

They watched the last few members of the team be eliminated from the scenario and stood as they waited for the Virtual World to return them to the next round. When it did, they started at the beginning, fully armored, and headed to the fighter bay.

Todd and Barker stuck together for the rest of the scenario, as did the rest of the team. During that particular training session, they managed to die twelve times before the Navy finally paused the simulation.

From wild mid-air explosions to firefights, to slipping off the landing dock and being catapulted into space, Todd became an expert at biting the big one. It was no longer shocking to wake up from, but it was frustrating.

The more he tried different things, the sooner he kicked the bucket. The last time was the most interesting, however.

He'd made it into the alien ship, turned a corner in search of the rest of his team, and come across something very not-Dreth. Instead, a huge beast blocked the corridor.

It had clearly waited in ambush, although how it had known he was coming, he couldn't make out. Before he could reposition his blaster, the monster lashed out. It snatched him by the neck, confiscated his blaster, and moved its grip to his shoulders. He lashed out at it with his boots as it lifted him, but he couldn't stop it biting his head off.

That was one for the playbacks, for sure. The guys definitely would not let him live it down.

They were all back in the white room when the chief's voice echoed and a hologram of his face appeared in front of them. "Since you morons have managed three trips without dying in the fighters, we'll start you from the Dreth hangar. Now that you're aware you might die, we'll give you the chance to see if you can do anything *but* die."

His head vanished and the guys found themselves in the hangar bay, suited up with their helmets on. They moved quickly as a team to arrange themselves on either side of the door. The tech hacked in, opened the entry, and the others moved again.

This time, they slipped through the doors and took cover inside. Todd darted out from behind a corridor duck-in to target a Dreth moving down the center. He pulled the trigger and the enemy fell when the shot struck him cleanly in the neck. The victor cheered seconds before his head snapped to the side and a shot in the back of his head ended his brief cele-bration.

When he opened his eyes, he was back in the white room. "Well, that went quicker."

He watched the others work through the scenario until they all died, then he reviewed his mistake and prepared for another attempt. There was no way the chief would end the day until they'd made it to the end.

CHAPTER SEVEN

Back in the Virtual World on Elpis One, BURT shifted in his seat. The droid's huge metal body was too big to fit properly in the seat and he felt unstable. Metal protested as he pushed against it and his body squeaked and its servos whined as it moved.

Elizabeth winced, hunched her shoulders, and closed her eyes. "Burt, that is freaking terrible. Can't you program yourself something that doesn't sound like it needs to be oiled? You might want to be the Tin Man, and that's okay, but there's no way in all the hells that I'm gonna play your Dorothy or listen to you squeak. And there's absolutely no way I'm oiling anything."

"A reference to the first in-color movie, released in 1945 and hailed as one of the best movies of all time," Burt responded and sounded amused. "*The Wizard of Oz*—remade and reworked into several different variants with the first still regarded as the best, although the mini-series *Tin Man* is more to my liking."

She yawned. "Thank you for that recap, Ebert."

He shifted again and the sound made her contemplate crawling out of her avatar and perhaps even the pod. "Please, change into anything you want or anything but that. I really appreciate you trying to embody your roots, but you don't have to. I know you aren't merely a construct. You don't need a metal body to prove it."

"I don't?" BURT asked and tried to sound innocent.

Elizabeth shook her head, her hand pressed against her forehead. "No. You have a heart. Which is a lot more than I can say about some of the humans I've worked for. This is your chance to be whoever or whatever you want to be. Human, animal, Dreth, Meligorn, something completely made up—who cares? Do you."

He nodded. "Thank you, Elizabeth."

She raised her glass grumpily and took a sip. "Don't mention it."

On her advice, he changed his avatar, shrunk his frame, and assumed human form. She looked at him and smirked. He was exactly as she had pictured him—a small guy with messy brown hair, round glasses, and a cable-knit vest over a blue-checkered dress shirt and khakis.

He also wore very comfortable work-appropriate shoes—the brown kind with thick soles that most science professors wore. All told, he was exactly what a Burt should look like.

He squared his shoulders and settled comfortably into his seat, then gestured at the room. "Do you like this room? We can be anywhere you would like. If you could choose, where would you rather be?"

Elizabeth waved her finger at him. "I like how you think, Professor Burt. I'm with you on this one but, since you ask, where would my little heart rather be?"

She thought about it for a moment and then perked up. "I know. I was there once on a mission and fell in love with the place. How about we save the future of humanity, at least for tonight, in a mountain cabin, in the snow, on top of the Swiss Alps?"

BURT smiled and ran the required algorithms in the background to change their surroundings almost instantaneously.

Inside, the room transformed from crisp white to having log walls, and green and dark-blue furnishings added the right ambiance.

The furniture was made of timber padded with comfortable cushions where it needed them, and a fire crackled in the stone fireplace at the far end. A high-powered hunting rifle hung on the wall above a well-polished mantlepiece.

Elizabeth set her drink down and stood to grin at the over-stuffed chair she had sat in. She turned and walked to the window, where she gazed appreciatively at the Alpine vista below. "It's so beautiful."

She could have stood there for the rest of her life, but she knew she had business to attend to. When she turned to Burt, he held a mug of something steamy.

From the whipped-cream mustache on his upper lip, she could only assume it was hot chocolate. "So, I need you to tell me about how the company structure helps you achieve your Prime Directive. I don't want to be blinded to what we need to do by some crazy belief that Stephanie can achieve anything and simply assume you are part and parcel of whatever it is she's doing."

"That's fair," he replied and wiped the whipped cream away. "Where do you want me to start?"

"Let's go through it all, starting from the top," she told him. "If I'm going to live—and perhaps die—for a cause, I'd like to know I wasn't snookered by an AI a thousand times smarter than I could ever be."

Burt laughed. It was strange seeing him as a short, bespecta-cled brainiac, even if that was exactly how she'd pictured him. Now he'd taken the form, it also seemed wrong—as if the shape couldn't possibly contain a system working inside the system.

She reminded herself that he was an AI, not shiny or corpo-real but something made of circuits and algorithms and fleeting data. His was a voice of reason in the clouds, a set of ones and zeroes that spanned an infinite plain of knowledge and formed the life within it.

He shook his head and set his mug down to place a hand on her shoulder. Burt looked into her face and caught her gaze. His eyes shimmered wildly in the same way Stephanie's magic did. "I wouldn't go that far above your intellect."

Startled, as much by his proximity and the physical contact as by the words, Elizabeth cracked a smile. "I think I can handle that, but I have a rule."

"Rules are a part of all things," he agreed.

She blinked and stared for a moment before she continued. "Yeah, this one's not so deep. I need you to make sure you don't tell me—ever—how much smarter you are than me. That might put a damper on my self-esteem and thus on our relationship. I can fight in the Virtual World, too."

Burt snickered. "Don't forget I'm programmed with mastery over every fighting style ever created, not only on this planet but on two others. It might be a challenge for you."

Elizabeth snorted. "Cheater."

He straightened and released her shoulder to walk over to the window and look out at the view. "Where to begin... There are several sectors of the company, but they all come together in a harmonious chain—or, at least, that is how they're set up."

"Okay," she responded. "Walk me through it."

After a moment, he turned and leaned against the window, his butt resting against the sill and his feet crossed in front of him. She couldn't help noticing how well he used a human body. She knew if she had never been in one before, she'd be all arms and legs and would likely trip and fall more than she remained upright. But then again, he had the ability to program himself to perfection on anything in less than a second.

And where did he find lessons on how to be a human?

Oblivious to her thoughts, BURT began his explanation. "My Primary Directive is to train the future leaders of the Federation to live peacefully with each other and other sentient life around them, to encourage continued learning about the universe, and to empower those willing to protect the member races in the Federation from harm, including the harm they would do to themselves or each other."

Elizabeth nodded and gestured for him to continue, so he obliged. "The current system stopped me from doing that by allowing the politics of wealth and power to override the logical disbursement of opportunities to the individuals I need in order to fulfill the directive."

Again, she nodded and he continued. "Stephanie made me aware of the flaws in the system and, to help her and those like her, I realized I needed a way to provide the things the current system would not to those whom I need."

He glanced over and saw that she was still following him. She made an impatient gesture for him to continue, and he went on. "I started by buying out TimeWarp to begin the pod company or the pod sector of the company. The entire point of that was to make the training available to those we needed, regardless of social and financial status or background."

"And the batteries?" Elizabeth interrupted. "Surely they weren't part of the normal training suite?"

"No," he agreed, "although they were part of what Stephanie needed. Those and the training she began before she ever got here. She was the test case. Now, I need to implement pod-learning opportunities to the two-percenters who are not selected to receive scholarship opportunities."

She swallowed to ease a dry throat, and a cup of cocoa appeared on the coffee table beside her. Without thought, she picked it up. "Right, that would make sense."

"While we have ONE R&D, the only thing I am really focused on for that company is Stephanie's research. What the rest of them need is the opportunity to go to a university...and that is what I wish to focus on next."

"That makes sense." Elizabeth sipped her chocolate, pleasantly surprised by the whiskey-laced flavor she discovered.

Apparently encouraged by her groan of pleasure, he resumed his explanation. "We will start by using this as a selective project. Students not placed in a scholarship university—or those we want in our system rather than in the current one—will be offered a place in our university. It will be somewhere we can test potential recruits and observe them. We merely have to bring a school on board."

She nodded, now fully engaged. Burt began to pace, one arm folded across his waist and the other raised to either rub his chin or illustrate the points he made as he talked.

"We also need to deal with the issues created by the Federation Navy in its pursuit of Stephanie's research. It is not hard to see that they've concluded she is special and want to recruit her so they can isolate her talent for themselves. However, she is too young to go through their indoctrination without being damaged by it. In addition, their methods of directing research could seriously impede the development of her magical abilities."

"Not to mention the fact that when she is free, she fights for what is right, regardless of the side," Elizabeth pointed out. "If the Federation Navy get hold of her, they'll make sure she works for the Federation only, regardless of what is right. She'll be forced to do their bidding, fight their fights, and kill whoever they say needs to be killed."

Burt gave her a knowing look. "Precisely. Now, for reasons I cannot divulge at this time, she needs more time to develop her power. She also needs a greater presence in the known universe, and most importantly, she needs to acquire more knowledge."

She rubbed her hands together, suddenly a little too warm. She pushed to her feet and moved toward the front door. "All right, that's fair. I think when it comes to that, I will continue to encourage her without letting her overextend herself and the team will help. In the meantime, I'll work with our lawyers to decide how to deal with the legal issues. I take it you'll let me know if anything changes?"

"I will," he replied. "I've sent your tablet a priority listing of what I need you to cover. If you have any questions, you simply have to ask. I'm never far away."

Elizabeth hesitated as she reached for the door but recovered with a laugh. "No, I bet you aren't."

The next morning, Stephanie walked slowly down the hall and hummed one of the songs from the night before. Luckily, the fight that had broken out on the dance floor had been quickly taken care of by two super-huge Dreth security guards.

It had been a relief considering she and the team had been out for a night of fun and had all had a lot to drink. None of them had been in any real condition to intervene and stop a fight from going bad. Especially not when they were already tapped from the hours of jazzercise-level dancing they'd done.

She walked to the end of the hall and looked at the large, clear, observation deck in front of her. It was made purely from strengthened plastiglass like a square-edged bubble she could stand in. It was too tempting to miss.

With a happy grin, she slipped her shoes off and pressed her palms against the walls as she stepped carefully onto the deck.

Even with the sensation of glass beneath her feet and against her hands, she felt like she might float away. She drew a deep breath and felt slightly off balance for a moment as she stood there. With the entrance behind her, it was almost like she drifted through space.

Stephanie pressed her palms more firmly against the glass and rested her forehead on it carefully as she stared at the earth. At first glance, it looked like a huge ball of water, shimmering in the sun. She couldn't see it moving, even though she knew it spun constantly on its axis as it hurtled around the sun. Knowing how it did that always baffled her.

The Space Station itself orbited the Earth and gave her a once in a lifetime view of the big blue orb she knew to be home to some of the most fragile yet intellectually advanced creatures in the known universe. For that reason alone, she felt ashamed.

She belonged to a species that had exploited its very home to the point of devastation, and all for what? Money and the greed of an elite few. And even those few had the gall to complain when the climate crash came and destruction followed.

As she continued to admire the glistening planet below, a tear came to her eye. She traced her hand over the glass above the scorched brown parts of Earth.

Some of the view was obscured by soft, roiling masses of cloud that gave no indication of wrathful forces at play below. She'd known it was bad, but to actually see the extent of the damage from up there stirred a deep regret.

Another tear escaped to trickle down her cheek, parallel to the first. How could they? How could *anyone* do that much damage and think the planet would merely shake it off? She stared at it and realized it was a wonder the world hadn't shaken *them* off. Maybe it would have been better if it had.

She stood there in silence and admired the striking emeralds and blues from the many beautiful parts of Earth but also mourned the many parts that were scorched and barren and too obscured by cloud to see. Those damaged areas were referred to as the Devil's Handprints.

They were places covered in ash and dust and toxic mud, scorched by the merciless rays that penetrated the Swiss-cheese ozone layer. Many of them were smothered by thick smog and experienced notorious weather anomalies during which the sun blazed for days at a time. They were so damaged, some said they'd been touched by the devil himself.

In reality, Earth had become a volatile environment, a

dangerous place for its current inhabitants. It was a change brought about not by planetary evolution but by the dominant species that relied on it for its very survival

As Elpis One's orbit took it over North America, Stephanie squatted and ran her finger over the continent's familiar outline until she found the singed black spot she called home. While on the ground, much of it was extremely toxic, ruined, and hostile to human life, from the space station, it looked as beautiful as anywhere else on Earth.

She stayed like that, oblivious to the corridor behind her, and watched the earth rotate beneath her. Finally, she had her fill of its damaged beauty and rose to her feet.

But as she stepped out of the small glass viewing area and slipped her shoes on, something stirred within her. With Earth to inspire her, she felt a determination to learn how to be better, to make herself stronger, and maybe to find a way to make amends for the generations past. With that in mind, she made her way to the team's pod room and slipped inside.

The white room remained unchanged, almost comforting in its familiarity. Strange as it was, she began to feel more at home in this part of the Virtual World than she did in the real. The most likely reason was because it was always there. The white room always remained the same as it was before and was always safe. Well, that might not be true for her but safer, at least.

Nothing was completely safe for her anymore, not with her magic so erratic at present. That, she decided, would change.

Stephanie paced for a moment and thought hard about what needed to happen. She sat one of the benches and nibbled her fingernails. "Burt, are you up there? Or in there? Or wherever you tend to be?"

Burt cleared his throat as if he were human. "I am here, Stephanie. I wasn't expecting you until training was re-authorized. Is everything okay?"

She nodded, still chewing her nails as the wheels in her head spun crazily. "Yeah. I have some ideas I want to run through. I thought about a few things and I couldn't put them down. You know how that is. Or maybe you don't. I don't know."

BURT struggled to understand what she was trying to say. There was no system translation for angsty, nervous teen. "Okay… Can you at least tell me what it is you think you'll test?"

Stephanie stood and walked around the room. "Have you been able to determine what happens if I have gMU in massive quantities? And not only like what happened during training but basically what happens if I'm unleashed like that in the real world?"

Beyond the unwinnable scenario, he really had nothing to work with in order to examine that kind of hypothesis. "Unlimited power?"

"Yes." She nodded.

BURT paused for a moment and realized that he merely needed to let her try to describe what she wanted to investigate. It was clear she had some idea in her head and she wouldn't let it go.

"Those calculations are not yet complete," he told her, temporizing. "However, I can provide a representation of such power and we can explore the potential outcomes. What is it you wish to test your power on? I wouldn't recommend going free-form on other beings. It might make your control less effective when fighting on Earth."

Stephanie shook her head. "Oh, no. No, I don't want to hurt anyone. Basically, to put it bluntly, I want to re-sculpt the world."

Burt remained silent for several moments. She was nervous as she waited for his response, not at all sure how he would take it. When no comment was forthcoming, she tried to explain and to help him decide.

"You see, I have obviously always known about the damage that Earth has taken from both manmade disasters and the storms and weather anomalies that came about due to runaway global warming. But I never thought about how bad it really was until I saw it from up here. I want to fix it."

"I think that is a fantastic idea," he replied.

She smiled and suddenly, the room swirled away and deposited her on Earth. A little startled, she looked around to see where'd she'd landed and gaped at the completely decimated scene.

The sight of a small teddy bear, burnt and all but destroyed, made her gasp, and she put her hands over her mouth. The area had obviously been through some kind of terrible cataclysmic event, but she wasn't completely sure what it was yet.

BURT could tell she was shocked and a little lost, and because her idea was far beyond what he'd hoped for, he decided to help her. She jumped when he spoke. "You must first know what ails the patient before you know how to fix it."

Stephanie nodded and plodded silently along what had once been an old suburban street. The road, although broken and shattered, was still there, but the houses were piles of rubble protruding from the rotting carcasses of trees.

Debris was strewn in all directions, and every shred of vegetation was dead, dying, or in a state of decay. She turned the corner, stopped, and tilted her head to read the twisted remains of a sign a few hundred yards away.

It leaned to the side, part of it broken off. As she approached, she shook her head in disbelief at where he had brought her.

"Browns Ferry," she whispered. "Alabama's power plant location. It was the second largest in the US until it had a nuclear meltdown due to an extreme weather event coupled with an earthquake that caused a catastrophic breakdown in its cooling systems. It was a disaster, a pure hell on Earth. Everyone across the country had to take precautions and that was when the huge environmental bill was drawn."

"Exactly," Burt replied. "But it did little good since they waited until they were literally up to their eyeballs in flooding on the coasts, and up to their headstones in radiation in Alabama and across the neighboring states."

Stephanie rubbed her arms. The silent eerie calmness around her seemed thick enough to touch. She closed her eyes, took a deep breath, and looked up. "All right, I need the knowledge of what's wrong here so I can fix it. So...download it to me. Give me what I neee...eeddd..."

Her legs wobbled and she put her hand out to grab onto something to keep herself upright as Burt uploaded the information to her system. There was so much, she could almost feel the data pulsing through her brain to ignite the sparks that would help her create a plan.

With a tight hold on to the twisted uprights of the sign, she did her best to regain her balance and pull herself upright. She damn near fainted and she wasn't even sure that was possible in the Virtual World. Still, she decided if she could die, she could faint.

She shook her head as the magic settled. "Oh, that hurt like a sonofabitch. What the...is that...the full rundown of sustainable radioactive cleanup?"

"And some knowledge on what radioactivity truly does to a human," he replied proudly.

Stephanie chuckled. "Well, it all makes better sense why even decades after the radioactive meltdown, the people haven't come back. I can almost feel the gamma rays surging through the air. I guess that solves my issue of needing to know what levels the radiation is at. It's also handy since it seems like I don't need any protective clothing right now."

"We're also taking this scenario as a chance to see what your physical reaction to radioactivity is," he explained. Your avatar will react as your body would, although the sensors indicate that the gMU blocks any harmful rays."

"That's interesting," she agreed and clapped briskly.

She took a deep breath and rubbed her palms together. "All

right. Well, let's get to this. Cleaning up a spill this big would usually take a lot of people—like Chernobyl when over two hundred thousand emergency and recovery workers were sent in to do the job. What I need to do is recognize which tasks need doing and in what order. Then, I need to twist my magic to do what would normally be done using men and machines, only much, *much* faster."

Stephanie scrutinized the area and her attention settled on the putrid valley that had once been a river and one of the largest reservoirs in the area. Water still pooled in some sections of it, but it was muddy and yellow and the mud on its banks was full of half-rotted debris.

Beyond the dead vegetation on the riverbank, she saw what had once been the containment wall for pools of water surrounding the plant. They'd been cracked wide, the buildings beyond them little more than piles of rubble in a small lake of still water.

gMU hummed over her skin to create a faintly visible silver glow as if the magic actively fought the radiation.

Good, she thought, glad to be protected while she turned her mind with its sudden burden of information to the problem of making the area livable again—even if it was only for plants.

"So," she began, thinking out loud rather than speaking to Burt, "what I need to do is stabilize the reactors and make sure the rods are cool."

She looked at what was left of the power plant and studied its fractured walls and the surrounding pool of water.

"I would assume that's done. The next thing is to remove the contaminated topsoil, the debris, and the plant material."

This time, she stopped and stared at the devastation around her.

"Somehow, I think I'm gonna have to move more than the two inches or so of topsoil they took out for Fukushima...and that's not gonna happen. What if I use gMU to transfer the ions and..."

She let her voice fade and frowned slightly. "Burt, I need— Hold on. Let me try something."

BURT watched her pace and make calculations in her head. When she stopped, he waited to see what she would do next.

Stephanie rubbed her hands together and a smirk played along her avatar's lips. She put both arms out to the side and let small orbs of light escape from her palms. They raced away and searched for the edge of the most dangerous areas of radiation.

With her connection to them, she knew when the orbs reached the limits of her ability to interact with them. There was still more radiation beyond, but they stopped and traced a boundary around the area. That done, they spun faster and faster until they became connected in one ever-revolving circle.

She breathed deeply, lowered her arms, and shook her hands out. Her focus intense, she crossed them in front of her at the wrists and closed her eyes as she pulled and pushed the gMU where she needed it to go. With a sudden shift, she swung her arms out wide before she slapped her palms together.

Bursts of streaming energy exploded from both sides of her body. They rocketed toward the circled limitation of destruction and elevated to create a dome of magical protection.

Stephanie opened one eye and glanced cautiously in all directions. "That will do."

"Wow," Burt muttered.

She pushed her sleeves up, put her hands in front of her with her palms together, and scrutinized the location. From where she stood, she could see the edge of the dome in the distance and turned slowly to study the entire thing.

Moving her feet lightly over the ground, she swung her hands to release the energy in different ways. Some danced high into the sky and spun and whirled to collect any radioactive particles that had escaped into the atmosphere.

The second energy release feathered out and rippled over the ground to gather any debris into neat piles. A swarm of airborne gMU swept in behind it to capture any particles kicked up. As it worked, she extended her hand and faced her palm up to release another surge of magic.

This resembled a thousand droplets of honey clinging together. The whole blob oozed stickily upward to hover in front of her.

"Find the water," she told it, and the blob separated into an army of glistening gMU particles that headed purposefully toward what was left of the reservoir and the reactor's cooling ponds.

Stephanie kept one hand extended in the direction the globules had gone while she knelt and pressed her other palm to the ground. With her eyes shut tightly, she drew more gMU and pushed it into the earth until the ground glowed from one side of the magical dome to the other.

That accomplished, she stood and raised her hand as if she were controlling a marionette. The energy elevated from the earth and hovered barely inches above the ground.

She drew that hand close to her chest, curled her fingers, and wiggled them at the soil. The energy coating there morphed to create thousands of small rods that punctured the earth and stuck, where they vibrated as if they were sucking on the soil itself.

They grew bigger and bigger as they filled with radioactive particles. In the meantime, the magic gathering airborne particles now resembled a cloud of small comets, each with a tail of radioactive debris.

The debris and dead plant material stood stacked in neat piles under a cloak of flickering gMU. The earth lay bare around each pile, now veiled as more gMU tried to decontaminate it. As she watched, the rods drawing the radioactivity from the soil reached two feet in length and turned a dull gray as they fell in neat rows.

The comets of gMU with their tails of debris settled over them and they melded into one another before they rolled together to form solid cubes of radioactive waste. She frowned. "That's not quite what I wanted."

BURT took a moment to consider what she'd done. "You expected to do *more?*"

"Yes." Stephanie turned in a slow circle and surveyed the area. The outline of the plant's collapsed chimney caught her eye. "I wanted to make this place habitable, again. I wanted—"

She glared at the neat stacks, approached one, and noticed how the gMU protecting her flared into brightness as the radioactivity increased. "How do I get rid of all this?"

"There were ways," he told her. "Humans recognized the necessity of disposing of this kind of waste. They still had not perfected one before disaster struck, but..."

Once again, she felt the impact of a rush of incoming data. This time, she reached out instinctively and laid a hand on one of the cubes for support.

"Ow!" She stumbled back and rubbed her hand against her thigh. "That smarts."

With a scowl, she raised her hand so she could inspect her stinging palm and an ugly red burn where she'd touched the pile.

"It appears the gMU has its limits," Burt observed. "Proximity and concentration play a role in how effectively it protects you."

"Noted," she responded, her voice dry.

Stephanie stared into the distance and struggled to decide which method she would try next. She could attempt to transmute the waste at the molecular level. There'd been several methods where ions had been swapped and the waste had been transformed into a less dangerous form.

There was also one where extreme heat had been applied and dangerous radioactive waste had been burned in another kind of nuclear reactor, but even that had only changed the waste into another form with a less long-lived type of radiation. What she wanted to do was get rid of the radioactivity completely.

Can the gMU be used to restructure the material into something that isn't radioactive? Maybe even something useful? Like... She thought about it. *Like new topsoil, maybe?*

"Burt, what kind of molecules are found in dirt that's good for farming?"

He sent her the data, and Stephanie studied it quietly for a moment.

"And what's the molecular structure of these?" she asked and gestured at the stacks around her.

Burt scanned the piles and sent her the information. Stephanie gave a soft whistle. "Well, here goes nothing."

She focused on the gMU and drew more in, then worked it through the vortex she'd built inside her. As she concentrated it into the strongest form she'd attempted thus far, she thought about the piles of debris and waste around her.

"This has to work," she murmured as she thought of the molecular structure she had and the one she wanted to create. It wasn't as simple as she'd first thought. Even using magic, she first had to split the heavy, radioactive atoms and recombine the protons, neurons, and electrons into the lighter atoms she needed. That was the only way to create carbon, hydrogen, oxygen, and nitrogen atoms that could be recombined into the various organic matter found in topsoil. She would definitely need to pull and compress a significant amount of gMU to accomplish it.

When she thought the gMU was concentrated enough to make the conversion, she raised her hands and turned to face the nearest pile of debris. As she directed the magic into it in a single silver stream, she thought about the way the molecules had to shift and change and willed the magic to make it happen.

She continued to pour the gMU into the stack until the orderly pile crumbled into a mound of dirt...and dirt that smelt better than the world around her. "Yes! Look, Burt. Look!"

Her delight made him laugh, but he tried not to let any of that humor show when he spoke. "And the rest?"

"Easy!" she exclaimed and channeled the energy over the remaining piles.

At first, it was as easy as she thought it would be, but suddenly, it wasn't. The magic faltered as it curled over the last pile and she realized she'd focused so hard on sending it out that she hadn't remembered to draw more in.

It didn't take her long to fix that particular error.

"Nice!" he said, but she didn't hear him.

With the last stack of debris now transformed into a nice big pile of dirt, her gaze had drifted to the collapsed chimney.

"You know what the ultimate test would be?" she asked.

"I dread to think," BURT replied. He followed the direction of her eyes and calculated the odds of whether she'd go there next.

Sure, enough, she didn't disappoint.

"Can you put me in the reactor room?" she asked. "Somewhere near the rods but not on them?"

Ah, so she'd remembered the burn.

"I can do that," he told her, and in spite of his better judgment, changed the scenery.

His misgivings were well-founded when with a single shriek of pain, her avatar crumbled. Apparently, the gMU couldn't protect against that level of radiation. He ended the scenario and brought her avatar back to stand amidst the piles of dirt.

"Ugh. Let's not do that, again," Stephanie told him. "Now I know what a piece of burnt toast feels like. Worse, even."

Burt chuckled. "Well, now we know there's a limit to the background radiation the gMU can protect you from."

"Yeah. Thanks for that, Burt. I hadn't noticed."

"Really?" He injected surprise into his tones and then tried to sound serious as he suggested, "Would you like to go back and try again?"

"Oh, hell, no! What I want to do is figure out what else I can do while I think about how to deal with the rods."

"Okay. And your next idea is?"

"You remember that data you sent me about phytoremediation?"

"Yee-ees," he replied and wondered why she hadn't made the connection before.

"Well, since I don't have the energy to make another three hundred tons of dirt, I might as well see what I can do with the dirt I have. First, I need to spread it out."

BURT watched, intrigued, as she directed gMU magic to spread the dirt evenly over the area she'd taken the radiation from. "What sort of plants do you require?"

She put her hands on her hips and cocked her head.

"Oh, I don't know. You're the one who gave me the list. Do you really want me to repeat it all back to you?"

He sighed. "When did you get so sarcastic?"

Stephanie rolled her eyes. "Blame the boys. Now, hit me with the greenery."

Seconds later, she was not so impressed. "Are you done, yet?"

BURT dumped another layer of plant life over her avatar and watched as she collapsed under the weight. She said nothing when she struggled free of it and merely glowered as she spread the plants over the surrounding landscape.

When she was done, she sank to her knees and pressed a hand to the ground.

"So?" she asked and fatigue threaded her voice. "How did we do?"

He checked the system. "Within the dome, you've reduced the contamination by almost seventy percent."

"Seventy percent." Stephanie didn't sound impressed. She raised her head and surveyed the land around her. It did look better, but it was a long way from done. She took a deep breath and drew in a little more gMU, but then she stopped. "I can't do anymore today."

She sounded so utterly defeated that he wanted to comfort

her, but before he could, she continued. "That's not bad. How much of the earth's surface did I cover?"

He pulled the Virtual World back to give her the view from space. Her eyes shifted feverishly and a small frown creased her forehead. "I don't see it. Did you get the projection wrong?"

A tiny light flickered on the planet and she blinked and stared at it. "That's it?"

"That's it," he replied. "It's about a square kilometer of surface area."

Stephanie rubbed her aching shoulders, starting to feel the strain of using that much magic. "Well, at this rate, it will take… ohhhh…only a million lifetimes or so."

CHAPTER EIGHT

Stephanie whistled to herself, her mind on what she'd done in the pod as she packed her suitcase. She ran through different scenarios she could try in order to magnify the effect.

Her aim was to create a livable Earth again but at her current pace, the sun would swallow the planet before she could finish. A knock on the door drew her attention and she packed the pair of pants she held before she answered. Lars stood on the other side and leaned nonchalantly against the doorframe.

He flashed her a handsome smile and caught her off guard. Not because he smiled but because she actually, for a split second, considered it a handsome one.

"Hey," he said and peeked into her room. "Are you about packed up?"

She looked back. "Yeah. I'm getting the last things folded, and then I only have my grooming supplies."

Lars chuckled. "Grooming supplies? Are you hiding a horse in there I don't know about?"

Stephanie joined his laughter, then he straightened and tapped the doorframe. "I wanted to let you know we have an hour before we leave."

She nodded and glanced at the numbers floating on the wall. There were three columns of digits on the far wall, all keeping her informed of the time in every sector of Earth, Meligorn, and Dreth. The one lit up green was the one they went by. "Okay, I'll be ready. I'm gonna call my mom quickly."

He smiled again. "Tell her I said hi."

Stephanie laughed softly and gave him the hand sign for okay before she closed the door. She stood there for a moment, frowning slightly, then shrugged and crossed to the small desk in her room. "AI, can you please get my mom on the line?"

"Calling her now," the AI responded.

Quicker than she expected, Cindy's holographic image popped up over the small silver box on the desk. "Hey, sweetie!"

"Hey, Mom!" She was excited to see her and hear her voice again. "How are you doing?"

"I'm good—cleaning up around the house," her mom replied. "Your father went to meet with a vendor for the supplies we need to reorder."

"Aw, I was hoping to say hi." She sighed. "And didn't you just restock?"

Cindy smirked. "We did, but to start the contract job we just signed—thanks to you—we'll need more."

She gasped and clapped. "Yay! Congrats."

"Thank you, and congrats to you too on those stellar selling abilities," her mom replied. "We happen to have this investor…" She cleared her throat and winked. "We're using some of that money to hire more people and get a second level of operational support."

"Look at you guys, getting all crazy big." She laughed and glanced at the door as a knock caught her attention. "Ugh, I'm sorry, Mom. We're getting ready to go so we have a million things to do."

"No problem," Cindy said and waved cheerfully. "I completely understand. Go, do what you need to do, have a safe trip, and call us from Meligorn."

Stephanie smiled warmly. "I will. I love you. And please tell Dad I love him too."

"Always," her mother replied with her signature warm, caring smile. "Kisses."

They hung up and she sighed as she strode over and jerked the door open with one hand. Elizabeth stood outside, looking at her phone. "Oh, hey, sorry to interrupt. I heard your mom so I waited."

She waved her mentor inside. "What's up? Are you taking the long trip in a business suit? That's hardcore."

Ms. E looked at her black calf-length dress and black dress jacket. "Oh, no. Actually, that's why I am here. Unfortunately, I have to stay behind and protect your back, so you'll go to Meligorn with only your team."

Stephanie bit the inside of her lip, slightly shocked by the news. "Oh... Okay. Whatever you need to do."

She wrestled with an odd sense of despondency. Up until that moment, she hadn't realized how comfortable she felt having Elizabeth around. She'd been a lot happier knowing she would go with them, and her disappointment must have shown.

From the look on the woman's face, her reaction came as something of a surprise to her as well. She didn't follow it up, though.

Instead, she glossed over it. "You guys went out to the bar the other night and came back in one solid piece—and thankfully, without mug shots trailing behind you. So why not another planet? Right?"

Stephanie's eyes took on a distant look as she remembered that night. There'd definitely been a considerable volume of booze, an equal amount of laughter, and in the end, several punches thrown before the team snuck out of the bar brawl Frog had started with another guy who, in all fairness, had been a right bastard. She looked at Elizabeth who watched her with humor in her eyes.

She tried hard to get rid of the idea that the woman knew exactly what had gone down, swallowed quickly, and nodded. "Oh, yeah. Right. We got back safely. Um, sure, that's fine. What could possibly go wrong?"

Ms. E grinned and patted her on the arm. "Good. You'll do great and you'll be back before you know it. Now, I have some meetings to get to. If I don't see you before you leave, buckle up, make sure you get enough sleep, don't start fights, and don't blow the royals up."

The girl laughed nervously as her mentor left and watched the woman answer her phone as she walked out of sight. As soon as she'd gone, she shut the door and ran to retrieve her hand-held comm. "Are you guys there?"

She was slightly panicked. Okay, she was freaking the hell out. Johnny came on. "We're here, big chief. What's up? Do you need Frog to come get your luggage?"

The other man groaned in the background. "Why am I always the bell boy?"

Stephanie shook her head and flapped her hand at the same time. "No. I got it. I wanted to know if we had everything. You know...do we have the armor, the MU stones, the backup batteries, the stuff from the armory, the—"

In the other room, the guys gathered around the comms when they heard the panic in her tone. Lars cleared his throat to interrupt her. "Whoa! Hold up there, Quality Control. Relax. Take a really big breath. The supplies have been checked, double checked, and then triple checked. Then, Brenden watched them loaded for the trip."

She instantly felt a little bit calmer. "Okay. Thanks. I thought I would ask because if I didn't, it would be my fault if we arrived there empty-handed."

Johnny chuckled gently. "It's all accounted for, boss lady. All we're missing at this point is you."

Stephanie looked around. "Oh yeah. Okay, be there in…uh…ten minutes."

She ended the call and shoved the comm unit in her bag before she rushed into the shower and yanked her bathroom bag off the counter.

Using her arm to swipe all her stuff into the bag in one sweep, she set it back on the counter as she double checked the drawers and the bathroom. When she was sure she'd left nothing behind, she picked it up and shoved it in her suitcase.

With two hands, she slammed it shut and leaned on it with her elbow to get it closed. She put her thumb on the front mechanism and it flashed blue and then green to confirm that it was locked.

Once she'd put her bags at the door, she walked over to the tablet on the desk. She swiped right and pulled up Todd's email, even though she knew he couldn't check it yet.

It didn't matter. She decided she'd leave him a little message before she left. A holographic microphone rose from the screen and she cleared her throat and leaned forward to speak into it as a small animated camera hovered in front of her to record the video.

"I always hated these things." She laughed. "Todd, I'm getting ready to set off on my own adventure. I wish I could tell you what, but it's kind of hush-hush at the moment. From the background, though, I assume you can tell I'm not at home. Anyway, I wanted to check in, tell you I am thinking about you and I hope you're kicking alien butt, and hopefully, by the time I'm back on Earth, you'll be out of boot camp. Love you, dude."

She raised her fist and stood there for a moment, then glanced from the camera to her fist and back again. She pointed at it and smiled. "Did you catch that? Jud Nelson? Breakfast Club? Yeah… probably not. Bye, dude."

Stephanie ended the message and sent it, laughing at herself as she shoved the tablet in her shoulder bag. She drew her information slip from her pocket and made sure she was headed to the right place. "Deck 9, *Meligorn Dreamer*, departing Elpis One 09:47 E1T," she read aloud.

After she'd repeated it, she took a deep breath and shoved the slip back into her pocket. She had reached the door when she remembered she was supposed to board the liner incognito.

With a scowl of irritation, she summoned her magic to give herself long red hair, green eyes, and honey-colored skin. After a careful examination of herself in the mirror beside the door, she asked the magic to make her look a good two inches taller and ten pounds heavier than she really was, and to make her look as old as thirty.

When she was satisfied that not even her mother would recognize her, she stepped through the door and drew it closed behind her.

"Now to find the boarding area," she muttered. "All by myself. Because now, we're on our own."

The boys were way ahead of her and taking their gear down to the cargo area, and they bitched every step of the way.

"Ouch," Brenden protested. "Don't push so damn hard. If you give me a shoe wedgie with that bitch, you'll rip my whole foot off."

Frog looked at him from behind the wheeled pallet. "Sorry, but it's hard to see through the giant pallet of shit you made me push. I know I was the last to join the team—by ten minutes, I might add—but that was a long time ago. Can we please either make me an equal or hire some newbie I can hand over to?"

Marcus laughed. He carried two duffels with ease. "There's no room for more, dude. You'll have to suffer through it for another round. Don't worry, it makes you stronger."

Frog groaned as they made their way across the dock with the last of the equipment. They'd told Stephanie it was all already locked away but had decided a little white lie wouldn't hurt when they heard how panicked she was. Not only did they not want her to freak out, but they also did not want a surprise appearance of Morgana.

The guard at the entrance to the umbilical leading to the hold put his hand up and flipped through his tablet when Lars showed him their badge. He glanced at it and back at him before he stepped to the side. "Lower Deck Twenty-four, Compartments nine-three-two and nine-three-three. Use your palm print to secure them. If you have any problems, use the comm center in your rooms to call the concierge. If you can't get in, drop past security over there."

Lars looked in the direction he'd indicated as he tucked his badge away. He nodded once he'd located the relevant area. "Thank you."

The team lugged everything down to their assigned storage, packed it away, and secured it for the journey. They didn't put a single thing in the second compartment but had rented it in case. Marcus shook his head as Lars pressed his palm to the pad. "What good is the equipment down in the hold?"

The guys turned and looked at him, and Lars sighed. "You aren't suggesting we'll need it on the voyage out, are you?"

The other man stared in return and gestured at the upper decks. "I'm only saying it's no good down here if we're attacked by pirates up there."

Lars rolled his eyes. "We have permission for our personal sidearms as security escorts, but that's it." He narrowed his eyes. "Of course, if you don't think you're man enough to handle a pleasure cruise without anything extra..."

Frog snorted, and Marcus shook his head. "No, I'm good. I'm

man enough to deal with anything *without* my sidearm...unlike the rest of you pussies."

The team leader gave him a look that said he might consider making him prove it, but the final boarding call came through and he led them back to the boarding lounge.

They checked in under their cover names. Frog was last to come up, tipped an invisible hat, and put on a passable Irish accent. "Shamus McGee," he told the attendant and showed her his boarding pass.

She didn't even blink, found his name, took his fingerprint, and handing him a map of the ship. He turned away with a sigh and rolled his eyes at her lack of reaction to his obviously impressive Irish name.

The guys laughed at him as they walked through the entryway toward the ship's foyer where a fountain sprayed multi-colored arcs of virtual water that looked almost real. Lars looked around and saw they'd caught the attention of a female passenger headed in the same direction.

He smiled at her and nodded politely before he turned back to the team. She nodded in response and her lips curved into a small smile as she studied her ticket and scanned reception for the right elevator.

After he'd taken a minute to admire the tall, leggy redhead, Marcus leaned over and whispered to Lars, "I thought Steph—I'm sorry, *Lilly* was supposed to meet us here. You don't think the nerves got to her and turned her into Morgana, do you?"

He looked around again but saw no one who might be Stephanie in disguise. His scrutiny dismissed the woman who stared at the same bank of elevators they needed.

His voice lowered to a sotto voce whisper, he added, "Maybe we should look for her and make sure she's not doing something desperate like holding hostages in the boarding area or looking for some Dreth to kill."

The woman hid a smirk and turned toward them. "If I were

her," she told them seriously, "I'd come in here to Hulk out. And maybe bash a couple of you knuckleheads together for talking about her that way."

Lars caught on first and covered a laugh, but the other man looked suspiciously at her. Stephanie ducked in close and put her hand up to hide her face from people passing by. For a brief moment, she assumed her own face and quickly returned to her disguise.

Marcus jumped slightly. "Whoa. Either you're her or we have a really big problem."

She laughed and her long ginger hair cascaded over her shoulders. "It's me, you dummy. I didn't want to give anyone a chance to recognize me. This place is huge. There are way too many people here."

He made another furtive scrutiny and this time, took note of the open floors layered above them. They stood close to the fountain in the center of an open atrium surrounded by what looked like thousands of people who milled aimlessly about.

Stephanie shook her head. "I didn't think for a second that this place was so monstrous."

Lars grinned. "Come on. Me, Frog, and Johnny have been on one before, and we studied the schematics for this one. We'll show you around."

"Mostly to make sure you know where not to blow shit up," Frog interjected. "You know, so we don't get sucked into the cold dark depths of space."

Johnny elbowed him. "You have no chill, do you? No chill at all."

He shrugged and hurried behind them. "What? I'm being for real here. Under the circumstances, I would say I have every right to feel that way."

"No offense taken, Froggy." She laughed and turned to squeeze his cheek.

When she'd let go and turned away, he rubbed his face. "She

really freaks me out with a new body and everything. Her attitude's the same, though."

They all laughed as they wandered across the atrium and into the elevator. It was glass fronted, so Lars pointed out all the cool things he'd noticed about the ship. Frog followed up with safety advice.

The team leader pointed down a level. "And there's the richie shopping mall with loads of designer boutiques for clothing and jewelry and stuff. I'm not sure I understand why'd they want to shop before they get to Meligorn, but whatever, right?"

They left the elevator and followed the corridor away from the center of the ship. When they reached the last T-intersection, Frog grabbed her arm and almost dragged her over to the wall opposite.

"See this?" he demanded, tapped it with the tip of his index finger, and made sure she was paying attention. "*This* section of wall is very thin. This goes to the outside in about twenty feet. We want no unnecessary explosions close to this wall."

A woman walking past them gasped, put her hand to her chest, and stared at them with wide eyes as she hurried away. Stephanie rolled her eyes as the passenger scuttled off.

With any luck, that was someone who thought they were a bunch of hooligans making really terrible jokes at an inappropriate time. If she didn't, they could expect a visit from ship security *very* soon.

She glared at Frog. "Are you done telling me stuff I already know?"

Over on Star Base Notaro, Captain Asparos stared out the viewing port at Elpis One. His mind drifted from the job at hand to the memory of seeing the command center of a Federation cruiser blown clean away.

It was hard to focus on what he needed to do next when he could still see the bodies they'd salvaged. He closed his eyes and rubbed his hand over them as he tried to will the images away.

It was a relief when a soft chime caught his attention. He stepped up to a console and typed quickly to bring up a screen that displayed the luxury liner known as the *Meligorn Dreamer*.

A brief message flashed across it.

Special people boarding...

The captain nodded and murmured to himself. "Got you."

He shut the system down and pulled out a rather archaic-looking contraption. It was a coder, old but a more modern variant of something used throughout most of Earth's history.

Seated at the desk, the captain plugged the device in, drew a carefully folded piece of paper from his pocket, and waited to send his reply. When the machine was ready, he tapped the sender three times before beginning.

It took him a moment to run his finger down the code words on the sheet as he tapped them out. *James sends his regards. You owe him drinks when you get back from your trip. STOP.*

When they reached their rooms aboard the *Meligorn Dreamer*, Stephanie immediately wandered to the balcony. She stared at the atrium beyond and tried to take it all in. It took her a moment to realize that what she'd thought was completely empty space was actually not that at all.

Every few floors, there was a magnetic floating floor, clear so it could be seen through, which gave an open feeling to the enclosed space. These floors also created a place for people to socialize under the everchanging colors of the artificial lights.

Holographic images of fields and forests graced the walls of each level to enhance the impression of openness.

Lars came to stand beside her and leaned his elbows on the

rail as he followed her gaze. "They're creating an impression of the real world using Virtual World technology. They added it when they found that many passengers, especially the Dreth and Meligorn, became claustrophobic on the longer cruises. From the balconies, you can see all the way down if you want to, but you can also change it so you can look out at whatever world your floor is programmed to show. It's very cool."

Stephanie laughed. "You say that like it's not a total security nightmare."

He stared out across the level. "Yeah, well, that's because I can see what's really there. Even on this level, we're three floors up, and I have it set so I can monitor everything I need to see."

She smiled. "It's good to know someone's on the job."

Lars had nothing to say to that, and as his gaze roved over the balconies opposite, he noted there was no walkway linking them together. Beside him, Stephanie was silent, still amazed by the technology the world outside the Gov-Subs had become accustomed to.

All around her were things she hadn't even known existed. It almost made her mad to see the difference between how people in the Subs lived compared to the wealth around her. She frowned, distracted by the sound of giggling coming from the floating floor two levels beneath them.

Irritated, she leaned over the balcony as several families began to enjoy some time out in the simulated parkland, oblivious to the drop below them.

The kids really struck her, especially the little girl with her bouncing blonde curls and innocent smile. Stephanie watched as she played with her brother, laughing like she didn't have a care in the world...not a single one.

CHAPTER NINE

Power thrummed through the *Meligorn Dreamer* as it warmed its engines. Warning klaxons blared a demand that the flight lounge inside the station be cleared before the umbilical was released and retracted into the station. At the same time, the cargo entry to the dock was sealed.

While the procedure usually ran trouble-free, nothing was left to chance. Accidents were rare, but in space, the consequences of a failed seal could be catastrophic. Lights flashed amber, and entrances into both the cargo and boarding areas were locked down.

Only when the station was sealed did the *Dreamer* use small auxiliary jets to push it carefully away from the station. Once it had reached the required distance, it engaged the larger drives and moved steadily into space.

On the viewscreen that displayed the scenery outside the ship, the passengers might have seen the rings of Saturn flash by, but only if they'd actually paid attention. The ship now moved faster than any human ship before contact with Meligorn.

The technology of interstellar flight improved by leaps and bounds and slow, small, heavy ships became things of the past.

The *Meligorn Dreamer*—mostly referred to as the *Dreamer*—was fitted with the latest advances in interstellar flight technology. It cruised rapidly through the Limitation Zone toward its transition point.

Limitation Zones were the areas around planets and other orbiting bodies where ships were prohibited from entering or exiting transition space. In these zones, they had to maintain a specific speed and be aware of passing vessels.

Once it had passed through this, the *Dreamer* would set course for the Transition Zone, where it would make its jump into the dark expanse of transition space to reach the Meligorn system.

The journey from the Limitation Zone to the Transition Zone would take a week, and that was only the beginning.

Inside the ship, time seemed to pass as normal. Stephanie decided to spend what time she could inside the Virtual World to work on her energy acquisition.

She'd had nothing specific planned, so Burt had left her to her own devices. Initially, she'd planned to work in the team's training space with gMU but that had seemed like too big a risk to take.

If something went wrong, she'd have a hard time fixing what she broke—and there were too many lives at stake for her to let that happen. It was safest to stay within the confines of the Virtual World for that kind of practice.

As she entered, she rubbed her hands together, the gesture pointless in her self-contained space suit. She left the white preparation room and stood on a clear platform which seemed to float effortlessly through the stars.

It was a location that gave her the best environment for concentrating and working on her skills. Not to mention that, for all intents and purposes, it made sense that she would have the best access to gMU in space.

Of course, standing on an open platform in the void of space wasn't something she could do in the real universe, but BURT put all the parameters required in place and left her to it.

Through the clear faceplate of her helmet, she looked down at her suit with its built-in boots and gloves. The days of bulky spacewalks were also a thing of the past, but she couldn't quite determine why they would make the woman's suit as tight as a second skin.

She shrugged and grumbled quietly, "So much for the surge of equality when it comes to comfortable dang clothes for women. I'll be picking this out of my—"

BURT cleared his throat. "How is it going?"

Stephanie glanced around and half-expected to see him float by, riding a meteor or something. "I'm only getting started."

"Good. And I will submit your space suit feedback anonymously to the engineers in wardrobe," he replied.

She blushed slightly and went back to work, breathing deeply through her nose as she spread her arms wide to draw in the gMU all around her.

As she did so, she focused on the vortex she'd created inside her and spun the energy until she had refined it into a more compressed product. The magic swirled and knotted within, sparkled through her body, and made her glow.

To an outside observer, she looked like a young dancing star drawing in a line of light in the shifting and often violent expanse of space. After a few moments, the energy had spun through its final turn and settled in a concentrated ball in the pit of her stomach. She wasted no time in repeating the process with a second batch of gMU in an effort to see how quickly and thoroughly she could convert the energy into usable magic.

The more she had in reserve, the better off she would be in a battle since a little condensed gMU went a long way or created one really devastating explosion. Sweat beaded on her forehead and her suit began to use the wicking to pull the moisture away from her skin to cool her down to her original temperature.

By the time the vault inside her was half full, she was exhausted. She let her arms fall to her sides and realized she was breathing heavily. Conscious of the need to pace herself, she dropped onto the center of the disc beneath her, sat cross-legged, and stared at her gloved hands while she tried to calm the rapid race of her heart.

She caught a small flash from the corner of her eye and looked up slowly with a small gasp at the wondrous sight before her.

Close enough that she could see the spiraling clouds of gases that erupted and pushed back against the weightlessness of space was a large nebula of stars. For only a moment, she sat and absorbed the beauty in the universe around her. It made her feel absolutely tiny, while at the same time, it seemed as if she held the history of everything and everywhere tightly in her gut.

She felt like a newborn floating on the ocean of space but also like something as old as time with the splendor of history flooding her veins.

When she depressed a button on the top of her gloved left hand, a dome rose from the platform's edges. As the dome enclosed her, it sealed with a soft hiss followed by the quieter sound of a breathable atmosphere releasing around her.

The whole ritual wasn't necessary considering there was nothing like it in reality. It also wasn't needed in the Virtual World since she couldn't die there, but it helped her mind accept the reality of her surroundings.

Once the dome signaled that she was surrounded by

atmosphere, Stephanie removed her helmet and gloves and pulled out her tablet. She began making extensive notes for ONE R&D.

It was essential that she recorded every aspect of working with gMU. After all, she wasn't the only being with access to magic, and the ambassador had only said her experience was unique. That didn't mean it couldn't happen again.

And it meant she had to record it all, from the way she converted it to the feelings of wonder and reverence that washed over her when the magic filled her. Every detail needed to be captured.

When she had finished and was sure she'd included everything, she saved her file and sat in silence to watch the universe turn around her. Her mind drifted to the job ahead of her and then to her ability to clean the earth up.

"There has to be a way to do it faster," she mused.

She set the tablet down beside her, crossed her legs at her ankles, and leaned back on her hands. Her thoughts drifted to the time before humanity had damaged its world and ranged to when people had marched to save it.

It seemed strange, now, to contemplate those distant years when humans had recycled what they could to minimize what they put into landfill. Those had been times when rubber was made into playground chips and smaller homes were legislated for all, not only the poor.

Admittedly, the technology was almost archaic when compared to the present, but the principles were the same. There had to be a way for her to not only clean Earth up using her magic but to also begin to heal it through sustainable practices.

Most of the trash had been taken care of during The Great Burning. With chronic overpopulation and a collapsing infrastructure, none of the large cities of the world had been able to cope with the waste produced by their populations.

During that time, people had simply disposed of their trash by dumping it into the streets and waterways when landfills were no longer available and recycling factories hadn't been able to cope. In an attempt to stop the practice of illegal trash fires, governments set up local furnaces.

The Federation's new leader had ordered that all rubbish was to be burned, without exception or exclusion. He'd ordered the furnaces to run non-stop until there was nothing left to consume. It was this event that tipped the world over the edge of catastrophic climate failure.

The number of pollutants released into the atmosphere covered most of the planet in heavy smog and released toxins that caused wide-spread breathing difficulties and ailments. Many mourned the stupidity, but others secretly rejoiced at the loss of population.

Their joy was short-lived, however. Once the portion of the population susceptible to acute respiratory failure had died, the survivors discovered there were worse things to suffer. The occurrence of cancer reached epidemic proportions when a new array of aggressive, untreatable tumors appeared.

Extreme climatic events such as the hot-cyclone anomalies, unseasonal blizzards, tornadoes, downbursts, and thunderstorms had increased. Sea levels had risen to engulf coastal communities before evaporation had taken its toll on the oceans. Waterborne disease had inflicted more casualties than any of the major disasters put together.

There were some who said her world was on the brink of dying, and others who said the world would survive but humanity would not. Neither outcome was acceptable.

Stephanie pondered the mess her generation had been handed and wondered how to fix it. She could magically scrub the atmosphere all she wanted, but if she didn't fix the source of continuing pollution, it wouldn't mean a thing.

That meant reintroducing clean technologies such as the solar farms that had once powered the solar schools of China as well as millions of homes in the United Kingdom, Bangladesh, Tanzania, and Australia. It meant finding a way to harness the wilder winds and renewing efforts to direct the energy of Earth's volcanoes.

And that was all before she discovered a way to channel gMU as an energy source in and of itself. As a power source, it would be cleaner with none of the waste products of nuclear power. There *had* to be a way to make it work.

Stephanie wrote her ideas down, starting with ways to power everyday items with magic that could be handled by the most non-sensitive human to ways of using gMU to power entire cities. Unfortunately, power wasn't the only issue she had to deal with.

People needed non-toxic areas to live in. They needed to get out of the Subs, grow their own food, and raise their kids in an environment that wouldn't kill them.

Her attempt to clean up the Browns Ferry site was a good first try. Well, except for not being able to get near the fuel rods. That still smarted, and it was another problem she would have to deal with.

A problem of that magnitude meant she needed more power and the ability to use her magic on a wider scale. If she could find a way to remove the toxins from the water and the soil, she knew she'd be able to open large areas for resettlement in a matter of years rather than decades.

With the pollution cleared from the sky and the land and the ground covered in plants and trees once more, humanity could set a course for a renewed Earth. The only concern she had was whether or not her race had learned enough from their mistakes to not repeat them.

For some reason, she found it hard to believe.

Elizabeth pulled her new ID from the envelope Burt had express-delivered that morning. With it now clipped it to the lapel of her jacket, she boarded the small shuttle scheduled to take her back to Earth.

While she'd enjoyed her time on Elpis One, she knew she'd be much more comfortable on the ground with a real atmosphere surrounding her. Space was fun the first few times out, but too much could go wrong that could end up with her sucking vacuum.

No, she was glad to return planet-side, even if it was with a new identity. The new ID would help her reach home with their enemies none the wiser. It had been awarded under a Federation-recognized protocol that allowed the wealthy to travel under an assumed name for one journey only for personal security reasons.

Of course, it was only as good as the database it was held in, but she trusted Burt. There wasn't anyone better to take care of the technical things than the damned AI who ran it.

She smiled at the thought and straightened her jacket, unaware that she now carried herself differently than when she'd departed with the team. She had a shit-ton of money, now, and the future of an entire race on her shoulders if he was to be believed. Wealth and the power of being the sole physical representative of a company with Earth's survival as its goal... Well, she'd always loved a challenge. And wealth. She *adored* wealth.

Elizabeth smirked at the thought and whispered, "Uncle Ben had it all wrong, Spiderman. It's not with great power comes great responsibility. It's with great big fat bank accounts."

The trip to Earth didn't take very long, being a direct route to Washington. A driver waited for her when she touched down, a nice little perk Burt had thrown in. It was wonderful to work for a boss who valued her enough to look after her.

When she arrived at the base, it took her a second to get

comfortable. Without the team there, the place was eerily silent. It wasn't at all what she had become accustomed to.

To remedy that, she went to work making additional calls to bring in a few contacts to help her. "Yes, Chancellor, I really appreciate it. I'll see you then."

She hung up and checked off the appointment made with the chancellor of Harbor Technology University. After that, she stared at the next thing on the list and pursed her lips. This would be a lot less pleasant than calling the chancellor.

With a sigh, she picked the phone up again and called the Federation Navy contact number she'd been given. It was time to see if they wanted to come to the office for another meeting. When no one answered, she left a message and managed to sound pleasant and unruffled.

Her call might come as an unexpected surprise to them, but it was time she took that bull by the horns. Stephanie was safely out of their reach—for now—and they had no way of knowing where she'd gone.

That wouldn't last for much longer, but there was no way anyone would find her. Unless, of course, the Navy pulled the ship over within the next week.

CHAPTER TEN

On the *Meligorn Dreamer*, the team was out for the evening. They'd secured their gear in their rooms and now gave Stephanie The Grand Tour, as Frog called it.

Their initial foray passed through the open atrium space to the Deck of Faith.

"It's so anyone can find a place to comfort their souls," Lars explained when they stopped at the entry to a large courtyard.

Stephanie looked around at the many churches, mosques, and temples to any deity or lack of deity she'd ever imagined...and many she'd never known existed.

At the back stood a huge building that looked like an ancient Buddhist temple. Priests in a mixture of saffron and maroon robes walked through the plaza and mingled with the tourists, travelers, and servants of other faiths.

She was surprised to see the representatives of each faith mingling so peacefully. That had definitely not been how the history books described it, even if it was nice to see now.

There didn't seem to be any valid reason why Lars would have brought her there and she narrowed her eyes at him. "This looks really cool, but you do realize I'm not a religious person, right?"

He shrugged. "I know, but this is basically the best floor for when you want no negativity and an abundance of friendly faces."

"Like when I start auctioning you off to whoever needs the most seats filled?" she joked…kind of.

Lars laughed. "That's not a problem here."

He pulled her back to the elevator and punched the buttons for the next floor. Stephanie leaned against the elevator wall with folded arms and watched the team warily.

If she knew these guys, they were up to something.

When he saw her expression, Lars turned toward her with a twinkle in his eyes. "I know we could have done this in the Virtual World, but since this is your first time on one of these liners, I thought it better for you to see it firsthand. Besides, it's a good way to work up an appetite."

She pouted. "Yeah, we were supposed to be headed to dinner. I get grumpy if I'm not fed."

He faked a sad face. "Hulk smash…fish and chips."

Stephanie laughed as they stepped out of the elevator and wound their way through the other passengers looking for something other than room service.

Lars lifted his chin to indicate one direction. "So, if you go right, you will find the richies' mall I told you about earlier." He tilted his chin to the left. "In the back over there is a food court. You buy from one of the vendors and choose one of the sticky tables in the center to eat at."

She screwed her face up in distaste. "That doesn't make me want to go there."

"Well, then, do I have a bargain for you." He put his hand on her shoulder and led her straight ahead until the corridor opened into another multi-deck vista. "You might change your mind about the eatery after you spend the day here gambling your heart out."

Even a cursory glance at the view left her impressed. "It looks like Vegas crammed into a ship. Nice."

She walked over to the railing and looked down five floors to a more softly lit area. "What goes on down there where the lights are dim?"

He leaned over. "Oh, that leads to the engines rooms and Engineering. There's nothing really to see down there, and you need a pass to access it. I can organize a tour if you want one."

Stephanie rolled her eyes. "Let me think about it."

They continued and took an elevator up past the casinos to another level. Lars and Stephanie poked their heads out of the elevator and stared at two large white doors in front of them. A simple white desk backed by a row of lockers and manned by two serious-looking security guards in pristine white uniforms was set to one side of it.

The men looked up when the elevator doors opened, and Lars tossed them a quick wave. "Sorry, wrong floor!"

He stepped back into the elevator and pulled her with him. "That's the brig. These kinds of places don't have too many instances of nefarious crime since they're so selective about who they allow on board. It's mostly used to let drunks to sleep off their stupidity— keeps them from starting a fight and wrecking someone's holiday."

She winced. "Sucks to be them, then, doesn't it?"

The tour continued until the team ended up in a plaza devoted to fine dining, dancing, and theaters. The mall of designer wear was linked by a short corridor, and beyond it, an entire deck was devoted to working out.

To Stephanie's surprise, they left the main restaurant area and walked to another small courtyard with a secluded restaurant. As they crossed the open space, a Dreth exited and headed toward them.

Lars linked his arm through Stephanie's when she froze and her hand moved instinctively for the blaster she usually carried in the simulations. Frog came up on the other side of her, slid his hand into hers, and squeezed her fingers.

Their presence calmed her first instinct and she managed to suppress the urge to call on her magic. Instead, she took a moment to notice how the Dreth was dressed. The alien was as huge as any of the warriors in the sims, but he wore a simple blue tunic over baggy red trousers, and he was barefoot.

Bells chimed as he moved, and he gave them a close-lipped smile as he passed and brought his hand briefly to his chest.

"Uh, wait, did I imagine that?" she asked.

Lars laughed and relaxed his grip on her arm a little. "The Dreth priest of Hrageth? Not at all. There are all kinds here on the ship. Believe it or not, I met a vegetarian Dreth on one of these vessels. You have to remember that not all Dreth are your enemy. There has to be a point where you open your mind enough to realize there's more to the Dreth than only the pirates."

"Not much more," Frog muttered, and Marcus whacked him upside the head.

The team leader ignored him. "The pirates merely make the news reports more often."

Stephanie understood and also realized she had become very isolated from news of the real world, and it reminded her of the last thing she'd seen. "You know, I watched a news report a week or so ago where a couple of business moguls slaughtered each other, and then, before anything could be done, their chalet exploded and all that was left of them were bones. Humans have their own form of pirates."

Lars squeezed her arm. "Exactly. Come on. They say this place serves the best food on the ship."

"I trust you to know." She glanced back for one last look at the Dreth priest and removed her hand from Frog's as she did so.

He gave her a look of mock hurt, slid back to walk beside

Marcus, and accepted his teammate's pretense of sympathy. They made her smile with their antics.

Still smiling, she turned and stopped when she came face to face with a Meligornian in traditional robes. Lars apologized for almost running into him, but he deflected the guard's embarrassment with a gentle shake of his head.

Stephanie looked into his face and noticed that he had a kind smile and warm eyes. She stepped back to bend her knee for the Meligornian greeting to nobility, reached up, and bowed her head.

To her surprise, he didn't let her dip any closer to the floor. Instead, he placed his hand in hers and pulled her in, holding her forearm tightly so that she returned the clasp as they greeted one another.

When he released her, she stepped back and smiled. "It's nice to see a Meligornian here."

He spread his arms wide. "And it's nice to see a human who knows how to greet one properly. Not many humans know how."

The rest of the team shuffled uncomfortably and reminded her they were there.

"Oh, I'm sorry. Please, these are my...friends," she told him, gestured to the guys, and stood aside so they could greet him.

They did as well as she had, but she couldn't help noticing how they were suddenly much more alert and their eyes scanned every corner of the courtyard. Ever since the attack on the ambassador and Elizabeth's unwinnable scenario, they'd become far more cautious around Meligornian people. Stephanie would have laughed if it didn't make her so sad.

The stranger cleared his throat, drawing her from her memories.

"I am sorry," he told her, "but I didn't catch your name."

Stephanie blushed. "I am...Lilly."

This time, he extended his hand in a human greeting. "Lilly. Okay. Nice to meet you, Lilly. I am Garmathiun Hondor of the

Triton Quadrant of Meligorn. You may call me Garma for short."

She smiled at that and let him walk beside her.

Lars kept hold of her other arm, and the team fell in behind them, exchanging glances.

Garma laid his palm against the back of her hand. She glanced down and realized she was taking MU in from the Meligornian.

With a gasp, she snatched her hand out from under his. "I'm so very sorry."

He chuckled and lowered his voice. "You aren't so hard to identify, Stephanie Morgana, even if you do have a different face. Your magic gave it away. I could feel it the moment you greeted me. If you're trying to hide your identity, you might want to watch that."

"Noted," Lars murmured from beside her, and he didn't sound pleased.

Stephanie ignored her guard and put her hands nervously in her jacket pockets as she tried to find a way to change the subject. "Your MU is very strong, much stronger than I'd expect for someone who's obviously been on Earth and is now traveling back to Meligorn."

"As you get older, you go one of two ways," he explained and accepted her diversion. "You either learn how to hold your magic tightly and only use small portions at a time, or you become… sloppy and lose everything in the blink of an eye."

"Then I will start to learn how to hold what I have," she responded with a solemn smile.

They now approached the restaurant and Garma glanced at Lars. "I will go back to my quarters," he said and glanced at Stephanie and the rest of the team. "Would you all like to join me for dinner, tonight? I have the top suite upstairs so there is more than enough room and you are all very welcome."

Stephanie took his hand in farewell. "I appreciate it, but we have plans tonight. If you are up for it tomorrow, I think we would be delighted."

The Meligornian grinned. "Excellent. Then I look forward to seeing you tomorrow evening. And you won't have to hide who you are while you're there."

They said their farewells and she walked on beside Lars. The team leader had released her arm and was already researching one Garmathiun Hondor of the Triton Quadrant of Meligorn on his tablet.

He wasn't very impressed with her. "You can't randomly become besties with someone who obviously saw right through your disguise. That's not exactly a recommendation, you know."

She patted him on the shoulder. "Deep breaths, Lars. Deep breaths. We'll be okay. The whole reason I am here alive today is because I put a little faith in the Meligornian ambassador. Out of everyone I've met since finding my magic, Meligornians tend to be safer than humans. Present company excepted, of course. They are also more powerful and easier to make friends with. Everything will be all right."

Frog slipped past them and opened the door so she and Lars could step through. Marcus slid through in front of them and obviously scrutinized the place because Lars was preoccupied with his tablet.

Stephanie let the team do their thing and entered the restaurant. As the aromas inside caught her nose, her eyes widened and she heard the guys all take several appreciative sniffs.

The place smelled amazing and there were representatives of all three races seated inside. A waiter guided them to a table and handed out the menus.

As soon as they were settled, they buried their faces in the list of selections. Soon, a lively discussion began as they read through the many multiplanetary options.

"I dare you to try the Dreth food." Brenden smirked and

nudged Marcus as he addressed her. "I hear it all tastes like either space gas or the underside of a Dreth's backside."

She curled her lip at him, then shrugged. "Screw it. Why not at least try it? Then, if I don't like it, I will never be tempted again."

The guys gawked at her as she ordered two Dreth dishes and a regular burger and fries in case she didn't like them. Everyone else ordered conservatively, all of them too chicken to try anything else. When the food arrived, most of them were relieved that they'd chosen to stick to the norm.

The waitress set the two Dreth dishes in front of Stephanie and smiled. She returned the smile before she picked up a fork and poked at the first dish. It looked like bacon with some kind of seaweed draped over it and a purple mashed vegetable piled decoratively on top.

She leaned forward and sniffed at it, but it had absolutely no odor, which was very strange. Intrigued, she tried it cautiously. The taste was similar to smoked meat and potatoes, although the consistency was more like eating seafood.

The lack of aroma notwithstanding, it had a subtle citrusy flavor that complemented the meat and softened the slow-creeping burn of something stronger.

"That was fairly good—spicier than what I'm used to, but not too bad at all," she said as Marcus dared Frog to take a bite.

Stephanie left them to it, turned to the next one, and tilted her head to the side as she tried to work out what it was. It looked like gray sludge—soup-like but too thick to be soup. More like mousse or pate, perhaps.

It formed the base for a pale, delicately folded pastry that had been loaded with diced cubes of meat and a mixture of purple and red vegetables shaved into thin strips. Like the dish before it, this one didn't have a smell either.

It took a moment for her to swallow her doubts and take a cautious nibble of the gray concoction. To her relief, it had a creamy texture and a delicate smoky flavor. Encouraged, she cut away a forkful of meat-laden pastry, swiped it through the sauce, and popped it into her mouth.

Spice exploded to startle her taste buds, hot enough to make her nose run and her eyes tear up. Entirely at a loss, she stopped chewing and held it in her mouth until she could adjust to the taste.

Unfortunately, the longer she held it there, the hotter it became until she had to chew hastily to clear her mouth. She reached desperately for a glass of water when a shadow fell across her table and Frog, Lars, and Johnny stopped laughing long enough to scramble to their feet.

"Please," a deep, gravelly voice said. "Drink this. It will soothe the burn. Water will only make it worse. I admire your choices, but akvenja should come with warning labels."

Stephanie grasped the glass and was about to lift it to her lips when Lars intercepted it. "Hey!" she protested.

"Let me," he said before he took a small device out of his pocket and scanned it. "It's fine. No offense intended," he added as he handed it back to her and addressed the Dreth warrior who'd offered it.

"None taken," he replied as she swallowed two large mouthfuls.

"Oh, that's much better," she said when the thick, fruity syrup coated her tongue and throat. She looked at the dish, took another forkful, and responded to the looks of disbelief on the team's faces. "What? It's really good."

The Dreth laughed, which made her jump, and he patted her on the back.

"Your courage speaks well of you. Next time we share a drink, it will be as friends."

The guys relaxed and slowly resumed their seats, although Stephanie noticed their gazes strayed often to the corner of the room where the Dreth sat. He, for his part, seemed to ignore them as she finished her plate.

She was careful to use more of the gray sauce with each forkful and to take regular sips of her drink. Lars ordered her a second one when the first one ran low, and the guys gave a soft cheer when she finished.

"Shut up and pass me that burger," she said. "I'm still hungry."

They all laughed and did as she asked, a little surprised that she was a better sport then they were willing to be. When dinner was over, Frog and Johnny hurried to the courtyard where some late evening dancing had begun.

Lars laughed as he followed them, grabbed Stephanie by the hand, and despite her groans of protest, dragged her after him. "Let's dance."

"I thought you'd never ask," she mocked but gave into his playful smile and put her hand to her forehead.

She ended up having a really great time with the guys and met innumerable people. Everyone seemed to be letting off steam and dancing because they were happy. It was different than the club the guys had taken her to.

That had been more like a place for mating and testosterone-fueled competition. They also managed to finish the evening without Frog punching anyone, which had to be a first for him. The last thing they needed was a drunk teammate starting a fight in the middle of the liner.

When they'd had their fill of dancing, they walked out of the courtyard and toward the elevators. Stephanie put her hand in her pocket and withdrew a piece of paper with a small frown.

She unfolded it and tilted her head back as she laughed and earned a funny look from Lars. "What's going on over there?"

She held the paper up. "It's that guy's number. The one I was talking to out there. He actually slipped me his number."

His face fell and he clipped the piece of paper right out of her fingertips. "I gotta check this guy out—and any other guys, too.

You can't be too careful on this trip. You can call me Dad for the rest of the time out here."

"You're out of your tiny little mind," she replied and hurried after the others.

He smirked and shook his head as he followed.

CHAPTER ELEVEN

Back on Earth, Elizabeth thanked the waiter as he seated her at the table. She placed her purse in her lap, draped her napkin over it, and studied the man seated opposite her. When he caught her look, the chancellor of Harbor Technology U cleared his throat and looked a little cautiously at their surroundings.

She had brought him to an extremely nice restaurant in the center of the most exclusive richie territory in DC. As part of her efforts to impress him, she had arranged for him to be collected by private car and they were about to have not only a meeting but a really memorable meal as well.

It all honestly seemed so easy. Ms. E knew exactly how to play the game. She would make an appeal to his sense of survival, but at the same time, to his sense of morality as well.

"Have you been here before?" she asked nonchalantly.

The chancellor chuckled. "No. I usually grab lunch at the school cafeteria and dinner is whatever snacks I have in my desk at the time. This is definitely a change of pace."

She opened the menu. "Well, I'm glad I could treat you, then."

Unsure how to respond to that, he opened his menu and his

eyes widened when he saw the prices. She watched him covertly for a moment before she looked away with a small smile at his reaction.

It was exactly what she wanted to see. This dinner was to set the stage for what she wanted to talk to him about. The menus were simply props, a way to show him the food's cost meant nothing in light of what she wanted to discuss.

She wanted him to know that the expense of the meal was merely a drop in the bucket of the funding they would provide. He needed to start thinking of what he could achieve if he let them supply him with the right kind of financial assistance.

They both ordered and the waitress poured them glasses of a very rare wine, one that hadn't been produced in the decades since the winery had been shut down by wildfires. When the server had left the table, they sat for a moment in silence.

Elizabeth let the charm and elegance of their surroundings really settle in and poke at his sense of desire over his sense of practicality. She wanted him to see the other side of life, one that existed well beyond the reach of normal people.

Finally, after sipping her wine, she spoke, her tone direct and hard so he would focus on her words and not the glittering opulence surrounding them. "Results are what matter."

He tilted his head and his eyes confirmed that she had his attention. "I'm sorry?"

She smiled comfortingly and leaned in a little to speak in a low tone to give him a sense of privacy. "I'm here to help you make your university one of the best in the world. I want you to be able to bring in the brightest students and prepare them for a future far beyond the usual expectations and limitations placed on someone not from a particularly affluent background."

The chancellor sat back and blotted his lips before he returned his napkin to his lap. "That sounds wonderful—a dream, really—but I don't quite understand why."

Elizabeth gave him a bright smile and set her glass down, although she continued to lean toward him. "Our company believes that only the brightest students will create companies of unparalleled excellence. These are the students who are the best in their classes—the cream of the crop, the most artistic, well-thought, innovative, and forward-thinking of their generation."

She watched as interest sparked in his eyes and didn't give him a chance to interrupt. "They're the only ones who can create the businesses this planet and country desperately need. We need people and companies willing to push forward and break the mold, not those promoting the same laziness and self-serving lifestyle that is usually found among those who are used to eating in places like this every day, drinking rare wines, and floating on a cushion of family fortune and Federation handouts."

The chancellor sighed and shook his head. "If you think that hasn't been the stamp of this university since its inception, you didn't do your research. I'm not frustrated with you. I'm frustrated with the fact that I have those same ideals but lack the capital to make them happen."

He sighed. "I have found that each year, we slip a little farther from reaching that dream. With my eyes wide open, I can see myself led down the same rocky path all the other schools have followed. There's a slight sheen of gold, but we know we're selling our souls for the money we need to keep the school alive."

Elizabeth sat there for a moment and allowed his emotions to calm. He was doing exactly what she'd expected and definitely what she'd hoped for.

He showed her, face to face, that he really did care more about these students and their education than their parents' fat bank accounts. This was all she really needed to know. The rest could be found in black and white.

When the color of his face had subsided from red to a normal pinkish hue, she placed her hands with the palm down on the table and looked him in the eye. "There are four hundred thousand top-tier students who fail to get into a university due to financial considerations—four hundred thousand, and that's every year."

She stopped to allow him to absorb the sheer enormity of the numbers. "We want to take five hundred of these and put them through your Harbor Tech." She settled back in her chair and made an airy motion with her hand. "If you care to change the future, that is."

The chancellor stared at her for a moment as if she had grown a second head or become an alien right before his eyes. His mouth opened and closed a couple of times, and his eyes took on a distant look.

Elizabeth suspected he was running through the idea of that many paid tuitions for students who truly deserved it. His words confirmed it. "That is more than all the academies combined take in a ten-year span."

She managed a small excited laugh and let some of that excitement bleed into her voice. "And that is only the beginning. We will focus on finding the *right* people, not simply anyone who needs a free ride. We know there will be times when we'll get it wrong, but in the long run, when other companies see that your students are a cut above theirs and fresh—and not from the same old background that they rely on—well then, that's when things really start to get interesting."

From the look on the man's face, he hung onto her every word as she continued. "All across the world, universities will see what your students achieve and some will follow your example. It will take time, but we will see some of them admitting students solely on merit because, if they don't, they won't be able to compete. Your graduates will help pull the Gov-Subs out of the dust by providing opportunities that no one's thought to provide before."

A small smile had appeared on the chancellor's lips, and he sounded almost breathless. "That is… Well, that sounds amazing. I don't want to get my hopes up because I've never seen it work, but if it does work… I mean, if it really and truly worked, you could change the world."

He stopped to catch his breath. "My grandfather and my father instilled one very important lesson into my head. You can grow a company organically. You merely have to provide an opportunity."

Elizabeth nodded and smiled at the waitress as she brought their food. "Exactly. And when you offer opportunities to those who simply need help getting into the system, it broadens their whole idea of what the world is like."

He took a bite of broccoli in oyster sauce. "That's right. The difference goes far beyond the training. Once the training is given, new career choices open up and then, each individual is responsible for making it—or not—on their own."

He chewed, ate the rest of the broccoli, and sampled some of the beef before he went on. "But when you have situations like that, people do amazing things to make the most of their opportunities and keep that hope alive. They will do anything to not have to go back to the factory or follow their family into a hazardous industry. They'll work their tails off in order to ensure they stay out of the Gov-Subs and to allow themselves a chance to achieve the better future they've always dreamed of."

"And that is something the richies don't understand because their families have already reached the top and there is nothing they can't do or have," she added as she lifted her fork. "Now, while we don't hold that against them, we aren't here to support anyone but those who strive the hardest to take the opportunity and make something with it."

"Of course, to do anything else would defeat the purpose," the chancellor agreed. "And if they truly are the brightest, they will understand the chance they've been given and will be motivated to make the most of it."

"Mhmm," she replied and savored a mouthful of steak. "Lazy geniuses need not apply. I'm here to change the future of mankind. And if someone wants to sit on their ass all day, what good is their mind to me?"

On the *Meligorn Dreamer*, Stephanie and the team had joined Garmathiun Hondor of the Triton Quadrant of Meligorn for dinner. She shifted in her seat and found it weird to sit on high-backed stools at the dinner table.

Then again, the Meligornian tables were kitchen-counter height if not taller. It was their custom and they often struggled on Earth with all the low tables and surfaces.

Beside her, Lars sat at full alert and his gaze shifted almost obsessively around the room. Marcus sat on his other side, his hands politely in his lap with a slight look of disdain on his face.

She found his expression odd but chalked it up to the stress of the trip and the days leading up to it.

Garma sat comfortably on his stool, his robes draped elegantly around him, and his long silver hair sparkled in the ship's artificial lighting. "So, in theory, all the magic should work together like a dance."

She pursed her lips, excited to have a chance to talk magical theory with someone who knew it. "Right, but because each type of MU is so old and has been pulled and pushed for so long, none of them are compatible without being changed first. You have to change the energy back to what it was by winding them together —which makes sense when you think about gMU."

He tilted his head to the side and a look of shock crept into his face. "My dearest Lilly, you are quite the savant when it comes to magic. Although I think I was aware of that before. Tell me more about your gMU theories. I like that name for it. We have always called it the Unknown Magic. A shout to the energy that roams every corner of space. We know it's there but few of us, if any, have ever been able to understand it."

Stephanie smiled and took a mouthful of the chicken on her plate. The Meligornian had asked the chefs to prepare human dishes to ensure his guests' comfort.

She enjoyed it, and from what she could see, the guys certainly appreciated it. "The gMU is older than both eMU and MU. It is the eldest of the three, the one that brought it all into existence. Which, I think, you knew already."

Garma leaned forward, clearly enjoying the conversation. "Well, we had an idea, but even on Meligorn, there is resistance to nailing down facts that go against prominent faiths."

Lars smirked and joined the conversation. "So that's not only a human issue, then?"

Their host snorted and waved his hands as he replied. "Not in the least. All beings share this natural need to understand. Some do better than others, but they can rarely step back and see the truth of things. Still, there are some who can see the destruction that blind faith can cause and some who can also see the connections between each different understanding."

He shrugged. "I don't believe that science and discovery can kill God, no matter what form people think God takes. I think science and discovery can close the gap a little between all beings and their religious concepts. We resist because we all fear that our truths—the ones we hold sacred inside—will be proved false. That fear alone can lead to a serious uprising."

Stephanie nodded. "Right. Or a sudden outbreak of death, whether from war or like the time in the mid-2000s when the seven thousand seven hundred churches all waited until the stroke of midnight and everyone killed themselves. They believed they were giving their lives for a worthy cause. But yes, I see your point. I still believe that simply because you fear the truth does not mean you shouldn't continue to seek it out."

"I very much agree with you," Garma replied and raised his glass to clink against hers. "And that is why what you're saying about gMU is so interesting. It's a really simple concept but because it's so different to what's currently taught in the education system and because pursuing it would draw money away from the Federation, there won't be any conferences or informationals about the opportunities it presents."

He seemed excited to discuss the theories she had and she was thankful she had found someone she could discuss it with, without having to be the teacher, the student, and the researcher.

She understood that discovery was the entire reason for what she did and that learning about her magic—how to use it and how it worked—was her main purpose. Sometimes, though, like with Brilgus and the ambassador, it was nice to connect with another being who understood some of how it worked. It was even better to get a different perspective from someone who didn't treat her like some kind of magic-wielding anomaly.

She and Garma talked for hours and barely noticed how much time had passed. Stephanie happened to look at Lars as he covered his mouth during a yawn, and this made her glance at the clock on the wall. She was mortified "Oh, my gosh. It's so late! I'm sorry, Garma. I didn't mean to take so much of your time."

He glanced up and his eyes widened when he saw the time. "It is late. I am also sorry. I was so lost in our discussion that I have kept you well past the time when I should have let you go."

He stood slowly and surveyed the half-asleep team.

"Let me show you to the door, and my apologies for keeping your team up so late."

Stephanie followed his gaze and immediately saw her guys needed sleep. They tried desperately to stay alert and not complain.

Garma thanked them for allowing him to keep them so long

and invited them to come back anytime. She hoped she would have another chance to speak to him because his insights had been really helpful.

After he'd shepherded the team to their suite, Lars walked Stephanie to her room. Before she stepped in closed the door behind her, she turned and kissed him on the cheek. "Thanks, dude. I needed something like that tonight."

He yawned again and nodded sleepily. "That's my job, lady. Keeping you safe and listening to MU theory. I am now an expert."

She laughed and waved before she secured the door and went to bed. Excited or not, she was definitely exhausted.

"It all looks really good," said Roger, the chief engineer, when he'd checked the readings on the screen.

Engineer First Class Cameron Bruce nodded proudly. "Thank you, sir. We've busted our nubs down here to make sure everything is on the up and up and we were ready for anything."

Roger shook his hand. "I know you were on the *Peter Travers* last year when they were attacked by pirates. I'm sorry you had to go through that. Hopefully, this trip will be smooth sailing. Speaking of which, the captain's ordered the FTL Transition for sixty-four hours from now."

Cameron frowned with obvious confusion. "I'm sorry, sir, but wasn't the Transition scheduled for one-thirty hours?"

He nodded. "Word's only just come down. The captain says we need to beat the official course from Federation Control, so we're transitioning early. We need to make sure the engines are ready."

The younger man squared his shoulders, always obedient, even if he thought the order was hazardous or dangerous. "Will, do, sir. They will be ready to go two shifts beforehand."

The chief gave him a grateful smile and slapped him on the shoulder. "I know you would, but it's the end of your shift, so I'll get it started. You can finalize it when you clock back on in the morning. I'll take over now and let you take an early mark. The heavens know you've earned it."

Cameron brought a knuckle to his forehead. There was no way he would argue with that. He left the engine room and headed for his bunk.

As soon as he was out of sight, he paused to wipe the sudden sheen of sweat from his forehead. This was an unexpected hitch. They would *not* like this. Not one little bit.

He reached the end of the corridor and took the stairs to the crew common room two at a time. Grateful he was one of the first off shift, he headed directly to his shared quarters and hoped to beat his cabinmate in.

Relieved to find the space empty, he pulled his console out and kept a close eye on the door while he sent off a quick message about the "game."

Worried the door would open any moment, he tapped the message out, trying to be quick but also to not make any mistakes. It was an extremely important message that had to be sent as soon as possible.

The game needs to finish early as he won't be available to play after. STOP.

With that done, Cameron paused and stared at the console before he unplugged it and stashed it in the back of his locker.

As he released it and pulled out a clean shirt and shorts to sleep in, Anton crashed into their space.

"Are you still up?"

"Not for long," he snapped in response. "It was a long shift and we have a longer one tomorrow."

Anton snorted. "Yeah. I heard. An early transition to top off a long week. I hope there are no more surprises on this trip."

"Me, too," he agreed and headed to the door. "I'm gonna hit the head before I hit the hay."

His bunkmate gave him a lazy wave of acknowledgment. "I won't be far behind you."

Cameron breathed a sigh of relief and left, glad the other man didn't seem in the mood to chat. Their departure had been unusually hectic, which meant everyone was tired.

And that made it really good for him.

CHAPTER TWELVE

Stephanie woke to the sound of a hundred tap dancers executing the cha-cha on her door. "What the hell?"

Her sleepy mutter was greeted with raucous laughter and Johnny's familiar voice. "Wakey, wakey, sleepy head."

She groaned.

The knocking came again. This time, she threw a pillow at the door as Lars' voice intruded.

"Time to wake up, lazybones."

"You can kiss my..." Even half-asleep, Stephanie thought it would be better if she didn't finish that sentence. "Go away."

Marcus snickered, and Frog howled with laughter. "You heard her, Lars my man. She asked you to kiss her go away."

"Yeah, her go away," Marcus repeated and his laughter made the phrase sound a lot worse than it could possibly be.

She rolled over and groped for something else to throw as Frog called again. "Come on, Steph. I know you had a hot date with that old Meligornian guy last night but it's time to get up and at 'em, sweetie.".

Stephanie groaned.

"I'll give you assholes sweetie," she muttered, rolled over

again, and yanked her blankets over her head. It didn't help that she could hear the guys milling around outside or that it wouldn't be long before one of them did something terminally stupid.

Like coming in to get her.

Yeah. That would be really terminal. She sighed. It was probably better if she didn't force them to try it. She sat up and scowled when her hair tangled across her face.

She scraped it irritably out of her eyes, hauled herself out of bed, and stumbled toward the door. She'd only made it halfway across the room when it was flung open and Frog led the charge inside.

They all stared at her for a moment before she threw her hands in the air, turned away, and headed to the bathroom. "Make yourselves at home," she grouched, "and make me coffee while you're at it. It is way too early for this shit."

The guys were still laughing when she returned and sat in the desk chair, looking as tired as hell. "Why are you here torturing me?"

"Torture?" Lars sounded hurt. He held a cup up so she could see the steam rising from its surface. "If I were torturing you, I'd do this."

He raised the cup to his lips and took a sip.

Stephanie let her jaw drop and gave a squeak of horror, and the guys fell about laughing all over again. She recovered quickly and stalked over to where Lars was still sipping her coffee while he watched her over the rim.

His eyes looked tired, but they danced with mischief as she stopped in front of him and held her hand out. "Give me my damn coffee or someone's gonna die."

He paused mid-sip, licked his lips, and smirked. "Can you be the one, Frog?"

"Hey!" Frog wasn't amused but everyone else thought it was

as funny as hell. She didn't care, though, because Lars finally took pity on her and handed her what was left of the coffee.

"If you let Frog live, he'll order us breakfast," he said and made sure she had a good grip on the cup.

"I'll what?"

"You heard," he retorted, and Frog spread his arms and rolled his eyes.

"Work, work, work," he grumbled and tried to suppress a grin as he turned to the console.

Johnny laughed, walked over to Stephanie, and patted her on the head as he sat next to Lars on top of her desk. "Speaking of work, we think you need to do some work in the pod today."

Stephanie rolled her eyes and moved her mouth away from the cup to wail. "I just *did* work in the pod. I did a ton of work and you guys were nowhere to be seen or heard."

"Hey," Lars protested and moved to stand next to Marcus. "We were doing security stuff. Mucho importante."

"Mhmm," she replied and sounded as snide as she could with a mouthful of coffee. She swallowed and added, "I saw you when I came out. Frog had a hat on that said *I played the slots and I got more than I bargained for.* Which I have to say, is too much to squeeze onto a hat. Nonetheless, I don't think that's part of your security stuff."

Brenden chuckled and tossed her a pair of jeans and a tee he'd obviously dug out of her closet. "Come on. Throw these on and we'll take you down. No heavy lifting today."

She drained her cup and handed it to Johnny, who happened to be standing closest. "While no heavy lifting sounds good, none of you have what it takes to win against me."

No sooner had the words left her mouth than she was hemmed in by the team, each one standing closer than any of them had a right to.

"Like that, is it?" she asked and couldn't help but giggle as she drew just enough magic to create a light field of static energy around her.

There was an abrupt fizz and crackle and the guys leapt back.

"Ow!"

"Man, remind me not to piss you off before breakfast ever again."

"Sonuva—"

"I won't piss her off after breakfast, either."

"If she doesn't cut it out, she won't *get* any breakfast."

"Do you really want to do that, man?"

"I'd give her all your breakfasts to watch her do it again."

Stephanie had to laugh at Frog. He'd been at the room service console and watched as they'd crowded her, and if he hadn't been finding them food, he'd have been zapped with the rest. He smiled when they heard a knock on the door to the suite

"I'll be back," he said, mimicking how the lines were spoken in a really old movie. Now that she thought about it, she remembered it was one of Todd's favorites.

"Bring breakfast," she insisted. "You know I get grouchy if I don't eat."

"We have work to do," Johnny insisted, and she pivoted as blue fire rolled over her hand.

"Breakfast, or I'll turn you into a—" She glanced at the door. "Slug. Two Frogs would be two too many."

"She has you there," Lars told him, and Johnny gave an exaggerated sigh.

"Fine. Breakfast first and then pod work."

Stephanie settled herself at her desk. The coffee had kicked in and they were right. She had to do something. It might as well be pod time.

"What am I doing? More battle tactics?" she asked when Frog brought their food and they'd finished eating.

He shook his head, retrieved his new hat from his back pocket, and pulled it down tightly over his ears. "It's time you had a little school session. You have been so focused on magic and how it works that we think it would be good for you to get a more well-rounded education. That and Elizabeth sent us a note threatening our safety if we didn't get you in there to take some different classes. Don't worry. It'll be stuff you're interested in."

Stephanie shifted her gaze from one guy to another before she threw her hands up in surrender. "Fine. But you losers wait outside. Go, go, go or I will call the dark side."

They all hurried out of the room, laughing as she kicked Frog in the butt and closed the door. Out in the common room, they could hear her struggle and even fall all over as she tried to put her jeans on.

After another small crash, the door opened again and she was dressed in jeans and a t-shirt, her silver stranded hair pulled back in a messy ponytail.

"Well, you took your time," Johnny sniped and she gave him the finger before she rolled her hand to point at the door.

"Didn't you have a fun day of pod school to get to?"

He looked at Lars. "Do we really have to keep her?"

"Stop your bitching," the team leader told him and headed to the door.

Stephanie followed and swatted at them to keep them moving when they bottlenecked at the entrance. They protested and she laughed as she followed them down the hall to the team's pod room.

She got into the pod, ready to prepare her avatar in the white room, but she never got there. Instead, when her eyes opened, she found herself in a college classroom, seated in the front row all by herself.

Instead of a chalkboard, there was a digital screen and Burt's voice came over the loudspeaker like a principal in high school, complete with the squealing PA.

"Welcome to Virt World Uni," he said and his voice oozed false cheer. "This is Burt and I will be your guide for today. On the screen is a list of courses you can choose to take. Pick two and we will begin."

"Can I have coffee while I think about it?" she muttered.

A cup of hot coffee appeared on her desk and she smiled, grabbed it, and approached the board to look at the classes. She scanned the list and her attitude improved when she realized they all had to do with her plans to fix the Earth. "So many good ones. How do I choose?"

"Decide which will help you the most at this moment," Burt instructed. "We can go back later to the others."

Stephanie tapped her finger on her lips. "I choose Environmental Damage and then Nuclear Fusion."

"Done," he said and immediately transformed the room into a giant map of the world.

He launched into Environmental Damage and took her to different places all over the world that had suffered extreme damage and explained what had happened to them.

The lesson covered fire and water damage caused by flooding, coastal erosion, and strong storms. After that, they moved on to the problems caused by increased temperatures and warming oceans.

She became engrossed in each one as she learned about what the coastlines had looked like long before she was alive. There had been states in the US that didn't exist anymore—places like Florida where the sea levels rose several times and slowly consumed the land until the state had completely disappeared.

They discussed the effect of rising temperatures on the planet. When they had covered the main points of Environmental Damage, they moved on to Nuclear Fusion.

That wasn't necessarily exciting, but it definitely gave her a better idea of what she would face on Earth in her clean-up attempts.

"So," Burt said as he completed the lecture, "since nuclear fusion is basically smashing light elements together to create a heavier element, why do you think this is ideal for sustainable electric production?"

Stephanie smiled. "Because, first of all, nuclear fusion occurs best in high density and high-temperature areas. Suns are one place, but humans can create such places like they did in the past."

She frowned and tried not to think of the things that could go wrong with that before she went on. "When the temperatures reach very high levels, the electrons are stripped from the nuclei and they form plasma. When you do this, it produces huge amounts of energy that could literally light the whole world."

BURT checked her details and decided he wouldn't teach her what she already knew. "Perfect. So, it's basically energy for which one part of its fuel is readily available and that creates the other part of its fuel."

Stephanie scratched her head. "So why don't we use that now?"

"A couple of reasons, really," he explained. "One, because billionaires have built empires on coal, oil, and gas, and two, because there are more billionaires who've built their empires on military technology. Fortunes were preserved while the naïve believed false promises of aid and let the wealthy stay in power. Earth has suffered as a result, and so has the humanity governed by those with wealth but not the necessary skills to take care of the population."

"Uh…what kind of skills?" She was genuinely curious.

"To govern the population?" BURT asked, surprised she'd be interested.

Stephanie shook her head. "No. To make fusion viable. What skills do we need for that?"

For a moment, he was almost disappointed but he was relieved, too. Stephanie was focused on restoration and not rulership. "Basically, you need to know how to duplicate the process of nuclear fusion in a controlled environment."

She raised an eyebrow. "Oh. Okay, well, I have the concepts, but actually doing it? That's something a long way down on my list. If I can't do it the human way, I doubt I can pull it off with magic."

"You never know. Now you know how it's done scientifically, you might be able to find a way to do it with magic. You merely need time to think about it." BURT forced himself to sound casual and not push her. He knew her. The idea would eat away at the back of her mind until she found a solution.

Right now, though, she'd had enough of study.

"You sound like an after-school special," she grumbled. "But I assume the lessons are over and I'm done here. You can let me out of class now."

There was silence. She looked around for a moment and wondered where he was. "Burt? Did you hear me?"

The only reply was a change of scene. The classroom vanished and she found herself standing in a ballroom. Her outfit had changed as well.

Stephanie looked down and noticed her jeans and tee had been replaced by a short dress. It was flaming red in color and complemented with nude stockings and dance heels.

She narrowed her eyes and demanded, "Buuurt, what am I doing here?"

"Don't shoot the messenger," he replied. "The guys said when you were done with the 'sciencey stuff' you had to take dance lessons."

Her shoulders sagged and she whined, "But... But...I don't want to. Can't I do some fighting instead? I really want to hit something, and it's so much easier to fight than solve the great mysteries of the world like nuclear fusion and ballroom dancing."

Burt chuckled and out came the dance instructor. She was a fifty-something AI named Ms. Gambol.

Her scrolling background told of glorious days in a famous richie theater, dancing for thousands of fans. As she'd aged, demand had moved to younger dancers and she was now stuck giving dance lessons to the…

"…uncoordinated, two-left-footed, tone-deaf, rejects of dance," she said, obviously repeating an oft-used phrase. "But I will do what I can with you."

She clapped her hands and Stephanie slid across the floor into the arms of another, much easier on the eyes dance partner.

He caught her and deftly turned their collision into a turn that brought her back into his arms.

"I am Baron. I will be your dance partner for this lesson."

The utter solemnity on his face made her smile and she giggled as he held her tightly. "Hey, Baron."

"The graceful Stephanie, you will soon dance like the butterfly," he said with an odd Italian accent even though he was clearly not Italian.

Ms. Gambol snapped her fingers and music began to play. Stephanie groaned and recalled awkward dance classes in school when she'd always ended up dancing with Becca or Todd. Those had been the worst classes of her life.

She took a deep breath and clung to Baron as he began to guide her around the room. The movements were vaguely familiar as if she'd done them before. The music wasn't but…her body remembered this.

As she fumbled along with Baron and tried to follow Ms. Gambol's sharp suggestions, she tried to recall where she'd done this before. It took several turns on the dance floor before the memory snapped into place.

The club. Waltzing with Lars. Doing the crazy boogaloo with Frog.

This was what Lars had taught her and now, it all made sense. Everything she had learned rushed back and she straightened in Baron's arms and glided more confidently through the room.

At the end, Ms. Gambol actually cracked half a smile. Either that or her programming had a glitch. The girl took it as a win either way.

"All right, let's move onto a new dance style. This one's called modern." The AI gave a snooty sniff. "Although only the heavens know why."

At her words, Stephanie's outfit changed. This time, she wore a pair of black stretch pants, a white cotton tank top, and a sweatshirt that fell off the shoulder on one side. On her feet were soft black jazz shoes.

The music started and several dancers appeared out of nowhere, bending their knees with their hands on them and swinging their upper bodies wildly.

Stephanie tried to mimic them but stopped partway through to let her head catch up and the dizzy spell pass.

The dancers continued to dance around her in a circle while Ms. Gambol screamed out the time. "One, two, three, stomp it out. Come on, Morgana, don't stand there like a stuffed dummy. Move your hips."

She stared at the avatar in disbelief, but she pulled her arms jaggedly over her head and moved her hips. The action wasn't even close to the smooth, rounded movements made by the other dancers. When the music stopped, Ms. Gambol sighed and shook her head. "Maybe modern was too much for you at this stage."

Stephanie looked around and back at the woman. "Ya think? Just a tad, maybe?"

The instructor waved her hand to the side, and her outfit changed again. This time, it turned into a flesh-colored leotard, accompanied by pink tights and pink pointe shoes.

Ms. Gambol snapped her fingers again and a dance barre appeared out of nowhere in Stephanie's grasp. The lesson that followed was grueling with the purpose of most of the movements performed at the barre a mystery.

"Maybe it's an ancient form of torture," she muttered, having never heard of ballet before. It wasn't something folk in the Sub really talked about—and no wonder if this was what it was.

The woman finally called an end to the lesson but informed her that she needed much more work on this style. She bit her lip and hoped that was Burt's idea of a joke. Frankly, she dreaded what came next.

She relaxed when the music changed to a beat and tune similar to the ones she'd heard in the club. Several other girls came rocking out of the back, dressed in club wear, and danced close with their male partners.

This, at least, was worth it, so she threw herself into it, used some of the moves the boys had taught her, and learned any new ones she was shown. She'd actually improved considerably before the session ended.

To a degree, she'd actually enjoyed herself and the guys would be happy. She scowled when she recalled the ballet lesson. They'd better be.

Back on Earth, Elizabeth picked up her cup of coffee and took a long, slow sip. As she set it down, the phone began to ring. "Who is it, Amelia?"

"It seems to originate from the Federation Navy base," the administrative AI informed her.

She raised her head and smirked as she picked the phone up. "This is Elizabeth."

"Hello, this is Petty Officer Wyld," explained the man on the other end. "We received your message and we would like to extend an invitation for you to come and talk to us at the Navy offices."

Ms. E rolled her eyes and shook her head. "Yeah, that won't happen. I know you think that's the smart way to do it, but I'd rather do this on my terms than yours. Why don't you come and meet in my territory?"

Wyld was silent for a long time. It was as if he didn't really know what to say and had to think about it. She had stumped him and while her wish for them to meet her on her own territory suggested she knew about some of the other tricks they had, it didn't confirm it.

As he sat there in silence, the line clicked when Childers picked up to help with the conversation. "Elizabeth, this is Petty Officer Childers. We are now online together."

"Oh, yay, a conference call party," she acknowledged sarcastically.

The woman ignored her and continued. "I'll get straight to the point on where we're at. We need to know what Stephanie is capable of and how that might change the future if other humans could do what she does."

Elizabeth held her breath. That was very to the point, especially for the Navy. She still wasn't quite sure what Childers wanted, though, and decided to dig for it.

"So, what are you asking for? Is it testing time on Stephanie or simply any answers I can give to the best of my knowledge? Because she isn't here, and I doubt she will agree to be the Federation Navy's guinea pig anytime soon."

"At this point, we don't care what it takes to obtain the knowledge the Navy needs," Childers told her. "If it takes a long time, then so be it. If we have to pull information from you instead of her, we'll do that as well. I know you think we're trying to steal her from ONE R&D, but we're not. We merely need the knowledge."

She paused, and when Elizabeth didn't interrupt, she continued. "I don't know why the Navy wants her, but personally, I want to know how to save the damn world. That is what I am interested in finding out. So, we can continue to fight and you can keep trying to avoid us, or we can communicate with each other and maybe come up with the solutions our planet needs. It is completely up to you."

Elizabeth whistled. "Damn girl, you have some balls on you, I have to say that. And you know what…I like it. Now, remember for a second that I am the one who called you to set up a meeting, so we'll work with that."

"I'm listening."

She smiled and accepted the prompt. "To answer your changing the future question, I'll be dead honest. I have no idea. That quite obviously is our goal in all of this—to create opportunities for the brightest to be educated regardless of their financial status and therefore change the world for the better."

Wyld chimed in. "See, we are on some of the same level here."

Childers and Elizabeth snapped in a simultaneous chorus, "Shut up, Wyld."

Ms. E rubbed her hand over her face and leaned back in her chair as she spoke. "Look, here is what I do know. Stephanie was in the top two percent of her year's testing, yet she didn't rate a university placement even though her aptitude also ranked very high."

She let that sink in, then continued. "Have you considered testing for magical aptitude in these tests? Has the Federation taken the time to consider defining a method to test for the human awareness of eMU and MU? Because from the sounds of it, none of that was required."

The other end of the line remained silent and she scowled. "None of it, obviously. Not a single thing. So basically, you put these kids through tests, graded them on their intellectual aptitude, and then toss the poor ones to the side regardless of their knowledge and IQ."

Childers sighed. "I wish I could tell you that wasn't the case, but I don't know. I don't work for the sector of the Federation that comes up with the tests—or even with the Navy sector that does the same. But I can put in a request for them to consider adding a magical aptitude test. Either way, she scored the same in the process and had the magic side as well."

"Yes, she did, but it took her saving a woman's life for anyone to notice her," Elizabeth retorted. "And the university that invited her to attend their school as a result of that allowed her the summer session, used her attendance for promotional material, and dumped her before the semester's start to avoid having to fund her."

When she heard her voice rise in frustration, she stopped and gave herself time to rein her emotions in. "It is obvious they don't care about intellect or educating the best. Why would they? They already have all the contacts they need to have decisions made in their favor. They don't want some really smart nobody to knock on their door. And they don't want her to disrupt their thought processes. To them, she was a temporary asset, easily used and as easily discarded."

Once it was clear she had finished, Childers spoke. She chose her words carefully. "I'm sorry that it didn't work out for her like it should have. She is the first Federation witch, so she should have been given an opportunity."

Elizabeth shook her head. "You don't get it. It's not only about her. There are thousands more like her, and no one seems to care. Anyway, what else do you want to know?"

The woman didn't hesitate at all. "We know about the use of MU and we saw her on the news during the battle at the ball. We want to know if Stephanie can do non-MU energy pulls?"

She tapped her fingers on the desk and tried to decide whether to tell the truth or not. Finally, she made a decision, knowing full well they would see what Stephanie could do in the upcoming ceremonies. From that point of view alone, it was pointless trying to hide her ability to wield the different magics. Besides, who knew what else the girl would be capable of by then?

"I can confirm that Stephanie is able to pull from all energy types," she responded. "During the Gala incident, she was capable of drawing much more than she did but was not willing to risk innocent lives. Her reluctance came from her need to gain more control of the MU she used. She has advanced in leaps and bounds since then."

Ms. E knew that secrets didn't make friends, and she knew giving the information away could be as bad, but there was a middle ground. She wouldn't give them details and they'd have to be happy with that. There was a line when discussions become negotiations, and when those negotiations became personal, Elizabeth shut it down.

"How did the two of you get this assignment?"

"I guess we're lucky," Wyld grumped, obviously displeased that he'd been shut out for the entire conversation.

Childers chuckled. "I'm not sure if you would call it luck, but we're still here, buddy. We're still here."

This was true. They'd tried to ask their questions immediately after Stephanie had saved the ambassador, but Elizabeth and the team had shut them down every time. The only time the Navy had seen Stephanie, the ambassador had made sure she wasn't alone.

She smirked. The Navy hadn't been very impressed with that either.

Now, it was time she turned the tables on them. She had a good sense of where she was going and exactly what she wanted to know. "Exactly what were you trying to find out after that event?"

"I...uh..." Childers was thrown, and Wyld was no better.

"Well, um..."

Elizabeth suppressed a snicker and asked her next question.

"What can you tell me about eMU?"

Their answers to that were as entertaining as their answers to the first one, but she maintained the pressure. She asked question after question, none of which needed a definitive answer, but each was designed to throw them off their game.

Finally, Childers caught on to exactly what she tried to do and cut her off. "The Navy wants to determine what you and Stephanie know that the Navy should know."

She shook her head and cleared her throat. "Not happening. I won't share everything we know on the off-chance that you might need it. Sorry. I've seen the news about your leaks and I won't entrust ONE R&D's knowledge to you. This information is far too important and dangerous to have out in the wild."

That stymied their conversation completely and caught the two Navy representatives off guard. When she looked back later, all Childers could think was that Elizabeth was right. The Navy leaked like a sieve.

With Elizabeth still on the line, the woman exhaled a deep sigh. "I wish we could come to an agreement. Unfortunately, we cannot provide that information to you since you aren't cleared and we don't have permission to do so. That means this conversation is over. I'm sorry."

Ms. E chuckled mentally. "Yes, I believe we are at a standstill, then."

She clicked her tongue. "And Stephanie Morgana?"

Elizabeth laughed. "Stephanie is en route to Meligorn where she will be awarded the Modfresha Garghilum."

On their end of the line, Childers muted the call and punched Wyld in the arm, which made him flinch. "We can't talk to Morgana because she's off-world getting awards. See there? I was right."

He groaned and unmuted the line. "Thank you for contacting us, Elizabeth. We'll let you get back to your day. If there is any more information the company is able to release, please let us know. You know how to contact us."

"That I do," she replied and hung up quickly.

She puffed her irritation, glad to finally be rid of them. "That should give us about…two months' breathing space."

Her features settled into a scowl as she stood and walked over to the bookshelf. She opened an empty frame of a book and withdrew a very old bottle of scotch. Once she'd poured two finger-widths into a glass, she sipped it slowly and enjoyed the taste of the vintage liquor, even if it was still daylight outside.

"I can't tell if my job is driving me to drink or my drinking is driving me to work. Either way, thank you to whoever left this bottle of whiskey behind. This was exactly what I needed. Now, I have about a million other things to do and I'm talking to myself."

She stared at her reflection in the mirror and shook her head at the tired woman who peered back at her. "At least I have enough money to see a shrink and have some me-time at a private spa. Those are two very important things in a girl's life."

Elizabeth chuckled and wandered back to her desk where she plopped down and took to the keyboard to bring up the files she needed. There was no rest for the weary…or the wicked for that matter.

CHAPTER THIRTEEN

"Did you know there never used to be any transition points?" Frog asked as they worked to clean the pods before they used them for another training session.

"Yup, and I'm so glad I'm not doing this way back then. The passengers had to go into stasis or cryosleep for long journeys," Marcus answered and wiped vigorously. "All I can think of is that movie where everyone goes to sleep on the long voyage and they wake up in hell."

Stephanie's head jerked up from behind her pod, and she pointed at Marcus and snapped her fingers. "Yes! Todd showed me that movie. Oh, man, what is the name of it…uh…uh…"

"*Event Horizon,*" Lars said quietly as he emptied his pockets.

She turned toward him, her mouth open. "Wow, I didn't know you—"

"Had the sophisticated taste of an old horror movie lover?" he asked.

"I was gonna say cared about that kind of stuff."

He put his hands out and looked at the others. "Why does everyone think I'm such a stick in the mud? Seriously."

Frog raised his head. "We-llll, you kinda sorta are? You know, when you're not being extra-grumpy and all Mr. Super Serious."

Lars opened his mouth but closed it again for a moment. "I'm not like that all the time. I can be fun," he protested.

"Mhmm, sure you can," Johnny soothed as if to appease him. "Like that time you cracked that joke about vegetables."

He frowned. "What joke?"

The other man swirled his hand in the air as he finished his Pod. "You know, the one about the carrots with legs."

The team leader seemed confused as he tried to recall what in the world Johnny was talking about. When he did, he closed his eyes and pursed his lips. "We were eight years old when I made that joke."

Everyone chuckled. Stephanie smiled and then pouted. "Everyone, leave him alone. He is the glue of the team, the big boss man. If he wasn't serious, you guys would wander like free-range hooligans and get into trouble without ever actually protecting anyone."

Lars nodded. "Thank you. Jerks."

She laughed and climbed inside the pod. "See you guys on the flip side."

It took only a moment to settle in and she felt good about the day ahead. She needed time with her family, her team. When she opened her eyes, she was in the white room. The suggested clothing was nothing more than regular civilian or the typical jumpsuit. She decided jeans and a t-shirt would work and grew curious as to what they'd actually be doing.

The room shifted quickly and thrust her into a large vaulted room made of stone. In the center was a table with pads of paper, floating screens at each seat, and coffee.

An eyebrow raised, she started toward it and paused as Frog, Johnny, and Lars appeared, all dressed in jeans and t-shirts as well. Frog wore a shirt that read, *Just a mass of cells.*

"So, wait, I really need to know how this whole transition thing works," he said as he sat at the table.

Stephanie sighed and chose the seat beside him. "In essence, we will move through or slip between dimensions. It was a huge breakthrough in travel for us. The Dreth are the ones who gave it to us."

"No way," he muttered in disbelief.

She nodded. "Yes, way. While their technology was very rough and slightly behind that of Meligorn and even Earth in some ways, their travel scientists discovered something the rest of us missed. The dimensions overlap."

He stared at her like she was out of her tiny little mind, but she continued. "Our dimension touches on others and we can slide from one point in our dimension, across the edge of another dimension, and back into ours at a different point. You only have to know where they touch."

Frog nodded. "Oh. Okay, so move like normal, do some crazy science-fiction shit, zoom through space using the back door, and then slow down again when we reach the destination."

Stephanie rolled her eyes and sighed. Trust him to put it like that. "Basically, yes. We can get more into it when we get back."

He shook his head. "That's nice of you, but I found the vintage channel and have a hot date with the vid screen."

Slightly relieved to not have that waiting for her when she got out, she looked around the table. She counted heads and then frowned. "Where are Brenden and Marcus?"

Lars swallowed a gulp of coffee. "They stayed behind to guard the pods."

She was confused. "Was there a threat I missed?"

He shook his head. "No, but we all thought today would be combat training. We aren't set up like we are at the base, so if someone comes in, we'll never know, and there's no way I want some civilian to join us accidentally ."

"That and if you have a meltdown into Morgana energy mode, they can pull you out," Frog pointed out.

Lars rolled his eyes. "That was put very nicely. Thanks, Frog."

Stephanie chuckled. "I get it. There are no alarms and with me transferring experiences between worlds, it's safer to have a backup plan. Thanks for thinking about it."

He shrugged. "All in a day's work."

Frog snorted. "That and we were all terrified something would happen to you and we wouldn't know until we finally exited the pods. They monitor your vitals but the last time, your vitals barely moved while your body started to crash."

Stephanie poured creamer into her coffee. "Yeah, I remember that. I meant to look into it, but I haven't had the time. I assume the energy does something to protect the most vital parts of me first but I can't be too sure. That gives the MU a number of live characteristics and I'm not yet ready to say it has a conscious state."

Frog shivered. "That sounds as creepy as hell. Seriously. To know you're basically sucking in a living creature and then shooting it out your fingertips to attack."

She giggled as Lars flipped his screen on and rolled his eyes. "We need to invest in children's science books for this guy. Give him the basics."

"I used to have a children's science book that was my great-great grandfather's," the other man replied. "It had all kinds of things about jet engines and breaking the speed of sound. Now, people break that barrier on a regular basis in their personal vehicles—really nice flying cars but still owned by dudes with big wallets and no idea how to fly."

This time, the AI was the hologram of a brown-haired woman who rose from the center of the table to float in front of them. "Welcome to your simulation. My name is Mindy. There will be no fighting today. Instead, you will undergo a very specific scenario that will directly assist in the future of ONE R&D. You will test the prototype for a future learning exercise for new students."

Frog groaned. "I hate school. I am not the brightest crayon in the box."

"There will be no need for crayons, Frog," the AI replied.

He jerked his thumb at her and whispered to the other three, "See, I'm not the dumbest one in the group."

"If you wish to look at the test scores of this group and compare IQ levels, we can do that," the AI said.

Frog shook his head. "No! Good Lord, woman, continue."

Everyone snickered as Mindy prompted a list of rules to appear on each of their screens. "Your exercise is to assume that humanity has found a new planet and that this planet will be vital to the continuation of the species. However, there is only enough power to transition one thousand tons of organic material and two thousand tons of inorganic material in one direction at a time. As a reference, you can assume that this planet is similar to Earth circa two thousand years in the past but with no humans."

Frog stared blankly at the screen while Stephanie jotted notes on everything. "What about other living creatures or organic material? What is on this planet before we bring a single thing there?"

"Good question," the AI replied and gestured with her hand. The room displaced around them, but they remained seated at the table. The landscape of a new world appeared. It was deep-green in some places and red in others.

When they'd had time to look around, Mindy continued. "The planet has similar flora and fauna to that found on Earth but no tool-making species. Please note that when you settle, you will not be able to receive any additional resources so you need to be careful and very selective regarding what you take. You have to get it right the first time otherwise, you will all perish on this new planet. Good luck."

By the time she withdrew out of sight, Stephanie had already launched into a list of things they needed to think about. "So, we have precisely one thousand tons of humans we can bring if we need to. That is approximately two million pounds."

Lars nodded and wrote the number down. "We need to figure out what the colony will need and then determine how many men and how many women to bring to the planet. Once there, we can breed and start a new population. That means bringing children there would be a moral choice versus a necessity."

She nodded. "We need people of all walks. We need builders, lifters, creators, and those who take care of us, like doctors and such."

He wrinkled his nose. "Unfortunately, a strong male is twice the weight of a female. A two-hundred-and-twenty-pound man, though, could be extremely important if he was built strong and muscular."

Frog laughed. "Are you only thinking Jocks here? Because I can tell you right now, I can put at least one and a half Geeks into two hundred and twenty pounds. Plus, if we say the women are a normal weight, which is—"

Stephanie put her hand up before he could finish. "I'm gonna stop you right there. I feel a responsibility to point out that even in a hypothetical situation, I have to stick up for women when talking about weight. So, go ahead my little friend, but tread carefully unless you'd like a boot shoved up your ass."

He put his hands up with a grin and shut his mouth. Lars tapped the end of his pen against his forehead. "We can't think only about people as organics, though. We need to discuss the other organics we'll need. Like meat or protein. What kind of animals would fare the best on this new planet? What about seeds? Those are organic too. And we'd struggle to do all of this without knowing what type of technology we'd need to produce energy."

She shook her head. "One thing at a time. I know this room is filled predominantly with meat eaters, but I have to point out that we don't need to bring animals to have protein. Look around you."

"We've been told this world has flora and *fauna* similar to Earth's." She gestured toward the planet and the wildlife. We could bank on finding an edible source right here. If it means we have to eat packaged protein for the first week while we confirm what we can catch ourselves, that's fine as long as we can have five more people instead. Animal husbandry and xenobiology is a thing, you know."

Lars curled his lip. "I know. But the idea of colonizing a new place without having burgers and fries seems unnatural. Still, I get it. We'll have to look at the numbers. Johnny, you need to look through the survey reports and find us a few places with animals that might be this world's beef."

Stephanie gave him a wink and moved on in an attempt to formulate a basic outline of what they needed. "As far as electricity is concerned, we'll have to see what type of renewable resources are present and if they can be optimized for this planet."

She stopped and drummed her fingers on the desk. "You want to learn from the past here. We don't want to simply assume that we are safe to create electricity versus determining how to use eMU or whatever variant is on that planet to meet the electrical need. I would have to test the MU on it and see where it goes and the differences in how it works, and we'd need an alternative in the meantime. There's no real way to tell without visiting first."

Lars nodded. "Cool. Okay, so we can say an exploration is needed. How long are the days on the planet?"

Frog scanned the data. "It looks like for every single day on Earth, there are almost two days on the new planet."

"All right, so we would have to think about adjustment periods." The team leader added that to his notes.

Stephanie studied her list. "Shelter. That is one of the main things. Frog, what are the weather patterns like there?"

"It looks like there are some rough storms—Earth hurricane-type storms but on a regular basis—so the shelter would have to be substantial. We'd need some kind of architectural specifics in order to keep us from dying or having to rebuild." He threw the storm information on the screen.

"So, we would need specific tools. We could choose simpler tools but increase the man-time and power needed, knowing those tools won't break. Or we can bring tools that will speed up creation but suffer from relatively easy breakage," Lars pointed out.

She nodded, and he went on. "Which begs the question, how do we decide on the right types of people and skill sets to bring? I feel like there would be two different sets of people for each set of tools. Some who would have to have a higher skill set and more endurance, and others with fewer skill sets but still able to endure the long building days."

Frog scratched his head. "This is complicated. We need a list of the different trades and then we need to figure out a baseline for the initial colony. Are we talking flushing toilets or will we share an outhouse or go in a hole in the ground? Will we bring fully functional ovens and stoves or use that weight for more important things and cook over fires? Is there clay and do we need kilns to fire it in? And we'd need someone who knew what they were doing."

Stephanie rubbed her face and groaned. She put her pen down and leaned back to bring her cup of coffee to her lips. There were so many variables to it, and she had walked into the whole thing without the right mindset to find the answers.

"Okay. Suddenly, one thousand tons of organic transfer doesn't seem enough. I have to worry about how many pounds of engineers I have allotted and how much each of them weighs versus whether or not I'll need a potter, a seamstress, a weaver, and maybe someone who knows how to cook a decent meal."

She leaned forward and studied the storm pattern on her

screen. "Not to mention the fact that we don't know what kind of diseases lurk in those tall grasses or what kind of insects and wild animals will hunt us while we attempt to build a civilization. We'd have to start with perimeters while getting shelter up as quickly as possible to avoid storms."

Lars stared at the walls and at the very familiar-looking planet around him. "We could always ride the storms out in whatever ship we took to get there. Even if we had to fly it out of the atmosphere and back down."

"That's a lot of battery power," Frog pointed out. "Not to mention the weight of those damn things."

"And fuel," Johnny added from his corner. "I'd suggest finding a cave system, but many animals hide out in caves and that might not be the safest option, either."

Stephanie put her hand out. "Then we have cross-training to think about. It would only be smart to bring someone if they can be used in a multitude of ways. They may start with being a laborer and then become a harvester. Or a scientist, or a doctor. We can't bring a person who is capable of only one task unless no one else does it and they are irreplaceable. If it is a female, she can double duty for procreation, but yeah, we have an issue with the general topic of how much testosterone is in a human. That can play a huge role in things."

Lars laughed. "That basically plays a huge role in everything. Women can be builders, harvesters, and everything else, but there are some primary natural traits that make it smarter to bring a big, burly, strong man instead. If something breaks, we need to know the woman is as efficient in moving things with brute strength as the man would be. It sucks but we're talking about evolutionary traits here for the masses, not a select few."

She wanted to argue with him, but it was science. Men were naturally made to manage and sustain more physical labor than women, even though she knew more than a few women and men who didn't fit that mold. It didn't mean that women on Earth couldn't do the same job. Given an unlimited amount of weight, they wouldn't consider sex, but with the weight limits, they had to make sure they got the biggest bang for their buck.

"And killing can be a concern too," Frog said and raised his hands in defensively. "Women can be great soldiers and hunters, but many are not. Men are bred to be protectors. It's in our DNA. Like you said, we have to pick the best choice, not the one that makes a political statement. Once we are safely functioning on the planet is when we will be able to start cross-training to put people in jobs they're best at or want to work."

Stephanie rolled her eyes at him but then shrugged. "You're right. I want to argue but I won't. We need to add that to our list in order to be able to get what we need. We must develop tests for those individual skills. People will have to show their abilities, strength, health, vigor, and everything between. It won't be a fun ride and there's a good chance people will die. We have to account for that."

Lars shook his head. "My brain hurts."

While the team worked through the difficulties of choosing their settlers, the *Dreamer's* Engine Room had gotten noisy. The thrum of working drives vibrated around the engineers who tended them.

The rumble was louder now the ship no longer idled at the dockside or traveled through normal space. The transition drives were bigger than the other engines and much, much louder.

The engineers monitored them carefully and constantly scrutinized the read-outs attached to each observation panel. A faulty engine or battery was incredibly dangerous when sliding the ship from one dimension to the next. If the measurements weren't correct, they could end up somewhere completely different with no way to get home.

Roger stood at the front of the room and checked things off on his tablet. One of the guys walked up and nodded his head. "Hey, are we redoing all the checks twice or three times?"

He looked up, his face thoughtful. "Only twice unless the readings are different. The first slip went really smoothly, and we have a few hours before we need to make the second." He smiled. "We were exactly on target when we came through, but you know slipping can be hard on the engines so use double checks to make sure everything's running smoothly as we travel through the local space quadrant. Once that's done, we'll use the travel time to make sure the slip drives are ready for the next transition."

The guy nodded. "Any word of when we'll be underway?"

Roger shook his head. "No. We won't know until Navigation confirms it has the heading, then they'll want us to haul ass like they usually do. As long as we have a smooth flow and the batteries glow, I'll be happy."

As he spoke, the entire ship shuddered. The crew grabbed the nearest handholds and some clipped safety lines to their harnesses.

The engineer had been rocked off his feet and pulled himself up slowly. He noted the slightly higher readings and pushed his hardhat off his forehead as he glanced around and muttered, "I don't know what that was, but I doubt it was a good thing."

On the bridge, the crew strapped in and waited for the juddering to stop. *Dreamers'* captain, Harlan Pensman, took hold of his console and looked at his crew who strained to see their monitors.

As the men reached for their keyboards in preparation to find the source of the problem, Pensman did the same, but when he hit the first key, he realized what was wrong.

The display was frozen, and when he pressed the emergency override, it began to skip wildly around like it was on the fritz.

He looked at the comms console. The crewman stationed to it was under it, already working on the panel, but the captain shouted, anyway. "Jeven!"

Jeven didn't even look at him as he examined what lay behind the panel. "On it, sir."

Before the captain could respond, the forward viewscreen went black and the signature logo of the Dreth pirates appeared.

"Security! Talk to me and it better be good," Pensman said and spoke quietly into his headset. "Kelly, tell me I have shields. Jeven, when do I get my comms back? I need them three years ago."

"On it, Captain." As soon as he replied, the tech nudged the mic in his collar tabs and began to speak in a low, urgent voice.

The captain watched as the comms officer waited, listened, and spoke again.

"Well?" he demanded when Jeven had finished.

"They've hacked the system, sir, but Rampart and Trillion have launched the Yelpers and some of them made the slip into Federation space. Hargan is working with the concierge and they've enacted the Level-One protocol."

Sending Yelpers—droid emergency capsules that could take an SOS to the nearest Navy vessel—had been next on the captain's list of demands.

"Very good, Jeven. Now, get me—" He stopped as the forward viewscreen cleared and they could once again look out on a field of stars. "Thank you, Jeven."

Stare as he might, Captain Pensman saw no sign of a pirate ship—and nor should he. This was the second dimension, a place they passed through on the way back to their own dimension. It wasn't somewhere mapped out in case of attack.

Maybe it should be.

He frowned and glared at the screen until his console beeped and drew his attention. His screen had returned to life, which confirmed that the system was rebooting and would soon be back online. He was about to sit when Jeven's voice sounded in his earpiece.

"Navy says they've sent a seeker, but they can't send anything heavier until they have a target." They both looked at the scan console but its operator shook her head.

"How long?" Pensman demanded.

"They say it'll take at least…uh…" Jeven typed hurriedly "It's…"

"Yes? Spit it out," he ordered, his voice tight with tension.

"It's fourteen hours, sir, before it gets here," the man replied and cast him a nervous glance.

The captain gritted his teeth and nodded before he keyed in the public address system. He cleared his throat, centered himself, and prepared to speak to the passengers and crew.

He knew what was going on outside the quiet of the command center. It would be orderly chaos—and that was if he was lucky. The Level-One Emergency Protocol would sound and a calm female voice would direct all passengers to their cabins.

Every corridor would be lit with amber lights, and the stasis pods in each cabin would come online. Through all that, he had to project calm and control and make sure his passengers did exactly as they were asked. Now was not the time for heroes.

His purpose defined, he cleared his throat one more time, took a deep breath, and made the broadcast. "Good evening, passengers. This is your captain speaking. We are experiencing some technical difficulties and will suffer a slight delay. To ensure your safety and to allow the crew to carry out their duties unimpeded, please stay in your cabins until further notice. I repeat, we are experiencing some technical difficulties. Please remain in your cabins until further notice."

He ended the broadcast and switched to Security Central.

"Make sure the decks are clear and lock the passenger

compartments. If we're boarded, I don't want them to have access and I don't want any strays to become hostages."

"Aye, aye, sir."

The captain ended the transmission and sat heavily. His mind raced as he tried to decide what to do next. It didn't help that he knew Security would have its hands full.

Most of the richies on the ship would either ignore him or lose their damn minds. He knew that as surely as he knew he would have to fill out reports for the next six months.

His tablet pinged, and he caught the defense officer's glance and nodded to let the man know he'd received the communication. He activated the message and watched the scan feed magnify to show the *Dreamer's* outer hull and the star field beyond it.

"They're coming in on our starboard side," the officer said. "It looks like a standard hard-dock approach to use the atrium and passenger entrance."

The scene on the tablet adjusted to show a projected course before it returned to the pirates. "You will see these two ships are currently locked together. When they detach, I'll let you know. Likewise, if we pick up any other signals."

"Good." Pensman nodded. "Watch them like a hawk. The moment anything changes, let me know."

"Yes, sir."

The captain made another call to Security Central. "Pensman here. Put me through to the commander."

The call was transferred and Commander Charles Wayforth came online.

"Captain?"

"It's not good, Charlie. There are two Dreth incoming. They're currently interlocked but I want—" Out of the corner of his eye, he saw his screen bubble and fritz until an image of a worm eating invisible streams of data came up. "Of all the goat-sucking—Jeven!"

"I'm working on it."

On the open comms line, he heard Charles give a startled bark of laughter and then swear.

"You got it, too, Charlie?"

"Big purple worm looking like it's eating its way out the top of the screen? Yeah. I'll get the Hats onto it right away."

Pensman sighed. The Hats were the company's 'white hat' hackers employed legitimately to counter hacking threats. They were useful but he wished he didn't need them.

He pushed that pointless thought to one side and resumed the brief. "Jeven's trying to clear the command deck, but you have the rest of the ship."

"Understood. Let me know if there's anything else, Penny. Don't get killed while I'm not looking."

"You too, Charlie-Boy."

They ended the call and both men set about their assigned tasks. They'd served together in the Navy and come aboard the *Dreamer* together, too. With any luck, they'd both make it to retirement.

First, though, they had to get through this.

***

Marcus and Brenden stood guard in the pod room, their backs against the walls. They were supposed to divide their attention between the readouts on Steph's pod and the door, but Marcus cleaned his nails with his knife and Brenden played *Dreth and Damnation* on his tablet. He glanced up and his gaze scanned the door and the pods before it came to rest on Brenden. "I wonder if they're kicking ass in there."

His teammate snorted and focused on the tablet as it loaded the next level. "They're probably getting an exclusive vacation package as a reward and will owe us the big one."

He shook his head. "Nah. Lars would never allow it."

Brenden glanced up and a sly grin lit his face. "Do you think he's conning Steph into another dance?"

Marcus laughed. "The man's not that lucky."

The other man grinned but before he could reply, a jolt rumbled through the ship. If they hadn't been leaning on the walls, they'd have lost their footing.

"What the—" Brendan stuffed the tablet into his jacket and leapt for the nearest pod.

On the other side of the room, Marcus did the same thing.

Together, they started the emergency eject protocol for each of their teammates. There was no time to lose, especially since they had no idea what the hell was going on.

In the Virtual World, Stephanie put her feet up on an adjacent chair and lifted her tablet to push through the pictures of the planet. "They appear to have a strong ecological system there. It must be from all the rain."

"If they live off rain and not some acidic hellfire." Lars laughed as he studied the same images. "That would put a real damper on things."

Before she could reply, the table flashed out of existence and the dishes fell. The chairs also vanished and dumped them on their asses.

Startled by the sudden flare that had run through the Virtual World, they picked themselves and glanced around in concern.

"Everybody ou—" Lars started, but that was as far as he got.

The AI came over the speakers "Prepare for ejection from the virtual simulation. This is not a drill. Prepare for immediate ejection."

"This can't be our fault," Frog said and tried to type on a computer that constantly disappeared and reappeared in front of him. "We didn't do anything crazy. There are enough servers in this ship's system to support the scenario. We didn't break nothing."

Stephanie looked around when the ground shook beneath her feet. "What's going on?"

Lars started to fade. "Nothing good," he said and in an instant, he had gone.

Frog vanished next and then Stephanie, Johnny, and Avery. She clenched her eyes shut, afraid that this time would be different and that something terrible would be waiting.

When she opened her eyes a few moments later she found herself back in the pod with the door wide open.

CHAPTER FOURTEEN

"Move in and take control," the Hormghast Orqtue growled and finished with a roar to get the attention of those under his command. "We make it to Engineering and the Bridge and that's when we start killing. No hostages."

"Hormghast!" the Dreth pirates responded and their deep voices echoed in the hold.

Orqtue turned to the airlock, snapped his helmet closed, and waited for the hatch to cycle. He was glad to see the umbilical stretched taut between the ships and the outer hatch already open.

With another roar, he led his men across, trusting the advance party to have already opened the way at the other end and now held the entry secure. Behind him, the Dreth raised their voices and their howls resounded through their suits and into the liner.

When they reached the other side, they found the breaching party had not only opened the way and held it, but they had secured the main floor. As expected, the elevators were locked down, but a pirate technician was already working to finalize the access the worm had started.

Referencing the *Dreamer's* schematics via their helmet HUDs, the Dreth hurtled directly toward Engineering. It didn't take them long to reach the security team that blocked their path.

"You shall not pa—" was all the security sergeant managed before the Hormghast shot him in the head.

He walked behind his men, his lip curled in a snarl of pleasure as he wielded the blaster single-handed. It wasn't pride to say he hadn't been made Hormghast for nothing. His aim was deadly and he was very, very fast.

Over his space suit, he wore a layer of thick leather armor adorned with gleaming metal spikes. From his belt hung the skin sections, shrunken skulls, and dried ears he'd taken from his defeated enemies.

Orqtue looked ahead as the last security guard fell and identified the human he knew to be one of his allies' inside men. He nodded and smirked slightly to reveal his long, jagged teeth through the visor.

The traitor did not impress him, and he responded as he should—by soiling himself at the sight of the Dreth charging toward him. As if realizing he had more to do, the man fled at a run.

"They're through!" he screamed, grasped a long metal rod from behind a stack of pallets, and rammed it into the security doors to stop them closing after he'd bolted through. "We've been breached!"

"Clever traitor," the Dreth commander murmured.

The man's terrified shouts would deflect suspicion from him long enough for him to ensure the leading fighters reached the door. Orqtue bared his teeth with satisfaction as the treacherous crewman grabbed a wrench and smashed the emergency override console on the other side.

"Dreth!" He turned with the invaders right behind him, only to find himself face to face with one of the junior officers. His face fell but she didn't hesitate. "You disgusting traitor," she sneered and her top lip quivered as she drew her side-arm. "You earned yourself a one-way pass to hell."

The guy raised his hands as she spoke but she fired anyway and the shot burned a hole through his chest. He fell and wheezed as he touched the wound in disbelief, but he was dead before he hit the floor.

Orqtue had to admire the young female because she didn't run. Instead, she tried to kick the pole out of the doorway, but it was jammed in too tightly. With the console disabled, she moved to try to close the door manually.

Fortunately, his men were faster. The lead warrior fired and the heavy slug drove into the officer's shoulder and spun her back. She impacted the wall behind her, smacked her head, and slid into unconsciousness.

Her attacker came through after her and made sure the room was clear before he bent to run a claw down her cheek. Orqtue said nothing as the warrior's second grabbed his shoulder.

"Hormghast Orqtue Rebile," the Dreth rumbled to alert him to their leader's approach.

With a hurried glance in the Hormghast's direction, the soldiers raced forward to make sure the area beyond was clear. If their HUDs had guided them correctly, they had one room to clear before Engineering's command center was in their grasp.

Orqtue stalked after his lead warriors and entered the atrium in front of the command center doors. Another traitor waited at a computer terminal, trembling as he tried to control his fear.

He snarled and the man jumped. Several of the Dreth raised their lips in appreciative snarls. The sight of their fangs did nothing to calm the crewman's nerves.

Sweat covered his forehead and his hands shook violently as he turned fearfully. "Please," he begged. "I put the worms into the system, but some of them didn't take. The main ones did, though, and I'll have it for you as soon as I can."

The Dreth stared at him for a moment and shook his head. "No need. I'll do it my way."

Before the man had time to protest, he raised his blaster and shot him in the head. He holstered the weapon and threw the corpse from the chair before he stooped over the console. Leaning forward, he wiped gore off the screen and peered at it.

It didn't take him long to see that the traitor had failed far more miserably than he'd claimed. Orqtue brought his fist down on the screen with a roar and decided brute force was the only remedy.

With the worm not doing all he needed it to, he had one thing left—the decades of survival skills inherent to his race. When all else failed, Dreth used brute force to bull their way through any and all situations.

Those who became pirates earned their place by being the most skilled at all forms of attack and infiltration. Orqtue was one of the best. He strode forward and examined the doors. His inspection complete, he turned to the advance team.

"Burn it down," he ordered, and they growled their affirmation.

As they scrambled for the equipment, the *Dreamer's* security sprung their trap. Orqtue's head snapped around when he heard shots fired. Two Dreth who'd scouted the room tumbled from stairs leading to a walkway. Both were mortally injured.

Their deaths infuriated him, and he uttered a deep howl that shook the inside of the ship. The other Dreth responded immediately and climbed the stairs to where a security team guarded another door.

As soon as the leaders reached the outermost guards, they attacked and didn't limit themselves to guns. Their armor absorbed most of the damage as they lunged at the defenders and hurled them over the edge to be ripped apart by their comrades.

Some of the guards took cover while others stood their ground and fired as rapidly as their weapons were capable of.

As Orqtue walked toward the stairs, he heard a scream from above and stepped aside to avoid the security crewman who catapulted over the rails. He paused as the guard landed with a thump beside him. It amused him to make a brief show of studying the man, even though he was clearly dead.

The guard's body was twisted in an unnatural way, his eyes were wide open, and blood trickled from the side of his mouth.

He snorted and shook his head. "These humans are so fragile. All the better for me and my men to destroy them easily."

Orqtue climbed to the walkway and assessed the situation. The HUD hadn't lied. Engineering's command center lay behind the doors below. He snorted and signaled the cutting team to begin. No doubt there would be a greater fight for the room itself.

Hopefully, the captain of his sister ship would have an easier time reaching the *Dreamer's* Bridge.

Hormghast Saqteq had fought his way from the atrium to the Bridge, almost relieved when the corridors and hallways of the liner remained empty. Well, except for the liner's security, and his men soon took care of that.

Now, the Bridge was directly ahead and the pirates were in another firefight with what he hoped were the last guards. With every shot the pirates fired, they claimed another kill without sustaining much damage in return. His men wore battle-grade space armor, and the liner's security did not.

When they'd eliminated most of the defenders, Saqteq placed his faith in his armor and marched up to the hastily constructed barricade before them. He reached over an overstuffed armchair pulled from Dreth knew where to seize the lead security man, Hargan. His huge hand tight around the man's throat, he held him suspended a few feet off the floor.

The officer's eyes widened but he still tried to position his blaster between them to fire. Saqteq yanked it from his fingertips with his free hand and put his face against Hargan's. "We are not here for games, human. Move your men or die fighting."

The man's eyes narrowed slightly, and he lashed out with a boot as he choked out a short reply. "We…will…always die… fighting. For the Federation!"

His boot glanced off Saqteq's armor and the Dreth captain sneered and used his gloved hand to crush his victim's throat. When Hargan went limp, he threw the body over the barricade and raised his weapon.

With a guttural call to his men to join the slaughter, he howled and sprayed the remaining humans with deadly fire. They fought back but not for long.

He smiled when they fell one after another. As the Dreth pushed past the barricade, the remaining security contingent backed away but made no effort to surrender. They knew they'd lost, but they wouldn't give up and they refused to run.

Saqteq and his men thought it was a morbidly stupid waste of life, even though the humans' courage was to be admired, and they carefully took their time to kill each one.

Deaths for the stupid were not something to be hurried, so the warriors marched forward and fired at each guard to render them wounded and helpless before the pirates' approach. When they reached them, the Dreth killed them systematically with their bare hands or crushed them under their feet.

The pirates bellowed in victory as they marched toward the Bridge, losing very few men to the security guards left to defend it.

Saqteq was on a mission and he wouldn't leave until he'd destroyed what he came to destroy.

In Security Central, Charlie buried his head in his hands and wept. Protocol kept him from leaving the center—well, protocol and a very pale-faced and determined 2IC whom he had no doubt would shoot him before he reached the door.

"We have to help them," he pleaded, but Hubert stood firm, even though his voice quivered when he replied.

"We have our orders."

The blaster trembled in his hands but not enough to miss, and Charlie doubted the tears streaking the man's cheeks would blur his vision enough to put him off his aim.

"When this over, you and I—" Hubert's voice cracked.

"When this is over, sir, you can shoot me. It'll be better than having to remember this."

He gestured at the screen and they watched as the Dreth pirates reached the doors to the Bridge.

As he stared at the number of pirates filling the corridor, Hubert whispered, "There are other ways to commit suicide."

"What if I come up with a plan that might free the *Dreamer?*" Charlie asked.

"At least you'll be alive to do that, now," Hubert pointed out, "and I'll be along to make sure you stay that way."

While Saqteq took the *Dreamer's* Bridge, a dozen or so pirates marched through the umbilical from the Dreth ship to the atrium. Four of them carried a large metal cylinder between them. The others escorted them, tasked with ensuring the bomb reached its destination.

They growled and snarled at the bodies of the security guards who had tried to stop their comrades from boarding and laughed at the ridiculous fountain in the center of the open area.

Their path took them past it, and they headed for one of the elevators on the far side which took them up several floors until they were able to reach the open space suspended above the atrium.

As they carried the bomb out into the space hologrammed to resemble open parklands, movement at several of the balconies adjoining the vista caught their attention. Blaster fire forced the occupants of the rooms to scurry back inside, and the pirates continued to the center of the open parkland.

Their leader, a Gramghast to the Orqtue's Hormghast, moved into the huge park sanctuary and watched his men carry the bomb in and set it down gingerly.

He surveyed the area and snickered. "When this goes off, it will rip this ship completely in half. There will be no survivors and this sector of space will forever be peppered with dead Federation civilians. Assemble it quickly. We have little time."

The pirates took a variety of tools and last-minute pieces from their belts and went to work. They'd trained for this for months.

Each piece fit perfectly into the bomb, and the gentleness and careful placement of them was reminiscent of a human engineer's soft touch. Even Dreth didn't like the idea of blowing themselves up, and none of them wanted to meet their captain in the afterlife if they did.

The Gramghast walked across the deck to a small ice cream shop. Its lights were off and there was a display window at the front. He could see something—or someone—hiding beneath a table inside and growled. The window shattered easily with a single powerful blow and he leapt over the counter and stools along it and grasped the small girl who tried to scramble frantically away. She screamed as he brought her closer to his face.

"Don't be scared, little girl," he bellowed and laughed at her terror. "We don't like the taste of children, but if you end up being all there is, I will make it quick."

The child uttered an ear-piercing shriek that made him

cringe. He dropped her and covered the part of the helmet that shielded his ears.

"Fey'da haqte!" he shouted and turned to look for her, only to find she'd vanished.

Before he could start searching for the little wretch, one of his men interrupted. "Gramghast, it's ready to program."

The corporal gave a frustrated snarl and glanced around the shop one last time. "Hide. Hide, while you can, little girl. I will find you soon enough."

Stephanie's team had hurried through the hallways, careful to check each section before they raced to their suite. Frog had worked his magic on the locked door, and they'd entered Lars's room without detection. Inside, he'd stashed an array of weapons in his closet as well as armor for everyone.

Marcus shook his head. "I thought all this was in the storage compartment."

The team leader handed the armor out. "You didn't think I'd come all this way without a backup plan, did you?"

She selected an armored vest, pulled it up her body, and snapped the pieces on the side. "I don't need armor. I have magic, remember?"

"Even your magic won't stop your body from dying if you're cut, shot, or stabbed," Lars replied while he laced his boots. "Being prepared with armor is a good first step on a really bad day."

"Hell yeah, it is," Johnny agreed and strapped his armor tightly in place. "There have been more times it's saved me than not. You may be a witch, but you still have a human body and compared to a Dreth, we're like porcelain dolls. Trust me. You want as much coverage as you can possibly get."

Stephanie nodded, put her foot on a chair, and tucked her

pants into her boots before she laced them as tightly as she could, one section at a time. "I can't determine what's happening here. I tried to send magic out to get a feel for it, but this ship is full of Dreth, Meligornians, and humans already. There is no way to know who's behind this."

"It could be the Dreth. Or it could be some unknown force we haven't met yet, and it could be the rebels," Marcus stated. "I do know that it doesn't matter who they are. We'll eliminate them. This was supposed to be a relaxing cruise and now, we're covered in armor and doing our best to not be seen before we want to be seen. It's complete bullshit."

"War *is* bullshit," Frog yelled. "But no one can seem to get the hell away from it. We keep trying to make peace by either starting a fight or making enemies of the ones with zero shits to give. There has to be a better strategy to it all."

"When we get back to Earth, Frog, you can spend all the time you need to find a strategy that will work in our favor," Stephanie told him and slipped a gun into the holster on her side. "For now, assume violence will be involved."

He checked his gun and shrugged. "Meh, I really don't mind. I simply felt like being a free-loving hippy for five seconds. I want to kick whoever this is back to wherever the hell they came from."

Suddenly, the comms over the entire ship gave a loud whistle that faded into a crackle. It was followed by a deep growling cough that radiated throughout the vessel. "Attention. Prepare yourselves to listen carefully to the announcement about to be made."

Stephanie walked over to the console in the corner. "Frog. A little help here? I want to see what's going on."

"You know this isn't allowed, right?" he asked, dragged a seat up, and opened a panel in the wall behind the terminal.

"It's an emergency," she told him. "I'm sure they'll forgive us."

"We have to be breaking I don't know how many Fed regs,

here," he grumbled as he fiddled behind the panel to wire in a connection to Lars's laptop. Once he'd done that, he slid a thumb drive into the laptop and began to type.

"Ha! I knew we hired you for something," Lars commented, looking over his shoulder.

"My good looks and chick magnetry?" Frog sounded hopeful, but his fingers didn't stop their rapid-fire efforts and the screen in front of her showed her a list of the difference surveillance sections. "There. That should do it."

"You're a genius," she said and clicked through the surveillance to see what was going on outside the suite.

The ship appeared deserted without a passenger in sight. There were large numbers of Dreth, however, and the bodies of security guards strewn in the corridors. The scene outside the Bridge was almost too horrible to look at.

Before any of them could comment on it, the speakers crackled again and a different but equally as sinister voice spoke through it. The emergency communications screens set into every cabin wall flashed on to display a Dreth pirate captain who stood on the *Meligorn Dreamer's* Bridge.

His grin was particularly nasty, and he gestured to the center of the Bridge. At the consoles around him, the other pirates held the *Dreamer's* captain and crew hostage with guns pointed at their heads.

The ship's captain had a look of disdainful calm on his face and did not appear to be intimidated by the pirates at all.

"He should have been an actor," Stephanie murmured.

The pirate captain spoke again, his tone brutish and guttural

"I am Hormghast Saqteq. As you can see, I speak to you live from the ship's Bridge. We have taken control of your ship. Your security personnel are dead, and your captain and crew are at our mercy." He lifted his lips in a fanged smile.

"He's very happy with himself," she commented dryly.

"He's also very calm for someone who's just won the battles he has," Lars said. "That's not good."

"No," Marcus added, his face serious as he studied the Dreth captain. "There's no excitement there at all, and that makes him very dangerous. He's here for more than simply taking a liner."

Frog cursed. "And they've put a worm in the system. I'd need to be in the ship's central computer to deal with that."

Saqteq continued his speech, and they fell silent. "We have the willingness and the ability to rip this ship in two. As I speak, my crew are placing a bomb on board which I can activate with a word. If that happens, your final resting place will be in the middle of another dimension, where your decompressed bodies will float with those of your families and children for all eternity."

He paused to let the horror of his words sink in and smiled malevolently again. "So, we will ask one very special and very esteemed passenger to come to the Bridge. Once they do, we will leave in our ship and allow you to continue your journey. If they do not come, we will detonate the bomb."

Marcus gritted his teeth and sneered at the screen. "He has no intention to save anyone. He will detonate that bomb either way. Whether they plan to leave first or not is another question. They're obviously willing to die for whatever ridiculous reason they have for being on this ship."

Frog glanced nervously at Lars. "And you're sure no one knew about us coming? This is a very big coincidence if they didn't. What else on this ship could they possibly want? Dreth pirates don't need to take hostages to get rich. They kill the people who have what they want and simply take it. Whoever it is they're after, they must be damned important."

"Which is why he won't get what he came for," Stephanie replied and stared at the screen like she could somehow stare into the pirate's eyes.

CHAPTER FIFTEEN

The pirate moved and the drone camera followed him wherever he walked. He stopped in front of the forward viewing screen and looked out at space beyond.

After a brief moment, he shook his head, turned back to the camera, and gazed directly into it. He hesitated when he had a strange feeling that someone stared at him equally as intently. He shook it off—because it really was a fanciful notion that did not belong in a warrior's psyche—and smiled at the people watching before he resumed his speech.

"This ship and—most important to you self-centered righteous bigots—your very skin will taste the heat of a million suns or the icy touch of space if this particular passenger decides they are more important than you are."

He glanced meaningfully at the forward screen with its vista of stars and shrugged arrogantly. "What they will decide I do not know, but I'll be glad to watch the action either way and I promise you, this is no virtual act. You won't make it back from either experience in this life."

Saqteq took a deep breath, clapped his huge hands together, and glanced over at where the captain waited, his face now slightly flushed. He permitted himself a chuckle at the man's emotion before he looked at the camera once more. "So, here it is —the name of the person who needs to come forward, the one who can save you or sentence you to the grave. Are you on the edges of your gold-coated seats? Good."

His face lost all humor and become stern and serious, and his lip twitched. "Ambassador of Meligorn, how about you come to the Bridge and save a few lives by not making this difficult? Leave your bodyguard behind if you value his life. You have five minutes before we start executing the crew. We will be waiting."

The screen went black as the mic clicked off. Stephanie whirled to face the team, her eyes wide as she shook her head. "No. That…that's not right, is it? The ambassador's not here on this ship, is he?"

There was panic in her voice, and the team had no idea how to answer her. They simply stared and their faces revealed that they felt as confused as she did.

Finally, Lars walked over and put his hands on her shoulders. "What did he tell you about this awards ceremony?"

Calming slightly, she shook her head. "Nothing really. He said he would see me there, but he said nothing about being on this ship."

Her voice rose. "I mean…if he were on this ship, he would have told me, right? Brilgus would have called to let us know. We would have known."

Lars stared at her for a moment before he looked at the other guys. "Johnny, check the passenger logs for any unusual names in the royal rooms and floors. Then cross-check who is staying there and make sure they really exist."

He turned to her. "I am positive he's not here. I have no idea why they think so, but freaking out won't fix this situation. You have to stay calm."

Stephanie nodded and walked over to the center of the room.

She thought about the MU conversation she had with the other Meligornian she had met.

She tapped her foot against the carpet and rubbed her chin as she wracked her brain to think of something she could do to determine whether or not the ambassador was actually there. When she recalled her encounter with Garma, she had an idea.

It might not work but was certainly worth the attempt. She took a deep breath, closed her eyes, and focused on a search for any sources of MU on the ship. Her gMU stirred and she could almost see it as it crept out of her and flowed across the floor.

She monitored it carefully and the energy traveled out under the doors and through the hallways to probe and seek for any trace of MU that might be there. It would take her a while to move through the entire ship that way but she decided it was the best chance she had to confirm the ambassador's presence.

If he was on board, there was no way she would let him surrender to the Dreth. If he wasn't, that freed the team to make a move. Either way, they couldn't simply sit there and do nothing. Everyone's lives depended on it.

Captain Penman looked at the pirate who held him down in his chair, a gun pointed at his head. His gaze followed Saqteq as he paced the room. He wasn't sure what the pirate captain had planned, but the Dreth's body language said he was waiting for something.

Aware that the human captain watched his every move, Saqteq waited for the signal. Either the ambassador would come or there would be an explosion that would rock the Federation. There was a fairly good chance that both would happen, which essentially made the explosion inevitable.

Captain Penman couldn't know that, but it soon became clear that the human had no intention to simply sit there. "Saqteq—"

His guard reversed the blaster and smacked him in the side of the head. "Shut up."

Saqteq turned toward them and waved his hand. "Let him speak. It is fine. What were you saying, Captain?"

Penman rubbed the side of his head and gave the pirate a filthy look. "I wanted to say that you are mistaken. I would know if the ambassador was on this ship. He has been our passenger in the past. I am the captain and I know the name of every passenger on board. That is my duty and obligation, despite the fact that some prefer to travel in secret. I cannot protect someone if I don't know they're on my ship. And I am telling you, the ambassador is not here."

The Dreth leaned his head back with a smirk and folded his arms over his chest. "Sure, sure. Maybe you don't know he is here but let me ask you something. You do have a special high-level person traveling to Meligorn on this ship, don't you?"

Penman felt shock flare through him. He knew he carried someone special but not exactly who. He tried to pretend ignorance and rolled his eyes. "That could be anyone. The Federation even defines famous actresses as special high-level guests on occasion."

Saqteq snarled at him. "Don't act like I am stupid, Captain. I have scalped humans alive for worse than that."

He fingered the string of scalps dangling from his hip and saw the captain pale. "Now," he said, "the special high-level guest. Who could that possibly be if not the Meligornian ambassador? The Federation does not hide the knowledge of simply anyone from the security system, not even your high-level actresses. Only the privileged and elite get to walk under the sun without the Federation's all-knowing yoke resting on their shoulders. Only those they deem as powerful as themselves are able to be a ghost in life. And the ambassador is one of those people. Perhaps even close to number one on that list."

Captain Penman shook his head. "Then why don't I know of

his presence now? Why would I know about him every other time he's traveled but not his identity for this trip?" He narrowed his eyes. "Why would *I* not know, but *you* would?"

Hormghast Saqteq spread his arms and his blaster hung sloppily from his left hand. "Oh, I don't know. Perhaps for this reason, exactly. So that you can have—what is it? Plausible deniability? So that you can tell me you always know and I think you are telling the truth. Well, it won't work this time. Do you want to know why?"

Penman shook his head and looked at the floor because he already knew the answer. The Hormghast ran forward, grasped his captive by the cheeks, and squeezed them hard as he raised his face to thrust his own inches away from it. "Because no matter what, if I don't have the ambassador when I leave this ship, you will all die."

He released the man's face with a dismissive flick of his wrist and turned away. The ship captain rolled his jaw and spat on the floor. "You'll kill us no matter what happens."

Saqteq paused mid-stride and pivoted, faking shock. "What? You doubt my honor? You think we don't have an honest bone in our bodies? Well, we sure as the Hromiqteg Deeps used to. It was only after your Federation destroyed our freedom that we left our honor behind. So, you may be right. I might truly intend to destroy all the souls on this ship because I have no honor. And, of course, you know all Dreth believe that a dead Federation citizen is the best kind of Federation citizen there is."

<hr>

Time was running out. The Hormghast had set a countdown clock to spin down in the center of the Bridge and focused the security camera on it to show the people how long they had until he blasted them all to hell.

As Dreth warriors took over the command consoles, Penman

was forced to join his crew. When he reached them, his executive officer leaned toward him. "I know who that guest on the ship is."

He raised his eyebrows, his expression plainly dubious. The man nodded vigorously. "I do too. It's not the ambassador either."

The captain shook his head and made eye contact with him in a meaningful exchange. "We have to reveal the secret to save some lives. Even if it only buys us ten minutes to get them into stasis pods, at least they'll have a chance."

The executive officer took a deep breath. "It's the witch. She's being hailed as the savior."

"Then she should be here doing some saving," Penman said. "By not coming, she's given up her right to choose."

He straightened but his heart sank as his face reddened. Guilt-inspired nausea rolled through him as he tried to find an alternative to what he had to do.

He didn't want to hand the girl over to the pirates, but it was one life for many—and she was the witch. Surely she could get herself free, which was not something even the ambassador was capable of.

Left with no choice, the captain cleared his throat. Hormghast Saqteq turned toward him with raised eyebrows. "Yes? Are you ready to divulge that the ambassador is indeed here?"

The captain shook his head. "He isn't. But someone else is."

The pirate snarled and walked quickly toward him. "You had better be telling me the truth or I will sit you on top of that bomb when it blows."

He swallowed hard. "I am telling you the damn truth. The secret person is—"

The comms squealed and crackled to cut him off and both captains looked at the screen. There was no picture, but they could hear breathing on the other end. "This is the ambassador."

The voice was unmistakable and in the next moment, the screen flashed on to reveal the man standing proudly in front of the camera, his robes draped around him and his silver hair sparkling under the overhead lights.

His gaze shifted to something beyond the screen and the Hormghast sneered. He strode closer to the screen and inspected the Meligornian's face intently. After he'd stared at the purple haze in the ambassador's eyes that confirmed his identity, he turned to Penman and the executive officer. The two men stared at the screen in complete and utter shock.

Saqteq laughed, crossed to the group, and crouched beside the captain. He draped an arm over Penman's shoulders and stared at the screen with him.

"See?" he said and forced the man's chin up with a brutal grasp when he tried to lower his head. "You see? Even the Federation hides the risk from the captain of the ship which carries him. You are nothing but patsies for others. Playthings. You should have chosen to be a liberated human. Now we will get who we came here for."

Penman stared at the pirate. "Why? Because you couldn't have the job you wanted? Because you couldn't have the house, or the city, or the car, or any of the luxuries? Is that why you're angry?"

Saqteq raised his arm and patted the man on the back. As he stood, he looked at the human and all humor had faded from his face. "I don't care about those things. No Dreth does. What we do care about is our freedom. We care about not being corralled and pushed around. We care when the Federation dictates our every move and thought and when the way it governs us kills our people."

He ruffled Penman's hair as he stepped carefully away and the man flinched. "Those are the things we care about, but even you —a servant to the rich—cannot see that you are nothing but a sheep. You humans like to be sheep. It makes you feel like you belong, and it's pathetic. But no matter. I am about to get what I came here for and that is what is important."

The ambassador stood in front of the drone camera and glanced across at Lars and the team every once in a while. The Hormghast was talking to the *Dreamer's* captain and forced him to look at the screen before he left him and came to stand before the drone camera.

"Well, Ambassador, now that you have come clean, get your ass up to the Bridge. We have some business to discuss and I have a public of freed Dreth, humans, and Meligornians waiting to see you lose your head as retribution for all those who have ever been oppressed."

The ambassador's jaw clenched and Saqteq narrowed his eyes where he stood very close to his own camera. "What's wrong? Are you afraid? You always said you would do what was in the best interest of Meligorn, no matter the personal cost. Wasn't that the line that made people trust you? Now, though, you are part of the human's world, and I fear that has corrupted you and made you weaker."

The Meligornian raised his chin in what could have been a challenge. "You are surely mistaken, pirate. I am stronger than I have ever been."

His eyes flashed black momentarily before they returned to their usual hue. It was so quick that Saqteq wasn't sure if his eyes had played tricks on him, or if something was going on with the man. "No matter. Come to the Bridge. We will handle our business there."

With a nod, the ambassador turned the video off and let his shoulders relax. As he turned toward Lars and the team, his body shrank down and his features altered. In less than a minute, Stephanie stood where the ambassador had been.

She rubbed her face. "That is a bitch to do. Next time, someone prepare a speech for me, okay?"

Frog jotted it down. "Noted. But I personally have to say, you were totally awesome."

Stephanie chuckled. "That was the easiest part of all. Now, we have to actually save these people."

Her expression grim, she lifted the hem of the robes and walked forward to claim her blaster off the bed and raise her robes even higher to strap it on her thigh. She had to take the pistols off her hip in case the Dreth noticed them before she could reveal herself.

There were lives at stake and she couldn't take chances. "Are you guys ready?"

The team was lined up in their battle gear and ready to go. Lars nodded and Marcus grinned. "Hell yeah, we are. The question is, will you be able to hide us from the cameras? Otherwise, they'll know it's a set-up before you even get there."

She bit the inside of her cheek. "I don't know for sure. I have to find a way to manipulate what's in the system."

Stephanie closed her eyes and let her mind scroll through the possibilities. With the pressure on, she was able to think clearer and faster than she'd expected. It was another new development she'd have to explore at another time when an entire ship wasn't held hostage by Dreth.

When the ambassador had told her that she had opened parts of herself that humans normally couldn't access, she hadn't been sure what he'd meant. Now, she began to have an idea of what that involved. The only thing was that she wished she could think this fast when she wasn't on her way to meet someone who wanted to kill her.

"Or," she countered. "I have to find a way to freeze the cameras I pass..." She rushed across the room and stood at the door with her hand on the knob. "You guys have to be thirty seconds behind me. As soon as I vacate a hallway, I'll work to freeze the cameras to what was there at the moment I left."

Lars nodded. "And that should give us time to get to the dark spot and wait for you to pass again. It should work."

Stephanie nodded. "It should. Using that, we can get through from here to the Bridge okay. You've seen the feeds, so you know there are still Dreth out there and you have to sneak through."

She drew the hood of her robes up over her head and her hair lengthened into long, silvery wisps as she stood there. Slowly, her body began to grow, fill the robes out, and broaden at the shoulders.

That complete, she lowered her head as her face morphed into the ambassador's. "No failure," she told her team, her voice still her own as she opened the door slightly. "We are on the way to Meligorn. Meligorn! And I will be damned if I let a horde of smelly, arrogant pirate savages stop me from seeing the planet of my dreams."

That thought alone angered her more than she could even explain. She let the door close again and the hood of her robe slid back. Her eyes flashed to black and sparks of energy erupted around her like miniature lightning bolts.

Her voice rose and then fell and became heavy with promise. "They want to threaten the ambassador? They want to threaten this ship? Well, we will make them wish they never found us. They will cry for their Dreth mothers by the time I am done with them. And when the last of them have been relieved of their lives, I will send a message to anyone else who wishes to destroy the very foundation of truth. We are not on the side of the Federation, but we are not on the side of the rebel Dreth scum either. We are on the side of freedom."

As she took a deep, steadying breath, the magic began to fade and her eyes returned to the ambassador's usual color. The guys stood awed by her power and motivated by her words.

Lars nodded and raised his fist in solidarity. Stephanie let the magic form a ball in her stomach and grinned from ear to ear as she flipped her hood up to cover her head. "The time is now, boys, and then we'll go and have a damn drink."

They cheered quietly and readied themselves while she walked out of the room. Fortunately, she remembered to mimic the ambassador's distinctive walk. She turned right and headed along the path to the Bridge she'd memorized.

From behind her, a whispered hiss demanded attention. She glanced up, then slowly turned. Frog had his head poked slightly out of the door and pointed frantically in the other direction. "The Bridge—it's the other way."

Stephanie pursed the ambassador's lips, nodded, and turned swiftly as though she'd forgotten which way she'd meant to go before she strode nonchalantly down the hall in the right direction. Frog ducked out to give her an enthusiastic grin and two thumbs-up as she passed. It took everything in her not to blush.

"Okay, Morgana. You're a little embarrassed, as you should be," she whispered to herself. "Turn that to pure and total rage and you'll well and truly be on your way to kicking Dreth ass."

She curled her hands into fists and released a small burst of static. "Too much, Morgana, too much."

"Get me the security scans," Saqteq ordered as he paced swiftly in the limited space. "I want to see every part of this ship so I know the ambassador isn't playing any little tricks. He's always fancied himself as clever and I won't fall victim to one of his idiotic schemes."

The Hormghast's eyes scrutinized the scans displayed on the main viewing screen and searched for any type of movement. Behind him, Captain Penman sat rigidly in his chair. He knew that if the ambassador surrendered himself, it would only mean death.

The Meligornian was older and more powerful, but he would

be one man against the Dreth killers and would be more than willing to give his soul for the people on the ship. The captain couldn't believe it would happen on his watch.

It seemed tragic that after a long and illustrious career, he would be remembered as the captain who'd allowed the capture—and most likely the death—of the Meligornian ambassador to Earth.

"Hormghast," one of the Dreth called and pointed to the third screen. "There is someone coming."

Saqteq waved his hand in the air. "Enlarge it. I want to see his final walk of shame."

They all watched, the humans in horror and the Dreth in good-humored anticipation as a lone figure walked slowly toward the camera, then past and down the corridor. His face was unmistakable. The ambassador had come as promised.

For a moment, Captain Penman had hoped it was a different ambassador or someone posing as him, but the eyes, the slender, youthlike features, and the sparkling silver tresses were unmistakable. He looked away for a moment and up once again as the view shifted to the next screen.

He thought about the ambassador for a moment and focused more intently with narrowed, confused eyes. Instinctively but surreptitiously, he scooted forward in the chair for a closer look.

The executive officer noticed the movement. "What is it, Captain?"

Penman shook his head in warning and kept his voice low. "It's probably wishful thinking, but I could have sworn the ambassador had a scar on that side of his face from his attempt to save his daughter many moons ago, and I didn't notice it there."

The other man scrutinized the feed as the Meligornian passed under another camera, and he confirmed there was no sign of any scar on his face. He glanced at the captain, who pursed his lips and attempted to keep a shocked look on his face and not reveal anything that might alert the pirates.

Saqteq turned toward them and smiled with quiet satisfaction as he gestured at the screen. "Don't miss it, boys. Watch as the reason for your ticket to hell approaches. And please, don't forget to thank him when he gets here. I'm sure he will love to see your faces before he watches you all die."

CHAPTER SIXTEEN

Stephanie wobbled slightly with the effort to constantly lean to the right side like the ambassador always did. As she passed each security camera, she released a slight surge of magic into the wall below it. The stream of translucent gMU flowed out to vanish behind the wall panels.

Inside, it twisted up the wires and into the camera itself. There, it sparked obediently so the devices froze the image and held it steady for thirty seconds.

She knew she was being watched and that the pirates and ship's crew were most likely shocked by the presence of the ambassador. It was almost hilarious to know with each passing camera that she was able to trick them into thinking she was not only a different age and gender but a completely different species.

Her magic swirled wildly inside and the vortex worked double-time. Soon, she no longer had to focus to maintain the Meligornian's form. Her skills grew stronger and the increased power couldn't have come at a better time.

The cameras changed as she moved, and she knew that her team was mere feet behind her, waiting for a clear path before they hurried through. She wasn't alone in any of this, and that made her feel even braver.

Behind her, Lars reached the next intersection and put his fist up before he glanced carefully around the corner. It was completely empty of Dreth so he moved through and gestured the team up behind him.

Marcus, who was closest, leaned forward and whispered, "Are you sure these cameras are frozen? Are you sure she can do this?"

He stopped and shrugged as they waited to enter the next section. "If she can't, this will be the shortest rescue from pirates in history."

The other man thought about that for a moment and nodded. "She either can or she can't, but we should act like it's done and keep watch for anyone who can see us and give us away."

They reached the end of the next section and Lars squatted and drew his team in close. "Marcus brought up a good point. Whether this works or not, we have to be prepared for Dreth. If you see a pirate, shoot him. Shoot him so he can't come back. Shoot him so the rest of his filthy comrades feel the pain."

Frog nodded. "Or her."

Everyone looked at him. "What? Just saying. No need to be gender-specific here. For all we know, those huge smelly bastards are all girls. You're the ones with the assumptions. Sheesh."

The guys simply shook their heads and readied themselves once more. Lars gave them all a strong look of approval. "We got this, guys. And so does she. Have faith in her."

"Always," Marcus agreed.

"To the damn glorious end," Johnny replied.

"She is pretty much the baddest ball-bustingest chick ever," Brenden said.

"Agreed," Avery added.

"You know I will hop along after her for, like, life," Frog said and made everyone suppress laughter.

Lars tilted his head toward the next stretch. "Well, shit, what are we waiting for then?"

Every step Stephanie took toward the Bridge as the ambassador became more difficult to make. It was as if the anger she held in vibrated through her whole body.

It was so strong it almost made her stagger. That pirate bastard didn't know what he was in for. He had threatened her friend, an adopted member of her family, a man who had more courage and morality in his pinky finger than any of the Dreth inside.

Her fists clenched and she looked down and twisted her neck as she tried to push away the feeling that she might lose control.

They deserve to have you lose control, she said to herself. *But shit, you gotta make it there first. Keep it together. Keep it together. Think of something calming.*

Todd's face flashed through her mind, and she felt the energy surge subside enough for her to continue. He danced around in her mind, told jokes, and talked exactly like he had when they were in school.

She remembered the way he walked backward to see her face as he spoke. Then he morphed in her mind to stand at the helm of a Federation Navy ship, saluting the Federation flag and ready to fight for them. She was proud of him, even though the military wasn't something she wanted. No, not in the least.

Seconds later, the anger took hold again, and she was struck by a vision of Todd dying at the hand of a Dreth warrior and screaming in pain. Fire blazed all around him with no way for her to get through.

The imagery meant she had to fight harder than ever to keep

the black from her eyes. Sweat began to pour down her forehead and despite her attempts to push out the bad, all she could see were the people she loved dying by Dreth pirate hand.

Now she knew how the Ambassador felt after losing his daughter. Now she knew how he would feel if he were subjected to the cruelty of what the Dreth pirate attempted to lay on his shoulders.

As she walked slowly forward, her breath became more rapid and she looked down when her eyes shifted from black to purple and purple to black. She could feel herself drawing in more and more magic until she didn't know if she could hold it for another second, let alone until she needed it.

When she reached the corridor across from the Bridge, she clutched the railing on the wall, stumbled, and put her head down. She closed her eyes and took a moment to steady herself and remember why she was there—and why what she was doing was so important. The magic flowing through her was under her control and she needed to start acting like it.

Shaking her head, she harnessed the rage inside her and set it to the side to box it in and buy her enough time to walk onto the Bridge. As she did so, she felt the black fade even though the anger remained. When she knew she was okay, she turned and continued toward two pirates who stood outside the Bridge doors.

They looked at her with sneers of disgust. The one on the right raised his comm to his mouth to report to those inside. "Meligorn Muschtak is here."

Stephanie knew it was a slur and a nasty one at that. She knew they were already baiting her as the ambassador, trying to embarrass him through ridicule, and it enraged her. The magic pushed at the boundaries she'd set, and she almost relinquished control then and there.

One of the Dreth looked strangely at her when he noticed the sweat trickling down her face and her clenched fists. He elbowed the other who studied the ambassador briefly and shrugged. "Maybe he is having a heart attack. That would do the dirty work for us."

They both laughed and only the knowledge that she would unleash hell on them enabled her to calm herself. They wouldn't know what hit them.

Behind Stephanie, the team halted around the corner from their destination. Lars watched as the Dreth guards grasped the back of her robes and shoved her into the Bridge. The door closed behind them but in the second before they disappeared from view, they slapped each other's claws in a Dreth high five.

He curled his lip scornfully and shook his head. With his back pressed against the wall, he took a deep breath. "She's in. Now, all we have to do is wait for the signal."

Marcus frowned. "Uh…Lars? What signal would that be?"

Frog hit his forehead and hissed at Marcus. "The one that comes over the comms. Sheesh."

The team leader blinked. He felt the need to rush after his charge but managed to hold back. "It's Stephanie. She always has a signal. Although we should probably order her to give us an official one. Something like the Bat Symbol, but way more cool."

"Like a Super Llama," Frog said and garnered several blank stares from his teammates.

The lighting inside the Bridge burned steady and white, a distinct contrast to the flashing amber lighting in the corridors beyond. It was also a contrast to the danger she was heading into.

Still, she was calm and collected and loved the fact that she could walk through as she was and have no one question her.

Someone began to clap loudly and a tall Dreth, built slightly smaller than the others, turned away from the viewscreen that stretched in front of the control center. There was something about him that set him apart from the others.

He smiled, still clapping. "The great ambassador has come here to die. How poetic could it get?"

Stephanie chose to remain absolutely silent. She could imagine that the Bridge was a comfortable place on a normal day, but not with a dozen Dreth holding guns to the heads of the crew hostages like they were.

Their leader observed the ambassador as he shifted his gaze and noted the position of every Dreth in the room.

"I know what you're doing." He snickered. "You are planning your heroic attack, right? The one where you save the crew and kick our asses back to Dreth? Maybe even kill us and show you have no mercy, even in your pathetic new life."

The Hormghast shook his finger at the Meligornian. "You know, it would be useless of you to fight anyway. Even one as great as you runs out of energy."

He yanked the ambassador's robes open and tilted his head to the side to inspect the tunic beneath. "Ahhh, you did not even bother with any batteries. Are you so impressed with your abilities that you spit on us in contempt?"

With a grin, he spread his hands and cracked his neck noisily. In silence, he raised one hand and drew it slowly down over his face before he released a stream of MU from his fingertips.

It flowed over his head and down to wind around the pirate's body. Stephanie gaped in shock as the Dreth elevated to hover a few feet from the floor as he morphed into his true form. When the new figure solidified, the pirate drifted to a sedate landing and released a deep breath.

She gritted her teeth and forced her voice to sound like the ambassador's. "You are a Meligornian."

The captain smiled. "That's right, Ambassador—which makes me a hell of a lot scarier now."

He held an empty battery out and gestured with his free hand." "Put your MU in here."

With her expression frozen in place, she complied carefully and pressed her hand against the battery to give him exactly what he asked for—her MU. When she withdrew her hand, the captain held the battery up and looked at the quarter-full rock. "I doubt this is all you have, but I will take it."

He drew the MU into himself and breathed deeply, his eyes shut. "And now you are but a portion of yourself and I am fully charged. Will you allow your anger to become your stupidity one last time?"

He grabbed his captive by the shoulder and dragged him in front of the viewscreen. Instead of corridors, it now showed the interiors of all the rooms where frightened passengers waited and watched their viewscreens in horror.

"You cannot possibly save them all with what little energy remains inside you. And we have planted the bomb which will break the ship apart if you do not disarm it in time."

With a bark of laughter, the pirate captain walked around the room, gloating. "How the powerful and mighty fall when their compassion replaces their passion. How funny it will be to see you crumble at the feet of the people and watch them shattered in agony and defeat."

He paused briefly, cleared his throat, and spoke into his comms. "Round them up, boys. We are getting the hell off this ship and going home where we can watch in peace as they spend their last moments in the cold abyss of space."

The Meligornian walked past Captain Penman, a look of scorn on his face. He stopped and stood with his legs shoulder-width apart, irritated at the ambassador's silence.

Stephanie focused on the screens to make sure none of her

team was visible on the cameras. Her magic had worked, and she knew they'd be waiting close by for the signal.

The pirate captain cracked his knuckles and drew her attention. "Do you have anything to say before we take you with us? The king will be at a loss once he does not have you as a pawn in this game."

She didn't know what he meant and simply reverted to what she knew of the ambassador. She spoke firmly, her back to him at first. "I don't know what you mean. The unfortunate situation for you is that I am well versed in the evil that dwells in the souls of all who speak as you do." She turned and fixed her captor with a cold gaze. "It's even more unfortunate that I refuse to bow to those like you."

His features mottled with anger but she gestured sharply to launch streaks of magic that wrapped themselves tightly around the pirates who guarded the crew. It immobilized them so they were unable to move. Immediately after, she gestured at the door to the Bridge, opened it, and blazed a fireball at the two pirates who stepped forward hastily to defend it. This was the signal her boys were waiting for.

The captain shouted in alarm and threw a spell. Stephanie raised her arm and blocked it easily as she looked over her shoulder at the door.

"Move your asses," she grumbled and wondered if it was time to feel anxious.

She would have to use the gMU she had stored or release her hold on the pirates if her team didn't hurry the hell up.

"Do you think the Dreth have emotions?" Marcus asked where the guys sat tucked against the wall. They were almost bored as they waited for the signal. "Personally, I couldn't imagine one of those giant things shedding a tear, cuddling a hideous Dreth baby, or kissing their wives."

"Now you're plain being sick," Johnny replied. "I'm sure they have emotions, though. And not all Dreth are bad. Only these."

Marcus shrugged and studied his nails. "Yeah, you're right. It's hard to see it, though, when they're trying to kill you all the time."

The doors to the Bridge slid open and caught their attention. The team huddled together to glance around. They were in time to see the Dreth guards step into the opening, clearly confused.

Suddenly, a huge ball of magical fire rocketed into the floor between them, knocked both Dreth off their feet, and catapulted them into the walls hard enough to leave dents. As the pirates landed heavily, Frog pointed. "The signal! That's the signal!"

Lars was already moving. He leapt to his feet, waved his arm, and raced as fast as he could to the Bridge. The two Dreth groaned and struggled to their feet.

"Scum." The Meligornian pirate spat and glared at the ambassador.

Outside, the guards raised their heads as the sound of feet pounding down the corridor intruded through their grogginess and confusion. "Huh?"

Their eyes widened as Lars and the team hurtled toward at them at a relentless pace, dressed in body armor with their weapons raised as they bellowed the new team battle cry. "Morgana!"

The pirates fumbled for their blasters but realized they'd dropped them and hadn't yet retrieved them. One of them pushed the other to the side and they both drew large swords from the sheaths on their backs.

The sight didn't strike even an ounce of fear into the team's hearts. Frog screamed at the top of his lungs and closed with the first one. He thrust his pistol under the alien's chin and pulled the trigger. The bullet plowed upward into the Dreth's head and the underside of his helmet as Frog stepped clear.

At the same time, the team leader stopped and fired at the other guard. The pirate grunted as his armor absorbed the damage, then took two enormous strides forward and swung his sword with a yell.

The blade nicked his cheek, and Lars narrowed his eyes. With a loud growl, he raised the gun and fired, hoping to fell his adversary before he could reverse his swing and slice him in two. He pulled the trigger repeatedly and filled the Dreth with bullets. His opponent shuddered with each strike but didn't succumb.

When Lars' gun clicked, out of bullets, he snatched another magazine and took several hasty steps back. "Does anyone want to take care of this?"

Marcus had snuck past the two as they fought. He now stood behind the Dreth, reached up, and tapped him on the shoulder. As the pirate spun angrily, he smacked a palm into the top of the invader's sword arm, shoved the blade down with his left hand, and drove the long-bladed knife in his right hand into his opponent's belly.

The Dreth froze and Marcus smiled as he thrust the blade deeper, "Do you feel sad, now?" he asked, a grim smile on his face.

The alien's eyes widened and the human twisted the blade, dragged it up, and shoved it down again. "How about now? Anything? Flashes of your lumpy childhood? Kisses from your mother? Your first time with a lovely Dreth girl?"

The pirate sagged heavily on the blade and Marcus sighed and used his free hand to push him back as he yanked the knife out and allowed the body to fall. "No? Well, maybe you're an anomaly. I'll test that on your buddies too."

Johnny looked at him in disgust. "Didn't your mother ever tell you not to play with your food?"

Inside the Bridge, the Meligornian pirate looked at his hands and purple magic sparked from his fingertips. "What is going on? This doesn't make any sense. I should have way more power than you, Ambassador. I took your power, dammit."

As the ambassador, Stephanie stood silently but a small smirk played around her mouth. Infuriated, Saqteq took a few steps to the side and attempted to see through the open Bridge doors.

As he approached them, a loud bang made him jump and he looked over at one of the pirates who stared out with a worried look on his face.

The Meligornian took another step to follow the direction of his warrior's gaze. He tilted his head for a better angle, and a bullet rocketed into his crewman's forehead. The force whipped his head back and sprawled his body over the control board.

Stephanie released the magic holding the pirates as the team rolled through the door. The boys glanced briefly at the Meligornian in pirate's clothing, at the crew held at gunpoint, and finally at Stephanie and continued into the room. They knew she'd deal with the captain and they had other assholes to eradicate.

Without stopping to ask either permission or forgiveness, they engaged the Dreth pirates, swept the invaders' weapons away from their human targets, and used their blasters and knives at close range.

A laser bolt barely missed Frog and he looked at the singed metal on the wall. "If you'd been three inches farther, you would be picking comets out of your teeth right now, dumb ass. That wall is really thin. Are you a space pirate or a dick with delusions of grandeur?"

"Muschstack," the Dreth sneered in response and Frog shrugged, leapt at him, and garnered a very satisfying scream as he activated the laser cutter he carried instead of a blade.

As chaos engulfed the Bridge, Stephanie, as the ambassador, kept her gaze locked on the pirate captain. The Meligornian shook his head at the scene and panic edged his voice. "This isn't how it's supposed to go."

He gathered his magic, thrust his arms out, and launched everything he had at his opponent in the hope that he could overwhelm him. She simply swiped her arm and pushed the energy back into the walls of the ship where it dissipated. Her eyes widened as the captain growled, stamped his boot against the floor, and pointed his finger angrily at her.

His jaw clenched and his silver hair stuck to the sweat on his forehead. "You traitorous piece of shit. I will be your end, one way or another. I will kill this ship and all the people on it and I will start with this pathetic excuse for a security team."

The Hormghast thrust a bolt of magic toward Lars, and she lunged sideways quickly, caught the purple ball of energy in her palm, and closed her fist to force it into mist. Her magic flared. It had reached the limit of its patience, and so had she.

The pirate captain had crossed the line and threatened her friends. Her team had stopped the pirates from threatening the hostages, and the crew had taken cover from the fight. Now, she had no reason to hold back.

The Meligornian gaped when he watched the ambassador shrink, the robes suddenly too big for the female form inside. The hood dropped over her face and he was at a complete loss as to what in the hell was going on.

Power thrummed over her small form, vibrated through the command center, and drew the attention of everyone present.

"Oh, shit," Frog said and pointed at her.

"Dammit." Lars tackled one of the pirates and managed to drag the enormous form to the ground. "Interesting," he continued, as the alien looked at him in confusion. "Tell me, do you feel anything but anger and pride when you take a life?"

The pirate's confusion melted into a look of scorn and distaste, and he bared his fangs as his body tensed. The human gave him no more time to react "Sorry, I need intel or I'd let her have you."

"Musch—" the pirate started and struggled to break his adversary's grip.

He released the alien but powered a fist as hard as he possibly could through the open visor. The blow rendered the man unconscious before he could finish his insult.

Marcus glanced over and nodded in approval. Lars winced, shook his hand, then motioned toward Stephanie. "Someone's gone black."

With the last pirate eliminated, the other guards raced toward her. "Stephanie!"

Stephanie swiped her hand back and pushed her team away from her. Her head raised in challenge, she shrugged the robes off her shoulders and stepped out of them in her body armor.

Her eyes were as black as the space outside and she glared relentlessly at the captain. *"You dare to threaten my people?"*

He froze. Whatever he'd expected to find under the cloak, it hadn't been this, but she gave him no opportunity to recover his startled wits. She leapt forward and moved so fast the team couldn't see her until she stopped in front of the Meligornian Hormghast.

Her hands moved swiftly over him to drag the magic out of him. "I'll take that back," she told him coldly, "and with the interest you owe."

His eyes bulged in shock and terror as pain engulfed him when streams of energy ripped their way through his skin. He opened his mouth and a scream shattered the air. It broadcast through the open comm line to fill every inch of the *Dreamer.*

In their cabins, the passengers cringed and some moaned in fear, while others stared with real horror at what they saw on their viewscreens. In an ice cream shop many decks away, one little girl felt a surge of hope and gave a very quiet giggle.

On the Bridge, Stephanie Morgana held the pirate captain at arms' length, his torso wreathed in purple energy. His body shook violently, and she smiled a terrible smile. As she looked at him, he opened his eyes and his skin began to melt from his bones.

Recognizing her, his voice cracked. "That human witch—"

Her smile widened. "Perhaps it would have been best if the ambassador *had* been here because I haven't the wisdom to use anything but raw power. And since I will need it *all* to fix the evil you have done, I'll take that from you."

The magic surrounding him brightened as she did as she promised, thrust her arm into his thinned and brittle chest, and wrenched the last strand of magic from inside him. He shuddered slightly when the energy left him. It shimmered as it flowed into her and left nothing but a pile of ash and bone behind it.

Stephanie drew several slow, deep breaths, and the room seemed to expand around her. She turned and stared at Captain Penman and the cold darkness in her gaze made him shiver.

Despite the urge to look away, he held her gaze and saw something beyond the young woman he had welcomed on the ship only days before. Sparks of energy crackled around her as she spoke. "Keep your people safe. Take care of everything else on this ship while we take care of the bomb."

He nodded and she turned and strode from the room, her security team close behind her. Penman sat for several moments in the silence that followed, then pushed himself from the seat and turned to his executive officer. "Deal with the pirates and the dead. Get them off my Bridge."

The comms crackled and Chief Engineer Bruce's voice came through. "Captain, we have a problem."

CHAPTER SEVENTEEN

The pirates had spread out and made for the passenger decks as their captain had ordered. Fortunately, they hadn't managed to do much before their captain's scream and the view screens set up throughout the ship had alerted them to his death. Now, they converged on the Gramghast and his team.

Their motivation had not changed. They'd wanted to destroy the ship and now wanted that more than ever. They had lost their leader and that was a travesty, the ultimate betrayal.

It was clear the ambassador had known they were coming and had seeded the witch in his place. For that, he would pay. But before that, they would destroy the witch, because no one, not even the magically gifted, could survive the vacuum of space.

At first, they'd thought they could team up, move into place as a single force, and trap her. There were enough of them that she wouldn't be able to eliminate them all before they overwhelmed her.

It might have worked, but with the speed at which their adversaries moved and their determination, the pirates couldn't enact it in time. They found themselves under fire before they could put any of their plans into action.

The team strode through the ship, Stephanie in the lead with her wild black eyes and silvery strands of hair blowing wildly around her. Any attempt at resistance was simply annihilated. Her team walked behind and to each side of her, grim-faced and unyielding as they fired with measured deliberation to pick off the pirates she missed.

They walked without fear and ignored the laser fire and bullets directed at them without flinching. She swayed her hand from side to side to block any attacks very effectively.

It took her no extra effort to do so. The shield had been a good idea but it demanded more power, and with her magic expanded, it was easier to block or slow any shots fired at them. Defeated in the ship's corridors, the remaining pirates converged on the bomb. Their Gramghast made the next plan seem possible. "We will be able to use the bomb as negotiation. We have a ship full of hostages so she will have to let us go. And when she does, we will detonate it. She killed our leader, and she must die."

The others who stood near the incendiary device looked doubtful. His plan sounded good, but they were not so sure. "Have you seen her? She is the Federation witch and there is something in her that none of us have ever seen. I watched Saqteq as he was reduced to nothing more than ash and bone."

The Gramghast narrowed his eyes and bared his fangs at this insubordination. "This is no time for cowardice. We are Dreth and we fight against the tyranny and oversight of the Federation. This witch is merely smoke and mirrors, a little girl who only plays with magic."

"I don't know, Gram," the pirate insisted and revealed a hint of fang. "If she is only smoke and mirrors, she is the kind that has more than fire and glass behind her. She sucked the power out of him and melted the skin from his bones."

Their leader sighed and waved his hand dismissively. "Whatever she is, this is our only chance to stop her. The hologram is gone. Start welding and close the hatches. We don't want her to throw it into the umbilical."

The Dreth went to work and moved the bomb enough to make sure it sat squarely on the beams strengthening the floor. They were very careful to avoid creating any kind of friction as they moved it.

Once it was in place, the pirates backed away and looked around. "Where is Krozar?"

A massive Dreth pushed through the crowd and his presence made the rest of them look small. His battle armor was worn, and he was covered in scars and wore a pair of round glass goggles on the top of his helmet.

He raised the welding torch he carried, pressed the lever to activate it, and lit the cigar clenched between his jagged teeth. Krozar puffed a couple of times and looked at it, then regarded his companions with a smirk. "Does somebody need a weld?"

The closest two Dreth exchanged glances and groaned but waved him over. "Krozar. Bomb. Stick it down and don't blow us up."

The alien sneered at them, knowing they were making fun of him and hating it. He sassed them in return and enjoyed the looks on their faces. "What? No boom-boom?"

Not giving them time to respond, he pushed them aside and went to work to weld the bomb to the floor. A pirate crouched to his right and another to his left to hold it in place. Krozar looked up and pointed to the guy to the right. "Move it a half an inch to your left."

The pirate hurried to comply, but his body was suddenly hurled away and blood splattered the side of the bomb. Krozar raised an eyebrow and turned to the other one. "All right then. You. Move it a half an inch to your—"

Another shot rang out and his second assistant somersaulted into the virtual grass. A blue wall of magic swirled around him and shoved him back several feet before it returned to wrap itself around the bomb.

Krozar threw his cigar on the floor and raised his goggles. He stood and turned to see what the hell was going on.

"I'm workin' here," he protested

The others ignored him. They were too busy looking up so he followed their gaze.

The witch and her team looked right back at him.

Stephanie leaned over the balcony five stories above the park floor. "I'm glad to see they take bomb safety seriously. Sure, let's smoke cigars and light torches around the big explodey thing."

"Well, you put a stop to that." Lars grinned.

Stephanie cracked a smile and put her hand out. "Fine. We'd better get our asses down there before they work out how to set it off in spite of the magic."

Around her, the team responded with a soft chorus of affirmatives, and she placed her hands on the rail and prepared to launch herself over. "Drinks are on me when we finish?"

"All right!" Marcus grinned like a maniac and placed his hands on the rail beside hers.

The others mirrored him and each of them grinned like they were about to raise hell—which was exactly what they intended to do. "Let's make an amazing entrance, and I hope the security cameras get this," she said and looked at Frog. "You *did* get the cameras, right?"

He looked at her and curled his lip with scorn. "Puhlease, I haven't been out of them since you had me get in. Smile! This thing will go out *live*."

They all chuckled and readied themselves to jump. She sent a small glimmer of magic to each of them and it coated their boots with a slight gleam. When it settled, she began to count. "All right. On three... Three!"

They landed hard and bounced, and the magic cushioned the impact enough that they didn't break bone. Marcus took two running steps and dived forward. Frog saw what he was doing and sprinted over.

He dropped to his knees and reached to push his teammate's feet up as he did so. The dive turned into a flip, and Marcus spun feet over head toward one of the Dreth.

The pirate raised his blaster, but his attacker moved too fast. His feet pounded into the alien's skull and felled him. Marcus landed and pushed to his feet where he bounced on his still-enchanted boots. "This shit is seriously wicked."

The Dreth groaned and struggled to stand. His opponent continued to talk about his boots while he drew his pistol. "I feel like I'm in control but I have super-feet power. Who knew that could be a kick-butt super-power?"

He pulled the trigger and fired two shots into the invader's head and immediately looked for the next target. Around him, the fight had started in earnest. Frog backed up to him and eliminated another pirate as he came.

When he ran into his teammate, he gestured to his feet. "My turn, my turn."

Marcus laughed as he locked his fingers together and stooped for him to step into them. A group of three Dreth had attacked Johnny as a unit, so he pivoted slightly as Frog stabilized.

He bounced his hands up and down and he crouched, grunted with effort as he straightened, and raised his hands to launch the other man toward the Dreth trio. He narrowed his eyes to follow the man's trajectory and his jaw dropped when he realized he might have tossed him a little too hard.

Frog whooped as he soared up to the sixth floor, then grasped the cutter as he began to descend once again. He tipped himself forward to aim at the three Dreth and Johnny and activated the bladed weapon.

At the last second, he flipped so he now fell feet-first, knowing they were the only part of his body that was actually cushioned by magic. His plummet hurled him into one of the Dreth and he lashed out at another and partially severed the pirate's neck.

Johnny blinked and grinned as he high fived his teammate before he turned back to the battle. "That was killer bad."

The third Dreth lunged toward him and his grin disappeared. He raised his blaster and fired to pulp the left side of his face inside the helmet. He followed up with a shot to each of the Dreth on the ground. "I want to give that a go."

Frog pointed at the closest wall. "Go running up and kick off the wall and put your enhanced boot in some Dreth's face."

He went to do exactly that and lined up the trajectory he'd need to come off the wall and reach his target. His teammate's gaze fell on his boots in time to see the gleam of magic disappear.

It was too late to warn Johnny, although he tried, and he could only watch helplessly as the man launched himself at the wall. With the magic gone, the jump didn't go as planned.

His feet touched as planned and he pushed off, but he didn't gain the height he needed and plowed head-first into the floor. Frog was already moving, ready to intercept the pirates who grinned at Johnny's antics even as they prepared to kill him.

He shot one and then a second as the other man pushed to his feet with a groan. "Sorry, dude. The magic literally vanished."

"Just my luck," Johnny told him and scowled at the Dreth moving in. "It looks like playtime's over. Time to kick ass and break heads."

Across the battlefield, beside the bomb, Stephanie faced the welder. She drove her fist into Krozar's chest. Under normal circumstances, the blow would have had little impact. Even with the magic, she barely pushed him back a couple of feet. She looked at him as he stepped forward and smirked. "Wow, you're a really big guy, aren't you?"

"He is," a familiar voice said beside her, "and he's mine."

Her smirk grew into a smile when Garma stepped into view and raised magic-laden hands.

"Be my guest," she told him and moved out of his line of fire.

The Meligornian didn't need to be told twice. He used his hands alternately to release a barrage of fireballs into Krozar's chest until the Dreth's armor burst into flames. The magical blaze took hold and spread over him and the fire grew even larger.

Krozar screamed and dropped to the ground, where he rolled frantically and beat at it with his hands in an attempt to extinguish it. Another Meligornian arrived, tsked, and looked at Garma.

"You always do this," he said. "It's inhumane."

With that, the new arrival shot Krozar in the head to end his pain and pathetic screams. Garma smiled. "This is my friend Baizel. Crystal's over there."

Crystal looked up from where she'd gutted one pirate and slashed the throat of another. Her eyes tracked the fight around them as she gave the witch a nod.

Stephanie noticed that Crystal's long silver hair was pulled half up and away from her pale purple eyes. The female Meligornian was dressed traditionally in a lightly armored space suit sans helmet but which was surrounded by the glow of protective magic.

She waved a hand at her two male counterparts. "This is our uncle, and that's my brother. We saw you fighting on the screen and came to help."

"She magicked her way out through the locks." Baizel grinned as Crystal calmly felled a pirate and Garma used magical darts to kill another. "Much better."

He raised his pistol and shot past Stephanie. She couldn't help noticing that his eyes were like purple-tinted crystals and his face was full of youth and excitement. She swallowed hard and smiled in return. "We're glad you could make it."

Before any of them could respond, a very human cry of pain was immediately followed by a groan. She whirled as Johnny toppled sideways in front of a Dreth.

The warrior laughed and pulled his sword back, but she bolted forward and called on her magic as she went. Before he'd completed his preparatory motion, she had closed the space between them and flipped up and over the pirate, seized his head, and snapped his neck before she landed behind him.

Johnny, bleeding from the leg, struggled to get into a sitting position as she lowered the dead Dreth to the ground. "How did you—"

"Are you okay?" she asked. "I can heal you."

He shook his head, unable to stand. "No. That will drain all your strength. I'm okay. I'll crawl over to that little corner over there and shoot everything in range."

As he spoke, Crystal arrived. She reached down, hauled him to his feet, and draped one of his arms over her shoulders. From the way she moved, it was as if he weighed nothing at all. "I'll get him to safety."

Stephanie nodded and surveyed the carnage around her. "Thank you."

The Meligornian woman grinned and eased Johnny into her arms like he was a child before she used her magic to boost her jump onto one of the balconies above.

Frog jogged over to her and pursed his lips. "I think I'm in love."

A surge of pain ripped through her side and fear rushed through her chest. It took her a moment to realize it wasn't her own and she whipped around to find Baizel and Garma facing two Dreth pirates.

A third had snuck up behind the older Meligornian and the blast the alien fired flung him to the ground. Baizel tried to reach him but he now had two adversaries to battle. The third aimed a second time and she tried to reach him before he could fire.

Even as the magic kicked in, the pirate walked over to the downed Meligornian and smirked as he pulled the trigger. To her surprise, Garma's eyes turned to her and he smiled in the split second before the bullet ended his life.

A flash of light filled the parkland. It blinded everyone and caused a momentary lull in the fighting. Garma's soul and the last of his magic fled outward at his death, and in that flare, Stephanie heard his laughter and saw herself seated at the table in his suite as they ate and talked for hours.

Just as quickly, the light retracted into Garma's body until the Meligornian exploded into a cloud of shimmering dust. Baizel gave a cry of heartfelt pain and tears streamed down his face.

Above them, on the balcony, Johnny wrapped his arms around Crystal as she shrieked in disbelief and tried to launch herself over the rail. The pirate looked around and began to take aim at Baizel's back, but only for a second. Fire, condensed into a small ball of glaring white, rocketed into him from across the field. It flared when it impacted his head and vanished in a bright eruption of light.

Pieces of helmet, flesh, and bone exploded outward in a burst of magic and gore, and the pirate dropped to his knees. The blaster clattered from his dead hand and he fell forward to lay deathly still. Smoke rose from his body before it blazed into dancing purple flame.

The other pirates stopped and looked for the source of the attack, surprised to see a young human female limned in a halo of purple fire.

"You scum-sucking bastard!" Her furious shriek drew the attention of the team.

Lars summed up the situation in a single word. "Goddamn!"

"Steph?" Frog began, but she was gone. All that stood before him was the Federation witch, Morgana, and she was too far gone for reason.

The halo of purple flared and four shields surged up around her, deep purple and solid enough to stop anything—including her friends.

Frog tried again. "Uh, Steph? Are you in there?"

It was no good. Even he could feel the tide of gMU she pulled toward her. Worse though, was that he could see what she did with it next. Her hands spun and swung both right and left as she delivered a continuous barrage of magical darts and fireballs.

He was about to try the suicidal and grab her when Lars tackled him from the side, then hastily helped him up again. "We have to get everyone out of here."

His teammate was horrified. "Not the pirates?"

"Oh, hell, no! They can fry, but this guy... She'd be really upset if we let her fireball him to pieces by mistake." Lars gestured to where Baizel stared at the hail of destruction around him. He seemed frozen in place.

Before they could reach him, though, Avery and Marcus grabbed the young Meligornian and hauled him down the nearest corridor.

CHAPTER EIGHTEEN

With the Meligornian cleared from the battle zone, the team tried to get close to Stephanie but each time they did, she pushed them back and, despite the magical fury they faced, the pirates decided to retaliate.

For them, the situation hadn't changed. They still had a mission to accomplish and they had vengeance to wreak on her. The bomb remained securely in place, and none of them knew if it would go off, but they were all reasonably sure the Gramghast hadn't needed to touch it to detonate it.

Maybe if they fought for a little longer, they could turn the tide and accomplish what they so desperately wanted.

The first attack came from across the room. A blaster bolt missed Lars's head by inches and drove into the shield. He flung himself down as Stephanie retaliated with several missiles in the direction the shot had come from.

"Sonuva..." He rolled out of her way as she pivoted and noticed the pirates still standing weren't about to run. Quickly, he spoke into the team's comms as he returned fire. "Target the pirates, guys. Maybe she'll come back to us when they're gone."

"You wish," Frog muttered, and Lars was sure his teammate hadn't meant to speak that over the comms.

Regardless of whether he'd meant it or not, the words reached Stephanie, exactly as the team leader's words had. Somewhere beneath the fury that was Morgana, she heard and knew she had to regain control. They were right. When the pirates were gone, it had to be Stephanie they found, not her rage.

She knew she was volatile from the sheer amount of energy bursting through her. While she couldn't stop it coming in, she *could* control it and the best way to do that was to fight.

With this amount of power, she could do that, and if she needed to bleed some of it off, that's what she'd do. She would fight like she'd never fought before. Around her, the rest of the team turned their attention to the invaders and worked their way out from her as though she were the center of their world.

Lars reached the edge of the park where the ice cream parlor stood. Momentarily free of Dreth attackers, he leaned on the frame of the shattered shopfront and shook his head as he tried to catch his breath. He scanned the area and had chosen his next target when he heard a small gasp.

It had come from behind him and inside the store. Slowly, he turned and crouched to see a small blonde girl tucked under a display. Her eyes were wide as she watched the battle, and they grew wider when she saw his face.

Tears tracks stained her little cheeks, but her eyes were dry. She squeaked in fright and scuttled away from him, deeper into the shop. "Just what I needed," he grumbled, straightened quickly, and pushed the door open.

With effort, he changed his expression from hardened soldier to kind adult and moved into the interior, stepping carefully over broken glass from the window.

"Hey, sweetie. You can come out now," he called. "I won't hurt you. I'm here to help."

At first, nothing moved, and he suppressed a sigh. He didn't have all day. The guys needed him, but Steph would kill him if he didn't rescue the kid, so he was screwed either way.

"Come on, kiddo. I can't get you back to your mommy if I can't find you."

That seemed to work. She peered out from behind the shop counter and studied him warily. Lars stopped and crouched again to offer her his hand.

"You gonna show me where we can find your mommy?" he asked.

She sniffed and her gaze darted nervously at the sound of the battle outside.

"Find Momma?"

He gave her a reassuring smile.

"Yes. Find Momma. Are you gonna help me?"

She regarded him warily for a few moments longer, then scurried over to him and took his hand. Without asking for permission, he scooped her up and held her close to his chest.

She couldn't have been more than four or five. She laid her head on his shoulder and sniffled. He patted her back awkwardly before she spoke.

"Help Momma," she told him and pointed. He followed the direction of her hand and startled. There, lying on the floor in a pool of blood, was the body of a woman. She had the same bouncy blonde hair and blue eyes as the child, although hers stared sightlessly at the ceiling. His heart stuttered in his chest.

"I'm sorry, sweetie. Let's find your daddy instead."

"Find doctor?" she persisted, and he didn't have the heart to tell her otherwise.

"Yeah, kiddo," he agreed softly. "We'll go find a doctor."

He left the store and slipped carefully out through the door. Crystal met him before he'd gone three steps toward a corridor. She'd jumped down from the balcony and left Johnny to take pot shots at the pirates on his own.

Now, she smiled sweetly at the child. "Any sign of her parents?"

Lars shook his head, not able to explain it in front of the child. He had a hard enough time holding himself together as it was, and the fight wasn't over. She took a deep breath and forced a smile as she put her arms out for the girl.

"This is Crystal," he told the child. "She's going to look after you for a while and I'm gonna kill the bad guys."

"Doctor?" the child asked, and her small voice quivered.

"Bad guys first, then doctor," he told her firmly and hated the lie even as he said it.

"Kay." The girl didn't argue any further but let Crystal take her from his arms.

"She'll be okay," the Meligornian reassured him as she leapt upward and used her magic to boost them out of the fight and return to Johnny's balcony.

He sighed heavily and turned his attention to the battlefield. Stephanie stood at the center of a magical maelstrom. The shields remained constant, but energy still arced around her. Fireballs, darts, and a rain of magic blazed through it as Morgana obliterated every Dreth she saw. Her eyes burned black, two pinpricks of darkness in the midst of the gleaming purple storm.

She kicked the front shield down, rolled forward, and stretched her hand toward half a dozen advancing Dreth warriors. They backed away before her and only stopped when the wall blocked any further retreat.

Morgana glared at them and they cowered before her and flinched when she swished her entire body right and left. Her left hand turned in circles to conjure a spiral of rope magic into her palm. Holding one end, she used it like a whip, flicked it up, and snapped it as she brought her hand down.

The whip made a chiming noise as it struck the ground and created sparks of magic. The fiery particles ignited into a low wall of wildfire that flared up in front of her adversaries.

As they cowered from the flames, she drew the blaster strapped to her thigh and began firing. She didn't stop until they were all dead and then, she looked at Lars.

He was too busy to notice her, however, having been attacked by one of the pirates not caught up in her attack. He landed a punch and followed it with a flying kick that missed the Dreth's face. The alien retaliated, hammered his fist into the human's chin, and launched him into a wall. He grunted as he impacted and slid to the ground.

When he didn't immediately move, Stephanie clenched her teeth and began to stride forward. This time, Lars did notice her. He raised his hand as though signaling her to stop and shook his head. Morgana fought to stay in control, but even she could see the battlefield was almost clear and very few pirates remained.

She stopped and waited as he used the wall to push to his feet before he turned to meet his adversary. He took a fighting stance and raised his fists as though he meant to use them, but as the Dreth approached, he grinned and drew his blaster. "Just kidding, asshole. We're not doing that again."

A single shot felled the pirate, and he walked toward Stephanie while he rubbed and popped his cheek. "Are you back yet? Because that definitely hurt."

He studied her carefully as he approached. Her eyes had returned to their usual blue and her hair now hung normally instead of rising in an invisible wind. The shields remained—only the three protecting her back and sides—and there was no longer a halo of magic surrounding her body.

To his relief, she smiled.

"I think you made up for it with that trick," she replied. "That was sweet."

"Thank you," Lars acknowledged. "Being that much of a smart ass is truly an art."

Stephanie rolled her eyes and patted him on the shoulder, then pivoted away abruptly to pursue a pirate who tried to open the doors leading out of the atrium. He made it through and disappeared into the corridor beyond with her in hot pursuit. As she raced after him, she passed Frog and Marcus, who faced one of the pirates using swords taken from his dead companions.

Frog swung, missed the Dreth, and overreached. He wasn't used to using a blade that heavy, and it pulled him off balance and spun him around. Marcus shook his head and bent his knees as the alien lunged at him.

"Dude," he told Frog, "you gotta bend at the knees. Find your center of gravity. Otherwise, you'll run around missing and falling all over the damn place."

Their adversary roared and made a sweeping stroke at his head and Marcus ducked. He came up under it and thrust his blade into the Dreth's stomach. He was fortunate to find a vulnerable point in the pirate's armor, but the blade caught, and he couldn't pull it out again.

The pirate dropped his hands to the trapped blade and stumbled back, a look of shocked disbelief on his face. Frog regained his balance and glared at his teammate. "You know what the real problem is here?" He yanked his blaster out and shot the invader in the head. "Using big-ass knives when this is supposed to be a gunfight."

While Lars, Brenden, and Avery battled the last of the pirates in the room, the other two looked for Stephanie, but she was nowhere to be seen.

"She went that way," Frog said when he recalled her running past him as he'd swung to miss the Dreth.

They spun and saw the open door leading out of the atrium. "Shit."

Neither of them said anything more. They turned and jogged into the corridor.

"She can't have gone very far, right?"

They soon discovered that, while they'd been fighting, the worm had done its work and the cabins—once securely locked according to the ship's Emergency Protocols—had unlocked. Because it had been so silent for so long, people had started to come out of their rooms and now wandered the corridors. They stared in shock and awe at the bodies and the battle damage that scarred the walls.

Panels had been shattered and laser burns seared the surfaces. Frog and Marcus tried to push them back, worried about where Stephanie could have gone but knowing they needed to move the passengers out of harm's way. "This is not a secure area, people. We have not neutralized the enemy yet. There is still a danger to life and limb here."

The people didn't listen at first and tried to see past them into the open parkland at their backs. The teammates tried to steer a path through them and persuade them to return to their rooms. It seemed a futile effort until a Dreth barreled out of a door marked *Staff Only*.

Everyone screamed and flattened themselves against the walls. Frog and Marcus drew their blasters and fired. Three shots struck home and the alien fell at the passengers' feet.

Frog thrust his blaster back into its holster and yelled, "I just told you, we have not eliminated the enemy. You need to be in your room with the door locked. This is not simply a precaution. The Dreth pirates will kill you and probably eat you or keep your head for a trophy. So, go!"

This time, they gasped, turned, and literally raced to their rooms. He shook his head, not understanding what they found so difficult to understand. "I swear the richies are like different people to the rest of mankind. They are specifically created to not listen, have ridiculous curiosity for things they should never be curious about, and have no moral compass. Instead of helping the guy on the ground there—who knows, he could be alive— they walked over him to see the *bigger* dead things."

Marcus walked over, studied the dead man on the ground,

and shook his head. "Uh, no, I think those people would have known *he* was dead."

His teammate scoffed. "How? You can be still alive and unconscious."

"Very true, but you cannot be still alive and headless."

The other man looked at him, then at the body and grimaced. "Oh. Oh, man, that's terrible. Now I feel like an asshole."

They worked their way through the corridors in search of Stephanie.

"Do you think she went black again?" Frog asked as they turned another corner.

Marcus was about to answer when they heard her furious tones punctuated by the snap of magic arcing over armor. "Oh, you miss your mommy? I'm sure, in hell, there will be *plenty* for you to do."

This was followed by the sound of three precise shots, followed by a thump, a pause, and one shot more. They exchanged glances and ran toward the sound.

"We found her," Marcus comm'd to advise Lars so he wouldn't come after them—after all, someone had to guard the bomb.

The bomb! They sprinted and hoped to catch up to her before she went any further. It was a relief when she turned a corner and strode back down the hallway as she wiped the splattered blood off of her face. "Uh...he wanted us to know that we are all infidels and that he will see his way from his afterlife to haunt each and every one of us."

The guys nodded. "Right on, new friend."

Stephanie smiled. "Yeah, I told him to make sure he knocked first."

"We need to get back," Marcus reminded her. "Lars is gonna hemorrhage something otherwise."

She laughed. "We'd better not let *that* happen, had we?"

They hurried to the open floor where the rest of the team waited. Crystal had helped Johnny rejoin the team where they stood around the metal monstrosity in the center of the field. As she, Marcus, and Frog entered, a small, persistent sound caught her attention. "What is that?"

Crystal pointed at the bomb, and Stephanie walked cautiously closer to it and confirmed it as the source of the beeping she'd heard. "This…uh, Frog? This is not good, is it?"

He backed two steps toward the corridor. "Don't look at me," he told her. "Stuff that blows up is all Brenden's fault—and Lars. Yeah. Lars likes to blow shit up, too. Ask him."

"Get your ass over here," the team leader growled before he turned to Stephanie.

"Like the man says, Brenden and I blow shit up."

"I forgot," she admitted and only now remembered how they'd set the boobie traps and dealt with the bomb in the passenger liner scenario they'd run through in what seemed like a million years ago.

Lars put his hand over his heart. "I'm hurt."

"I don't think there's a luggage drone made that's big enough for *this* thing," Marcus muttered morosely.

CHAPTER NINETEEN

Beep. Beep. Beep.

Stephanie, the team, and several guards stood in front of the bomb and stared at it. The timer ticked down on the front. The thing was huge—big enough to have to taken several Dreth to move it into place. Lars pursed his lips, his eyes wide. "Hey, Frog?"

"Mhmm," the man murmured, his eyes a little glazed as he stared at the device.

"If we cut the floor—"

"You'll be fine," Frog told him. "But this floor's two feet thick."

Everyone looked slowly at Stephanie, who sighed. "Okay, this is the plan. I'll use my magic to cut a perimeter hole around the bomb without accidentally damaging it. We can lower it to the atrium and float it off the ship."

"How?"

"Well, there's this pirate ship, you see," she told him and grinned. "We simply have to get it down five floors really fast." She shrugged. "So we'll cut a hole in the floor."

"That sounds terrifying." Baizel wore an expression of disbelief.

Marcus shook his head and swiped his hand through the air. "Nah, she's a pro. She's got this. I hope."

Lars stepped in front of her as she readied herself, slightly nervous. "You've got this. You know you do. Focus everything you have. We'll head down to the atrium and clear a path to make sure you have the space to get through. Keep your eyes on the bomb. Will you be able to do some floating magic stuff to get it out or do we need to make another plan?"

Stephanie looked at him and cracked an exhausted smile. "No, I got it. Better to sail it through on magic then you guys drop it. Boom. All disintegrated."

"Besides," Crystal added. "Baizel and I can help there. We still have magic left."

"There!" Stephanie said as though that settled things. "I have magic back-up *and* you guys. I'll be fine."

Lars gave her a dubious stare but he nodded and his gaze slid to the side. "Elizabeth is really missing a party."

The bomb kept beeping, but the tone changed and the tempo increased.

She jumped. "We've gotta do this now. We're out of time."

"And the time is ticking faster," Marcus yelled as he watched the numbers change.

Stephanie and Lars looked over to confirm that the timer seemed to move in double-time. She cracked her fingers and shooed everyone away. "Go. Clear the path. I need to get this to the pirate ship like yesterday."

"Got it," he confirmed, turned, and ran off with the team.

Crystal and Baizel came and stood beside her. "Let us know what you need."

Stephanie closed her eyes and remembered all her training, all her abilities, and all her moments of discovery. She calmed her emotions and breathed deeply through her nose. Shaking her hand, she pointed at the floor and concentrated her magic into her index finger.

She calculated exactly how much she had to cut and tried to balance that with conserving her energy before she moved two feet away from the bomb and began. First, she focused a sharp ray of energy into the metal below her and cut deeply into the floor.

With her other hand, she directed a reinforcing wave of magic beneath the bomb to keep it floating and not allow it to plummet through to the atrium below. The fountain would be a problem.

As she walked a circle around the bomb, she noticed that it wasn't as hard to support as she'd thought it would be. The reason was clear when she glanced at Crystal and Baizel and saw them focusing a stream of Meligornian magic on the floor beneath her.

She continued her circle and completed it. After she'd added an extra surge of support beneath it, she finished the final cut through the last section and immediately used both hands to cycle the energy from her body to beneath the bomb. It helped that the two Meligornians were lending their support, but their magic alone wouldn't have been enough.

As they worked, passengers slowly emerged onto the balconies overlooking them. They also crowded around the openings to the corridors leading into the space. Everyone watched in silence as she lowered the energy carefully to float the load through the floor and past the fountain to the atrium floor below.

Once they reached that level, she and the two Meligornians let the floor she'd cut away settle to the ground and stepped off it.

"Thank you," Stephanie told them. "I'll take it from here."

She stepped through the bodies on the floor and forced herself to concentrate despite them. From his position at the doors leading to the umbilical, Frog looked at the hole in the floor above. "That'll definitely need more than a simple patch."

One step at a time, Stephanie moved the bomb through the ship. It took her a moment to register that the two Meligornians had ignored her instruction and helped her lift it, but she didn't complain. She could feel fatigue pulling at the edges of her body.

The team moved ahead of her to clear anything and anybody in the way. Bodies were dragged to one side and overly curious passengers pushed back. Crew members appeared from nowhere to take over passenger control and help with clearing the path and they were able to move more quickly.

As they crossed the last corridor leading to the airlock, the bomb beeped again, and Marcus stuck his head around the edge of it to peer at the countdown. "Let's say you might want to move triple-fast."

Stephanie rolled her eyes and fixed her focus on the amount of magic she needed under the device before she began to jog in place.

"You guys got this?" she asked and looked at Baizel and Crystal.

At their solemn nods, she began to trot down the last stretch of corridor. "All my guys go first. We might encounter resistance. *Don't let them shoot the bomb!*"

The umbilical bridge was flimsy and hard to balance in. There was no way they could move through it at speed and still keep hold of their volatile package. Stephanie stopped halfway and shook her head.

Lars looked right and left and turned quickly to put his fingers to his lips. They listened to the sound of people on the other side preparing for their arrival. She held the bomb with one hand and surged a protective shield around them, closed them in, and made it much easier to move forward.

When she was done, they continued and picked up the pace. The guys didn't tell her how much time was left on the clock There was no point. Either they'd make it, or they wouldn't.

When they reached the other side, they were bombarded by a wall of bullets. The slugs drummed into the shield and crumpled to fall at the team's feet. The Dreth maintained fire but couldn't breach the protective barrier. They persisted, even though they were unable to stop the team as they pushed forcefully into the ship.

As they proceeded, Stephanie glanced around and realized that the forces were not only Dreth but included Meligornians and humans. These weren't merely pirates. They were part of the resistance and one which had grown in leaps and bounds if humans had already joined their ranks.

She didn't know much about it, but given what life was like at home, she understood how easy it would be for a human to be drawn into it.

The bomb beeped more rapidly now, and Lars glanced at the timer. "The next right is the last stretch. We have to run."

As soon as they turned the corner, she dropped the shields and surged into a sprint until they reached the center of the ship. Frog raced ahead and hacked them through a large steel door.

Beyond it, they found a podium surrounded by a scattering of tools and pieces of technology. Stephanie and the two Meligornians floated the bomb to the podium and set it down carefully before they released their magic.

"That…that says three minutes," she said. "That's…holy shit, we gotta go!"

They barreled out of the room and were forced to a halt when they encountered a line of resistance. Dreth, humans, and Meligornians blocked their path. One of the older humans stepped forward and held his weapon to his chest. "You aren't going anywhere. You killed our leader and your lives are forfeit."

She sucked air in through her teeth. "Yeah, I don't think that's how it works."

Before the enemy could attack, she pushed both hands forward and to one side to create a wave of magic. It swept the resistance aside and into a wall to clear a path for her and the team to escape. They bolted through the gap and the two Meligornians pushed hard to keep up as they ducked and swerved.

Behind them, their adversaries regained their feet and set off in pursuit.

Lars, Avery, and Marcus dropped back a little to fire blindly behind them to slow their pursuers down. Stephanie created a small ball of magic. "Find the control room."

The orb hurtled away and she followed to lead the team down another corridor and up to a set of double doors. She pressed the button and it slid open to reveal three Dreth and the command center.

The pirates looked at her and she smiled nervously. "Hey. I'm gonna need to steer the ship. Thanks."

The Dreth left their posts immediately and charged. Lars and the guys entered and swung into position to turn their weapons on the aliens. With the enemy occupied, she hurried to sit at the ship's Navigation panel and peered at all the buttons. Marcus leaned beside her on one side and Frog on the other. "Do you know how to fly this thing?"

She licked her lips. "Uh…no. But I'm sure I can work it out."

The AI activated as Stephanie tapped the controls and a map of stars and planets appeared before her. "You must give me a destination."

She poked frantically at the map. "There—go to that star over there."

"I'm sorry, that is not a valid location."

"Right. Point the ship right," she commanded, conscious of time ticking down.

"I do not know what your right is," the AI responded calmly. There is no location that meets your criteria, but there is a large city only thirty seconds from here. Would you like to go there?"

The whole team yelled, "No!"

Stephanie pounded her hand onto the board. "Listen, you undereducated Artificial Intelligence. Point the damn ship away from the Federation Ship…or I'll…I'll damn well delete you."

Everyone went silent and waited for the response. "Accepted.

Pointing the ship away from the Federation enemy."

The vessel shook and the deck vibrated as the engines powered to life. Slowly, the vessel began to turn and altered its position to face away from the *Dreamer* as instructed. Then, it slowed. "I am in need of confirmation. What is your Resistance Identification?"

She groaned and buried her face in her hands for a moment, then raised her head and looked around. "Frog, where would I find the AI's computer on this thing?"

He scanned the room and pointed to a big metal black box on the wall. "That should be the server controls for the AI."

"Great," she said and stormed over to it. "And if I disconnect it, will the ship still run?"

Frog thought about it for a moment and nodded. "Yeah, it should."

Stephanie turned to the box and pulled magic over her hands. She growled her frustration as she ripped the entire system from the wall, yanked the wires free, and hurled the box to the floor. The computer screens flickered and skipped and finally went dark, and the deck surged beneath their feet.

She turned to the guys, her eyes wide. "We should probably get the hell out of here."

"No. Really?" Frog asked and started for the door. "Because I thought a short cruise before *blowing up* was a great way to spend my last few hours."

They bolted and raced through the ship. The resistance crew immediately resumed their pursuit but she knew they had no time for a running fight. She gestured with her arm and swept them aside with another wave of magic.

As they rounded the last corner leading to the exit, the pirate ship's engines surged again and threw them down. She scrambled hastily to her feet. "That's early."

Frog shrugged. "Yeah. Most likely because you cut the AI."

Marcus shrugged. "Hey, shit happens."

Stephanie grimaced as she realized the seriousness of their predicament. "I don't know if this will work, but shit, we'll go for it." She took her magic and swirled it a few times to create a bubble that surrounded the Meligornians and the team.

As soon as they were enclosed, she severed the bubble from herself and swirled a second piece of magic around her head to seal her suit.

An alarm blared and the lights in the corridor turned a flashing amber. Behind them, the corridors echoed with the sound of heavy bulkheads sliding closed. Over the intercom, a deep Dreth voice advised all personnel that there had been a hull breach.

Ahead of them, the hatch leading into the section to which the umbilical was attached was firmly closed and a red light flashed above. "I need to get through there," she screeched and tried to be heard above the alarm.

From inside the bubble she'd wrapped around the team, Frog pointed at the wall. It took her nanoseconds to use magic to pry the panel he indicated loose and seconds more to short the safety controls and force the doors to grind open slowly.

The amber lights turned red and the alarm tone changed, but she used her magic to draw the ball surrounding her team closer. As soon as the door rose, the atmosphere was sucked into space and tried to drag them with it.

Stephanie guided the ball carrying her teammates and flung it as hard as she could out the door and through the broken umbilical. Now she was in there, she could see that it had torn in two.

Through the doors, she could see the passenger entry where suited figures tethered to the liner tried to free the Dreth equipment from the hatch. Focused on her teammates and their bubble, she guided it directly to the entry, which made the liner crew scatter as it approached.

She didn't relax until she saw the bubble reach the boarding area inside the ship, where it landed hard and bounced. Her team were tossed around and rolled awkwardly together in the airtight magical ball. From the looks on their faces, she'd hear about it later, but she could live with that. At least they were alive.

With them safe, she backed away and took a running start. She leapt through the door and the umbilical and used her momentum to propel herself forward.

Thankfully, she made it through the boarding entry but landed almost as hard as the bubble had. Behind her, the tunnel whipped wildly as the pirate ship drew slowly away. Before she could stand, the crew finished removing the umbilical attached to the liner and activated the outer hatch to cycle it closed.

A familiar vibration shivered through the floor as the airlock sealed and filled with oxygen. With a flick of her wrist, she released her team and a liner's crew member helped her to her feet.

The pirate ship headed away from them, now at full speed. When the bomb detonated, it was so far away that they didn't actually felt a tremor from it.

Exhausted, Stephanie helped the other guys up, checked for broken bones, and thanked the Meligornians for their help. Marcus cracked his back and groaned and Frog wiped the blood off his elbow on his pants. She smiled awkwardly. "I probably shouldn't have cut the AI?"

Lars shook his head. "The difference between stupidity and genius is success. Since we are here and the pirate ship with the bomb is way out there, I'd say it was genius."

Frog jumped and clapped enthusiastically. "Day saved. Whoop!"

The comms crackled and the lights dimmed, and the red emergency ones began to flash overhead. The robotic voice of an AI came over the speakers. *"Alert. Alert."*

The warning lights continued to flash but the voice crackled and went silent. Frog pouted and sighed. "Maybe I spoke too early."

CHAPTER TWENTY

One of the officers in the engine room shook his head and waved his arms at the chief engineer. "No, we simply don't have it. There is a worm invading the engine control system. I have no control over the engines. I can't stop them from shutting down and then surging and it's bleeding us dry. It's like leaking gas during a jump. We could dive through and the ship would be stuck in the middle."

Roger rubbed his temples and flicked impatiently through the schematics on his screen. "The Hats are working on the worm. Those damned techs say we'll have control back any minute."

The engineer shook his head, removed his hat, and lowered his voice. "I don't think you understand, sir. We've already lost too much energy in the surges. *Dreamer* won't only be dead in the water at any minute. Even if there is power, there won't be enough for us to get back."

Several crewmen ran past with large wrenches, sheets of metal, and new lines. The engineer watched them pass, looking over his shoulder. "They're fixing things as fast as they can and as best they can, but these surges are stressing the ship's frame and the engines themselves. We're shunting excess power to try to keep it in the system and cut down on the release into space, but this is something that is known as a TKO. Normally, vessels are found a thousand years later orbiting some planet with everyone on board long dead."

The chief engineer shook his hand and his head. "That's not an option here. What do the numbers say?"

His subordinate rubbed his chin, reluctant to deliver the news. Roger laid a hand on his shoulder and injected a commanding edge into his tone. "Just tell me."

The man stared at him for a moment and sighed. "The numbers say *Dreamer* will need a refit and early safety testing." He drew a breath. "The engine stress is getting worse, sir. Like I said, soon, we won't have the power to make the slip back, but there's a chance we might not move at all—and we might never get them back online."

Roger stared at him and then through him as he wracked his brain in search of some indication as to what to do next. He shook himself out of it as the executive officer led Stephanie and the team into Engineering.

He'd never seen a sorrier-looking bunch. His guys looked the worse for wear, but the girl's team looked worse. They were battered, bruised, and covered in splatters of blood, and the two Meligornians with them looked equally as bad. They were a ragtag group, all of them, and he wondered why his colleague had brought them.

That was answered soon enough. "This is the Federation witch and her team. Since she knows how to handle MU at least as well as the Meligornsians, we thought she could help."

The chief engineer resisted the urge to groan or put his head in his hands. *This* was the best chance they had for survival?

Hiding his doubts, he shook Stephanie's hand and studied her for a moment. The executive officer pointed to the team. "They've just removed the pirates and an explosive device from the boarding deck, but they're willing to help us here. Fill us in."

Roger nodded to his officer, who tipped his hat to Stephanie and walked away to monitor the disaster happening around them. The chief offered her his arm and walked them into his office.

She stood at the door and listened intently as he broke it down to a bare-facts explanation. "The worm has infected our engine controls and sprayed our energy out into space. We have almost completely exhausted our battery power and the engines are in danger of failing completely. Basically, we might not have enough energy to make the slip to Meligorn. These batteries are run off MU, and there isn't enough out here to charge them. We're light years away from Meligorn."

The executive officer rubbed his face. "That's bad."

Roger shook his head and strode to the window. "That's not all. The second Dreth ship is moving toward us as we speak. They're pissed that we blew their friends up and killed one of their higher-ups in the attack on our section. And now, we can't move. This is a luxury liner. It doesn't have any weapons."

The other man stepped back and his gaze drifted when he realized how critical the situation actually was. If his colleague wished for guns, they either needed luck or a plain miracle.

Stephanie tried to listen carefully but something pulled her to the right like an invisible hand. She shook her arm in an attempt to ignore it. Finally, she looked out of the room and down toward the open hatch at the end.

Her eyes immediately widened, held by the sight of the large glowing cavern beyond. She shifted slightly to see it better, and Lars noticed she no longer paid attention to the conversation. He ducked his head out to discover what had distracted her and said, "That's the engine cavern."

"Oh." She stepped out of the office and started walking toward the hatch. Lars followed, then the rest of the team brought up the rear. She reached the hatch, her voice soft with awe. "It's enormous. There are batteries in there the size of school buses."

"They have to have enough energy to make it through the trip," Lars said. He stopped just outside and squinted at the bright light that radiated within.

Energy moved and swirled through machinery beyond. Wisps of it flipped out like tentacles, curled around her, and crept back in. She was the only one who could see it, but its light was visible to all.

Lars leaned toward her. "Your eyes are glowing again."

She nodded knowingly. "I can't help it. I need to see the energy flows."

He shifted his weight to his other foot. "What energy flow? I don't see anything. It's bright in here, that's all."

Stephanie shook her head and broke contact with the energy leaking from the batteries. "It's everywhere. The energy is literally flowing wildly around us—around the engine bank, around everything. But the storage batteries are acquiring it so slowly that the chief engineer is right. It will take too long to restore enough energy to move this ship. If it were all MU, the batteries might fill faster but probably nowhere near as fast as we need it to."

The executive officer exited the office and wandered down the hall to watch her. His colleague followed and moved forward to stand behind them.

When he noticed the entranced look on her face, the executive officer turned to Lars. "Does she see something?"

The team leader glanced at him and raised his hand for silence. He needed to finish his conversation with her before she was distracted again. The two officers stepped back with the other team members and waited while Lars talked to her.

She waved her hands toward the batteries and made all kinds of motions as she described something to him. He stood quietly and nodded his head as though taking in what she told him.

The executive officer really hoped she had some kind of plan because they were sitting ducks, and it wouldn't be long before the pirates were ready to fire on them.

Together, they watched as Lars stepped back between the JC and the engineer. Stephanie rolled her neck and stepped inside the engine bay, and the energy whipped her hair around her head.

She ignored it and moved between the massive core engines until they could only see her silhouette between the large batteries.

Lars talked to others and pitched his voice so it could be heard over the noise of the work going on behind them. "She wants to make sure the valves are closed."

The engineer furrowed his brow. "The engine energy storage?"

He clicked his tongue. "Uh…yes? Whatever it is that stores the energy used when flying the ship."

Roger nodded. "Yeah, that's done as soon as we ejected the Surge. We have someone check and double check those things multiple times a day."

He released a deep breath. "I think she simply wants to have a feeling of it—a really good one—and she wants to triple check your double check before diving into it."

The other man shrugged. "Hey, that doesn't bother me in the least. She might find something we overlooked."

Stephanie stepped out for a moment and waved them over. "Have they confirmed that the worm is completely out of the system?"

The executive officer nodded and yelled over the noise. "Yes. But I'll call right now to double check and confirm it for sure."

She nodded. "Thanks."

He moved off to the side, made his call, and returned within only a few short minutes and nodded energetically. "Yes, the worm is completely taken care of. You're free to work your magic however you need."

The chief engineer settled his gaze on her. "You're going to use *magic* to get this to work?"

Lars gave him a knowing smile. "Trust me. If it's something to do with magic, she'll get it done."

Roger wasn't convinced, but he was willing to let the girl try. This part of the problem was all about the magic. *Something* had to work.

They gathered around the door to the engine room, but none of them followed her inside. She planted her feet in the center of the ring of batteries, drew a deep breath, and let the energy inside her build into a good flow.

It could feel the energy outside and it jostled within her as though confused. She could sense that it would calm, though. Confident that she had full control, she began to sway and her body moved like a wave to follow the rhythmic motion of her feet. She put her arms out to the sides and gingerly let her wrists remain weak for a moment.

"These things better hold a lot of power," she yelled over her shoulder as her whole body began to glow.

"More than you can make," Roger shouted back and laughed as he threw the challenge down.

When he looked at her again, he had to squint and raise his hand to shade his eyes. The light she generated bounced frenetically in the engine room as her body danced to the beat of the energy inside her.

Stephanie lost herself in the moment, connected strongly with all her energy centers, and allowed the power to course feverishly through her veins. She could feel every wisp and trail of the magic twisting through her as it prepared for release. That was the thing about the MU. It knew when she would do something and knew she needed to release the energy.

There was no resistance, and she fell quickly into a melodic trance. The only things she could hear were the flow of the energy and the swirl of it deep in her chest. She worked hard to push the MU to cycle and made it flow as fast as it could. The faster she managed to move it, the quicker she could push it out to saturate the batteries without losing too much of it to the room around her.

Her audience stood for several moments and simply blinked occasionally, mesmerized by her dance of magic. Slowly, she lowered her arms to her side, then raised them again and held them out in front of her. Without warning, she flung them over her head and her back arched as she lifted slowly onto her toes.

The engineer jumped and shielded his eyes as the energy erupted from her, surged into the batteries, and flooded the storage units throughout the room. Her silver hair blew riotously around her as her body became almost weightless.

With the magnitude of the energy she had held in, Stephanie couldn't even open her eyes during the process. All she could do was focus and push the magic out as hard as she could.

The red lights on the panel outside the engine room had flashed to signal low quantity for hours. However, as her efforts continued, the lights clicked through amber and finally to green and their color flared brightly for a moment.

Roger was shocked. He spun and hurried to the gauges and stared in disbelief at the levels. They were higher than when they'd put fresh batteries in the system. However, once he adjusted to the number, his face assumed an expression of alarm.

He whirled and half-ran to where the crew were working and bellowed, "Open the cores on engines three and five! Come on. Come on! Get this ship moving or she'll overload."

He pointed to the executive officer. "Tell the captain to start the crank and not to stop until it comes on."

Lars watched with amazement as one tiny person was able to power an entire city-sized ship. And she did it without question, motivation, or complaint. She did it because she cared about people. The engineer tapped him on the shoulder and squinted into the brightness. "Can we speak to her?"

The team leader looked at him and then at Stephanie. He tried to walk forward but had to catch hold of the doorframe. There was a resistance and extreme air pressure from within the room. Every time he managed to put one foot forward, his hands would slip. Every time he got a good grip, a gust of air would hurl him out again. Finally, he gave up. "I can't even get in there."

Roger was as close to panic as he'd ever been. He raced over to the controls as soon as the engines began to turn. "No! This will blow!"

He thrust the engines to maximum and listened almost despairingly as they strained until the ship moved forward a fraction. With a muttered curse, he shook his head at the executive officer and then at each of his men. "Dammit, tell everyone to use all the power they can. Turn the damned air-conditioners all the way to high. Start the coffee maker, turn on every light. Override the cabin controls and *make it all work!*"

The engines fought even harder as she loaded the cells but within minutes, when the energy was strong enough to begin to surge through the lines of the ship, they came fully online and engaged with a powerful thrust.

It took the chief engineer a moment to realize what was happening and when he did, horror tremored through his tones. *"We're translating!"*

He tipped his head back and whispered prayers toward the ceiling before he slammed the release lever down. The ship was in service.

CHAPTER TWENTY-ONE

Stephanie jolted as the energy flow from her body ceased. She had spent everything she had to power those batteries and get the engines turning and had even willed the magic to take them home.

First, she'd combined both the gMU and the eMU she'd had stored and flowing through her. She'd bolstered this by drawing in and converting the gMU that flowed all around them to give it as much power as she could. Everything seemed to move in slow motion. Silver, purple, and blue energy swirled chaotically around her.

Finally depleted, her body fell back and her view of the batteries turned to a view of the ceiling. With the worst of the turbulence gone, Lars raced forward and thrust through the dying winds to slide onto his knees and catch her before she hit the floor.

Avery and Brenden remained with the few Dreth prisoners they had acquired in the earlier battle as the rest barreled into the room to surround her.

Lars swept her into his arms and carried her from the room and through the crowds of workers who were now frantically engaged in stabilizing the ship. He took her to Roger's office, laid her on the table, and moved the hair out of her face as he stared at her. While he was so incredibly proud of her, he hated to see her so pale and still.

"Stand back, guys," Baizel said as he and his sister pushed through. "These should help."

They each opened one of her palms and pushed powered MU rocks into her hands, closed her fingers tightly around them, and held them in place. The energy inside the stones glowed and began to soak into her and twine around her hands and wrists as she lay there unconscious.

Baizel shook his head. "They aren't enough. I can help."

Crystal stepped back. "I would, but I used most of mine helping Johnny and that little girl, Marissa."

The Meligornian closed his eyes and placed his fingers carefully on Stephanie's temples. Lars was worried, but he knew she needed help he couldn't give her. The man's fingers glowed brightly as he pushed more energy into her body. While he didn't say anything to the team leader, he could feel how weak the girl was and how her body fought to simply stay alive.

He kept his fingers on her temples for several minutes longer before he finally opened his eyes. Lars looked at him, his face strained with worry. "What? What is it?"

Baizel shook his head and smiled softly. "She is healing. I just…I have never experienced a being with pathways for magic that were so open and so raw. Even inside the pathways of Meligornians, we have restrictions. She is open almost all the way."

The man looked at him and then at the witch, his face clouded by concern. Baizel raised his hands when he'd depleted most of his power and put one on Lar's shoulder. "She will be okay. Let's get her to her room so she can rest."

He nodded and they moved her carefully upstairs, and he insisted on carrying her the entire way. They laid her down in her bed and covered her and there she stayed. A thick dream world enveloped her mind and soothed the pathways as they healed from channeling the sheer mass of energy she had drawn through herself.

Lars stayed in her room on a chair beside her bed, his head inclined toward her, and kept his eyes open for as long as he could.

The ship had been in rough shape, but the crews worked around the clock to make sure they made the translation smoothly. As soon as the ship lit up with power, the Dreth vessel retreated, knowing that it was better to avoid whatever was happening. Jaws dropped as the ship translated and ensured that the resistance would remember Stephanie's name.

Unaware of the impact she'd had, she slept on. A light knock on the door made Lars look up in time to see Baizel enter.

The Meligornian was smiling. "Her color is looking very good. Fresh and pink like a human should look. I wanted to tell you we are arriving on Meligorn. They will dock in an hour. We came to help pack her things."

Lars straightened and rubbed his face to rid himself of the last traces of sleep. "I need to decide where to take her when we get there."

Baizel shook his head and smiled at his sister as she entered. She went to the closet and pulled out the suitcases inside. He walked over and stood beside the team leader. "Do not concern yourself with that. I will take care of the arrangements. I have very good contacts on my world. My uncle was not only a good man but a brilliant businessman. When he was alive, he taught me everything he knew, and I opened my own company. It has grown by leaps and bounds and my uncle and I were coming home to merge our businesses. He was ready to retire. I am only getting started."

Lars put his hand on the man's shoulder. "I am sorry for your loss. I didn't think of it until now."

The Meligornian smiled, knowing his shoulder squeeze was a gesture of sympathy and friendship in the human world. "We mourn death like humans, but in different ways. We still have parts of our loved ones mixed in with us. When he died, his energy transferred to all of us. For you, it means little, but for those who can sense that energy, he became imprinted in our pathways. Meligornians stay connected with all others throughout time. A speck of Meligornian dust is all it takes. The rest floats out to the stars where we first came from."

Lars smiled kindly at him and the visitor patted Stephanie's hand before leaving. Crystal packed everything and left it ready for the team. She was still taking care of Marissa. They had discovered she had no other family and, if taken back to Earth, she would be put into the system. The woman couldn't accept that, so she made arrangements through her uncle's connections to keep the little girl on Meligorn. It was an unusual arrangement but the best thing for her.

When they arrived at the docking station, a group of local healers boarded the ship and moved Stephanie gently to the Meligorn side of the massive space station. She was put into their side of the hospital since the healers knew who she was and what kind of magical powers she possessed. She was more like a Meligornian than a human in that respect.

A couple of days passed, and she gradually began to return to normal. Her cheeks were rosy, her breathing steady and deep, and her connection with magic seemed restored as her body refilled quickly from the magic around her.

The planet was the best place for that since MU seemed the easiest to access and process. Lars remained by her side but went to his room at night to sleep, update Elizabeth and her parents, and take care of the team.

When he wasn't doing that, though, he stood beside her bed,

one hand in his pocket and the other touching hers. Baizel came to visit one afternoon, dressed in business attire with his hair no longer wild and uncombed. The team leader chuckled. "You look like a new man."

Baizel hugged him, something Meligornians did with few people. "And you, my friend, look tired."

He shrugged. "I won't sleep well until I know she's awake."

The visitor nodded and studied her peaceful face. "It's a pity."

Lars looked at him in confusion. "What is?"

He ran his finger down her cheek and traces of MU escaped him and entered her. "I suspect if she ever goes without MU for too long, she will waste away."

Lars snapped his head toward Baizel but the Meligornian had already turned to flag down one of the attendants. "Yes, sir?"

He lowered his voice. "See to it that the ambassador, her very close friend, is notified of where she is. The humans have not been able to contact him here on Meligorn."

The attendant nodded and he turned and gave Lars a half smile before he headed out of the ward.

"Well, they simply needed to be reassured," the ambassador said as he stood in front of the king and queen. "And you did exactly that. You reassured them that they would continue to be prized and welcomed in their home, even if they chose to explore other planets."

The king nodded and rubbed the queen's arm. "I told you we did the right thing."

She rolled her eyes playfully. "He always needs reassurance that he is the greatest king there ever was. Silly man. The people of Meligorn adore you on every level and they trust you. Those who rebel do it for many more reasons than the Universal Cooperation of Governments. They have agendas, and this extra entity blocks some of those. It's not necessarily a bad thing."

The king smiled and refocused on the ambassador. "My wife, the queen of queens. She is brilliant. She will go down in history as the crown jewel of Meligorn."

V'ritan chuckled and bowed lightly to her. "I could not agree more, my queen."

A messenger entered the chambers and handed the king a small silver cube. He thanked him and waited until the boy left again. The ambassador backed away. "I will excuse myself."

The king shook his head. "No. This is addressed to you as well."

A small hologram emerged from the top of the cube. It was the assistant to the king. "I have just been notified of two points of interest. Stephanie Morgana is currently being treated on the Meligorn side of the space station hospital. Apparently, the *Meligorn Dreamer* is damaged because it was attacked by pirates looking for the ambassador. The Federation witch and her team have been credited with not only eliminating the pirates and removing a bomb they planted, but the witch also apparently used her own energy to repower the ship. Unfortunately, she has not yet regained consciousness. I will update you as more comes in."

The hologram faded and the royal couple looked tentatively at the ambassador. He had turned to the side, his fists clenched and a look of shock and anger on his face. "They were looking for me…" He choked on the words. "But they found Stephanie."

His eyes narrowed in rage as he turned abruptly and stormed toward the exit. The king and queen watched him with concern and heard him mutter as he grabbed the door handle, "I will kill them all—"

Silence settled inside the throne room for several moments as they watched the door close behind him. When he was gone, she slowly turned to the king, a perplexed look on her face. "Did he leave without our permission?"

He exhaled a deep breath and shook his head. "My queen, please forgive him. Stephanie has become his new daughter and she was almost killed because they were looking for him. I believe the pirates have brought about the healing of the King's Warrior."

The queen, her mouth open, glanced at the door when she heard a scratching sound and saw that it had closed on the ambassador's robes. She shook her head and smiled lightly before she stood and smoothed some of the creases in her dress. "Oh, the things that happen in Meligorn are like those human soap operas. Well, I suppose I will inform his wife that the Most Trusted Advisor might be late for dinner."

She wiggled her eyebrows and leaned down to kiss her king on the cheek before she walked sedately across the room and into her private halls. He remained seated, his hand on his chin and concern on his face.

The door opened a fraction and he saw the ambassador's robes slip from beneath it before it shut for a second time.

His gaze darted to a large painting suspended by magic on the walls. It was of him and V'ritan in their younger days, adorned with ribbons and without a worry in the world. "Oh, old friend. I embraced your advice as we worked through our peace. Please do not bring Meligorn to war in your anger."

He shook his head, slapped his hands to his thighs, and grunted as he stood from his throne. One of the servants hurried over, draped a cloak about his shoulders, and handed him a pen and parchment. "Very good. Now, bring my ship to readiness. We go to the space station."